ALTER

Also by Jeremy Robinson

Standalone Novels
The Didymus Contingency
Raising The Past
Beneath
Antarktos Rising
Kronos
Xom-B
Refuge
Flood Rising
MirrorWorld
Apocalypse Machine
Unity
The Distance
Forbidden Island
The Divide
The Others
Alter

Nemesis Saga Novels
Island 731
Project Nemesis
Project Maigo
Project 731
Project Hyperion
Project Legion

Post-Apocalyptic Sci-Fi
Hunger
Feast
Viking Tomorrow

The Antarktos Saga
The Last Hunter – Descent
The Last Hunter – Pursuit
The Last Hunter – Ascent
The Last Hunter – Lament
The Last Hunter – Onslaught
The Last Hunter – Collected Edition
The Last Valkyrie

SecondWorld Novels
SecondWorld
Nazi Hunter: Atlantis

The Jack Sigler/Chess Team Thrillers
Prime
Pulse
Instinct
Threshold
Ragnarok
Omega
Savage
Cannibal
Empire

Cerberus Group Novels
Herculean
Helios

Jack Sigler Continuum Novels
Guardian
Patriot
Centurion

Chesspocalypse Novellas
Callsign: King
Callsign: Queen
Callsign: Rook
Callsign: King 2 – Underworld
Callsign: Bishop
Callsign: Knight
Callsign: Deep Blue
Callsign: King 3 – Blackout

Horror Novels (written as Jeremy Bishop)
Torment
The Sentinel
The Raven

Short Story Collection
Insomnia

ALTER

JEREMY ROBINSON

For the voices in my head.

SURVIVAL

1

A tree branch is the first thing I see upon waking. Normally, such a mundane thing wouldn't garner a second glance, but as my eyes adjust to the shifting light around me, I focus on the twisting limb slicing through the air in front of me. The bark is smooth, as far as bark goes, like the hide of some hairless mammal. A hippo, perhaps. A few green leaves add color to its heathered gray surface.

As the branch grows larger, I stop seeing the bark and the leaves. All that remains is the limb's kinetic potential.

A sound like screeching brakes drives home the limb's murderous intent. The Cessna's two pilots' high-pitched screams reveal the state of their unpreparedness for what comes next: eternal supernatural life or nothingness. As my own scream builds, I realize I have yet to fully contemplate the issue myself. I've always been so focused on the plight of the here-and-now that I never really gave much thought to what comes next. Probably why I never finished that novel I started.

The branch shatters glass, its ancient strength hewing through the small plane's metal frame. The impact drowns out my voice.

But my fear is not just for myself. My heart aches for Gwen, who will lose her husband. And for Juniper, who is still so young she won't be able to remember me when she's grown.

A prayer to no particular deity flits through my mind as the sinister branch cleaves the pilots in two, popping their lungs and silencing their screams.

Take care of my family. Protect Gwen and Juni—

The end comes before I can finish.

I feel the bark on my face, its rough surface scratching, more like sandpaper than skin. And then the world bends and shifts. Light becomes oblong. Disorientation swallows me whole.

This is what it feels like to die, I think as distortion consumes me. *Is this my soul slipping away? Or the last surge of chemicals numbing my mind, now that it's been separated from my body?*

Then gravity reasserts itself.

I'm still in the plane.

Still strapped into my seat.

Still looking at the branch, now just inches from my face.

The limb stopped the plane, and is now lodged inside it. My face had brushed against its surface when my forward momentum came to a sudden stop, but the branch was unable to complete its murderous mission.

I have been spared.

Warmth drips onto my face, drawing my eyes back to the branch. A line of ants, carrying leaves down the tree, have had their progress stalled by rivulets of dark red.

Blood. The pilot's blood. It's pouring out of his torso's lower half, still strapped into the front seat above me. I can't see the top half. Red and white tendrils of his insides hang down like slick vines.

Above him, through the ruined windshield, a luminous jungle canopy shimmers in hues of yellow and green, and through the leaves, the blue sky.

We're not being held aloft by the branch. We're hanging from it, tail down. The plane must have swung down after stopping.

I need to escape.

But I've never been good at climbing, or anything else remotely physical, and the door appears to be fused to the branch. If I open it...

"Focus," I say, my voice quivering with fear. 'Observe, deduce, formulate, and react.' Those were the words my father often spoke to me as a home-schooled child. He was my mentor, teacher, and role model until he died. I'm not sure his personal scientific method of dealing with problems makes complete sense, but I've always understood the gist of it. Slow down. Think things through. Come up with a plan and see it through. If I survive, I'll probably teach Juniper my own version of the lesson.

My attention turns to the plane's ruined front end.

Past the branch, and the bodies, the windshield that no longer exists is my path to freedom.

Fingers fumble over metal made slick from blood. I try to ignore the gore. I've never seen its like before. But its surprising warmth and pungent old metal scent pokes me with white-hot reminders. When a drizzle of syrup-thick liquid traces a line across my chin and ends at the confluence of my lips, I yank to the side, but I'm held still by my restraints.

"Why can't I get it off?" I shout to no one, and then scream and thrash, lost in a moment of abject horror.

Movement silences me and draws my eyes upward.

Like a snail emerging from its shell, the pilot's insides curl out of his torso.

"No, no, no." The words are spoken with a flutter.

While the branch drew a scream from my lips, the hot innards of another human being splashing across my outstretched palms, and then my body and face, sends me into convulsions. I vomit the fish from lunch into the mess, twisting and pulling and slipping through coils of what I know are intestines, despite having my eyes crushed shut.

I heave again, and this time the roar of my expulsion has a kind of doppler effect, fading into the distance as my stomach lurches up. For a moment the pressure of gravity reverses.

By the time I realize the branch is missing, the plane covers the distance to the ground. Metal shrieks along with my cough of pain, expelled by the jarring impact. As the second pilot's insides begin stretching out for me, I'm granted mercy at last.

The plane's front end angles forward and then falls, coming to rest at a forty-five degree angle on the forest floor, as though we'd landed—poorly.

A heavy silence fills the cabin. In it, I can hear the hiss of leaves high above, the wind sifting through them. And then, birds. And insects. And other things I can't identify. My voice joins the living chorus a moment later, blubbering unintelligible noises as I struggle with the seat restraints again.

Slow down, some part of me drowning in blood manages to gurgle.

I turn my full attention to the buckle trapping me in a slick prison. My fingers slip over the button every time I try to press it. It was hard to remove when it was dry, a fact that had once given me assurance that it wouldn't come undone before I wanted it to. But I had never envisioned this scenario.

Pushing with both thumbs, using equal force against each other, and down, I depress the button. With a click, the seat belt retracts.

Freedom brings fresh waves of panic. My fingers slip over the door handle three times as I groan and croak, my breaths coming in uneven gulps. When the latch finally stops fighting me, I push on the door.

Bent metal resists.

Repulsion-fueled outrage draws a scream from my throat, loud enough to once more silence the nearby wildlife, and scratch my throat.

I kick the small door hard, again and again. My bones and muscles protest, but I hammer away until the door swings open.

Like a birthing horse, I slide from the orifice, bloodied, panicked, and confused as I fall a foot to the earth. I mewl like a wounded animal, thinking nothing coherent. I just want to be held. To be comforted. To know I'm going to be safe.

But I get none of those things.

Instead, the jungle calls out, reminding me where I am, reminding me that while I've survived the crash, death still looms.

"Good intentions or not, the depths of that dark jungle are no place for a man of your...physical abilities," Gwen told me upon hearing my plan to provide medical support to the tribal peoples of the Amazon. "There are plenty of people in the world that need help, including places with electricity and running water."

Her points were valid. Are valid. I'm lanky, have poor endurance, and am prone to insomnia, but just because something is hard doesn't mean it shouldn't be done. We've led a privileged life, and will continue to do so after my three-month stint is done. Giving back to the world that's given us so much is the right thing to do. And I believed I could have a real impact on people's lives. Healing in the Amazon is often mixed with superstitious folklore and questionable hygiene. Modern medicine cannot just heal people, it can transform lives. Entire communities.

In hindsight, I should have listened to her, but even she couldn't have predicted my first tour of the jungle I intended to make my temporary home would end in disaster.

Lying on my back, gore congealing on my clothing and skin, I stare up at the dancing canopy. Pinpoints of light twinkle through the endless green twilight, but I have been cut off from the sky. There's not even a hole to mark the plane's passage. I've been swallowed by a great beast, and will be slowly digested by its sweltering insides.

I roll to the side and vomit once more.

When I push myself up, stiffness—in my muscles, and from the drying blood—nearly keeps me down. Muscles quiver and spasm. Adrenaline is wearing off. Shock is setting in.

Unsteady legs hold me aloft, but I'm forced to cling to the now wingless plane. In every direction: jungle. Twisting trees. And vines. And leaf-littered ground, alive with marching ants.

I should have never come.

Don't give in to despair, I tell myself, and I try to channel my father's calm, problem-solving nature. "Show me the way home."

I've spent less time pondering the existence of ghosts and spirits than I have a supernatural creator. My job is to prevent death, usually through prescription drugs and ointments. I don't get paid to think about what happens when I fail. Desperate times, I suppose.

If my father still exists in spirit form, can traverse the astral plane and hear his son's voice, maybe he can do something to help? Impart some wisdom from beyond the grave? Maybe redirect someone's path toward me?

Of course, if that were possible, we'd all be talking to the dead on a regular basis.

The sound of approaching feet through brush makes me flinch.

A chill runs up my back and raises the hair on my neck.

"Dad?" I whisper, glancing around like I might catch sight of his apparition.

The footsteps grow quieter, but I have no trouble zeroing in on my rescuer.

With a pounding heart, I realize that if my father's ghost had anything to do with this, his goal isn't to save me, but to bring about our reunion in the afterlife.

2

Like all cats, jaguars are curious creatures. Where other animals might flee from the sound of humanity, many feline species are drawn toward the unknown. And the beast of a cat eyeing me from a gap in the low-lying jungle foliage is no different.

Round yellow eyes lock on to mine, unblinking. I've never seen such focus. Its ears are folded back, tight like the rest of its low-to-the-ground body. It moves with such slow fluidity, it's like watching a nature film in slow motion. I can hear the British narrator in my head, describing how the predator is about to pounce on its feeble prey, pronouncing jaguar as 'shag-yoo-are.' If not for the hunger in its eyes and the lack of a barrier between us, I'd find the creature beautiful. The only blemish on its sleek, perfectly made body, is a scar above its right eye.

I try to mirror the cat's pace, stepping back, but my body quivers as adrenaline flows once more. A half step is all I make it before bumping into the plane and yelping.

The cat doesn't flinch. I suppose it's accustomed to hearing its prey cry out.

But why hasn't it struck yet?

Before starting on the long path toward being a general practitioner, I was fascinated with animals and very nearly became a veterinarian. Potential income drove me toward healing people over animals, but I've never lost my interest in the Earth's menagerie. I've never interacted with a cat larger than a Persian, but I've always had a sense that, at the core, all cat species have similar personalities hardwired into their DNA, making them both beautiful to behold, and deadly.

Back on the plane, when I was sure death was certain and impending, I felt less fear than I do now. I would be, and then I wouldn't be. But this... The idea of being eaten alive has never crossed my mind.

But I won't be alive when I'm consumed.

That's why the jaguar hasn't attacked.

It's waiting for me to run. To turn my back. To provide it with a clear path to my neck, which it will grasp in its powerful jaws before breaking my spine. And if that doesn't kill me, the cat will apply pressure until I'm suffocated. Better than being eating alive, but still...

I risk a glance to the right.

In the moment it takes me to confirm that the plane's door is still open, the jaguar takes three silent steps closer, its shoulders pumping like pistons. The cat's yellow coat and paint-dab spots slide over its body, a living work of dark expressionism.

When I startle at the movement, the cat slows once more, continuing the game of life-and-death Red Light - Green Light.

I slide along the plane toward the door.

The jaguar's eyes flare. It's subtle, but I think it recognizes that the structure could separate it from a meal. The creature's nose twitches as it takes in the scent of my dead pilots, whose names I can't recall. Feeling like a jerk, I continue on my snail's-pace path to safety.

We move in tandem, me toward the door, the jaguar toward me. I'm going to reach the door first, needing to cover just another twelve inches, while the jaguar has twice the distance in feet to cover. But that doesn't mean I'll be fast enough.

Catch it off guard, I think. *Move before it does.*

That's my only chance.

The jaguar leaps forward, as though sensing my plan.

A high-pitched wail slips from my lips as I dive inside the plane. When I spin around and look back, intending to yank the door shut, it's clear I won't have time. The jaguar is nearly upon me. My hand slaps something firm. My fingers clench, and I hurl the object with a desperate roar.

The jaguar is as taken aback by my sudden about-face as I am. Doubly so, when the improvised weapon strikes its nose.

With a shrill roar and a few swipes of its extended claws, the jaguar defeats the three-pound human liver. Noting the cat's distraction, I continue to shout, as much out of self-defense as horror, and then I set about tossing the rest of the pilot's insides...outside.

The jaguar backtracks, confused by a prey animal that can shed internal organs at will.

Lumps of various shades of maroon slap on the rich soil, collecting dry leaves like breading. Loops of entrails thump on the ground, pasta to the meat. A human smorgasbord.

It feels wrong, offering up a man who was alive just minutes ago, as a meal. But he is dead and gone, and I am not.

It's just meat, I tell myself, as I kick the last of the insides out through the door. Then I offer one last roar at the big cat, grasp the door handle, and slam it shut. The door bangs and bounces back open. I leap for the handle, and close it again, this time more carefully.

The cat's eyes remain locked on mine through the window, its posture still one of attack. But I'm safe. I'm... My eyes drift to the plane's ruined front end. There is plenty of space for the jaguar to reach the plane's interior. But *it* doesn't know that. It's just a cat. The barrier that now separates us—from its perspective—is impenetrable. Well, it doesn't know that yet, but it will if it tries to assault me through the window.

That doesn't happen.

The jaguar's tongue slides out of its mouth, wrapping around its snout before being withdrawn. There's a moment of frozen stillness, and then...realization. It's tasted the bloody liver residue on its nose.

Ears perk up.

The cat stands to its full height.

And for the first time since we locked eyes, its gaze turns downward.

Mouth open and panting, the jaguar surveys the bounty with which it has been provided.

"Oh, thank God," I exhale more than speak.

The cat nudges a morsel of organ with its nose, tests the chunk with its tongue, and then snatches it up. Two quick bites and it's gone.

I cease to exist. Predator is now oblivious to prey. The cat lies on the forest floor, content to devour its meal.

Wrapped in a humid blanket of fetid air that smells of blood and feces, I watch the jaguar eat. With each mouthful of human meat, the cat becomes more lackadaisical, subdued by a full belly. While it avoids the intestines, it plucks up one organ at a time, sometimes swallowing the meat whole, sometimes tearing away chunks.

Muzzle red with blood and stomach full, the jaguar lolls onto its side. Cats are hard to read, but it looks pleased. Looks content. If big cats didn't sometimes kill for the sport of it, I might be tempted to step outside and pet the beast.

When the jaguar rolls onto its back, coating itself in the gore of its recent meal, I slide back from the window, hoping the creature will assume I've fled the scene while it ate. Slouching in the plane's rear seat, coated in blood, I try not to weep.

Try not to scream. Try not to move.

The smell is beyond horrible. I breathe through my mouth to dull the odor, but all that accomplishes is to remind me that strong scents can be tasted, too. I learned that lesson, standing over my first med-school cadaver. It's been long enough that I'd forgotten. A gag threatens to overtake me and reveal my presence to the jaguar, but I manage to free a handkerchief from my pocket. While it's not clean, it is free of blood, and helps reduce the scent, and the flavor.

Sweat trickles down my forehead. Over my sides. The jungle squeezes moisture from my body, wringing me out. There is water, and food, and clothing in the gear stowed in the plane behind me, but I dare not reach for it. Not yet. Not until I'm sure.

Hours pass. I spend the time reflecting on what I will do with my life when I'm rescued. I'd like to say I'm the kind of person who can shake off something like this and stay on mission, but that's not what will happen. I think I'll go home to Massachusetts, to my nice family, and double my efforts at the food pantry I started five years ago. Probably what I should have done from the start. It feels wrong, giving up before I've ever started, but after this I don't think Gwen would ever forgive me for staying.

And people in need are everywhere, whether it be the Amazon jungle or the suburbs of Boston. Coming here was a mistake, and motivated by a selfish desire to be part of something that wasn't just humanitarian, but also exotic. Something to brag about. A story to tell. The food pantry isn't glamorous, but it feeds the hungry and maybe even saves lives. And there's a lot I can do to improve things. Marketing expansion to improve donations. Drop off locations. Pick up locations. More volunteers. On top of seeing patients and family, there's a lifetime of work in the pantry.

Thinking about a future in which I'm safe buoys me for a short time.

Then my thoughts turn dark.

I see myself rotting in this tepid green hell. Plants grow out from my insides. Animals gnaw on my remains. A line of hard-working ants carry away the rest.

I see my wife and daughter, sad and confused. At first, they'll hope. But eventually, they'll accept that I'm not coming back. They'll move on. Without me.

I'm lost.

In the Amazon rainforest.

No one knows where I am.

I don't even know where I am. I could have been asleep for ten minutes, or two hours. I could be an easy thirty-minute walk from civilization, or an impossible thirty-day hike. I know a lot about animals and healing people, but nothing about surviving in the wilderness I was foolish enough to believe I could make my temporary home.

Hubris brought me here. Believing I could be some kind of noble savior. In the future, I will evaluate my motivations better. How can I truly serve others if I'm also serving myself, or my ego?

Night descends slowly, and the jungle that has seemed alive during the day, blooms into a chorus of nocturnal creatures. The cacophony becomes a kind of white noise, drowning out anything distinct, as fully as the leafy canopy blots out the moon. Wrapped in a cocoon of sound and darkness, I close my eyes.

And sleep.

Upon waking, I'm greeted by the early morning's light, a body in agony, and the unflinching gaze of death itself.

3

The jaguar freezes in the ruined, open front end of the plane with statuesque rigidity. I don't know if it hadn't noticed me or had assumed I was dead, but my sudden inhalation upon seeing it locks the cat in place.

Cautious eyes drift toward me, but the rest of its body language remains unchanged. Right now, it's not a hunter, probably because it has the top third of...*Matheus*—his name was Matheus—clutched in its jaws.

Matheus's face, locked in a rigor of surprise reflects how I feel, but I'm too afraid to express it.

When the jaguar's eyes meet mine, I just stare back, trying to not reveal my fear. Right now we're just two predators separated by more meat than a jaguar needs to eat in a month. That the cat has come back for more so soon means it's been a while since its last meal. But Matheus should do the trick. If the smell of blood in the air doesn't draw more predators, I should be able to walk away unscathed.

Unless the cat decides fresh meat would be better than day-old.

While my heart is thumping hard, perhaps hard enough for the jaguar's keen ears to hear, I fight to keep my outside expression indifferent. I lean my head back while maintaining eye contact, letting my language exude something like, 'I don't care. Take the meat for yourself. I won't stop you.'

The armrest beneath the cat's paw starts bending outward. It pushes against the downward movement, but that just makes things worse. When the armrest gives way, it takes everything I have to not scream. To not flinch away, or barrel my way outside through the closed door. But I manage it, because I'm sure that anything other than confident stillness will result in my demise.

So when Matheus lands in my lap, and the jaguar atop him, I lock up and crush the squeal in my throat.

The cat is less relaxed. It flinches back, irate.

Claws extend, and with two outstretched arms, the jaguar slap-scratches Matheus a dozen times, shredding what remains of his clothing and the skin beneath. The cat ends the barrage with two right hooks, the second of which breaks Matheus's neck with a crack and cants his head at an unnatural angle.

Fighting revolt, I push up on Matheus's partial corpse and am caught off guard by how light he is. The body rises like a sacrificial offering, arms dangling to the sides, head lolling back. The cat takes two more swipes at the body, nearly filleting my arm in the process, and after getting its footing on the two front seats, sinks its teeth into Matheus once more.

A growl from the sides of the cat's cheeks tells me it's time to let go. I pull my hands back and Matheus's remains hover above me. The cat turns its head, moving Matheus away from me, and it catches sight of me once more. When it does, the cat freezes in place again.

"Seriously?" I say, unable to contain my annoyance. "Just go."

When the cat's muzzle flinches into a snarl and its ears fold back, I realize the depth of my mistake. I relax my posture again, wondering what I can do to get the jaguar to leave.

Do nothing, I decide.

Going against my instincts, I slowly close my eyes.

Breathe, I tell myself, *slow and easy*.

When I hear thumping, my muscles tighten, but I don't move. Don't open my eyes. The sound is coming from the front of the plane, not approaching.

My muscles start to shake, but I keep my eyes closed.

When I hear a thump outside the plane, and then nothing, I count to ten.

They're the longest ten seconds of my life, knowing that at any moment, the jaguar could attack and disembowel me.

But it doesn't.

At the count of ten, I pry my eyes open.

Aside from me and the pilot's lower two thirds, I'm alone.

The panic I buried during the encounter grips me hard. Each breath is a quivering heave. Sharp tingling moves from my fingertips and up both arms. My heart knocks in my chest.

When I was thirteen, I was approached by a pair of boys, close in age, but somehow far older than me. The smaller of the two said he knew me, that he was going to beat me to a pulp because of how I treated him in second grade. I claimed ignorance. I didn't know him. I didn't go to Beetle School. I lived on the far side of town. All lies, but convincing enough to get me a 'I'm going to give you five seconds and then I'm going to fuck you up.' I was fifty yards away by the time those five seconds were up, and in another five seconds, I was out of sight. Upon rounding the corner, panic set in. I'm not a violent person. Never have been. Not even in second grade. I don't have the heart for it.

Still don't.

The panic I felt on that day doesn't match today, but I feel like that small boy again, not just afraid of the pain, but of the violence itself. Of the violence and wrongness of harming another person. I suppose that's the other reason I chose to heal people over animals. People don't deserve to be treated poorly. Don't deserve to be abused, or bullied, or harassed, or discriminated against. Not even the worst of us. Human life is sacred. To be cherished.

My stomach twists as the juxtaposition of this opinion coupled with the fact that I've now fed part of both pilots to a jaguar sets in.

As the muscle twitches slow, the tingling fades and my pulse slows. My thoughts return to the here and now.

Get out.

Take what you can and leave.

Before it comes back.

A vision of the jaguar returning to claim a larger meal, growing frustrated that the rest of Matheus and his fellow pilot are held in place by seatbelts, and opting to take me instead, sets me into motion. Accessing the storage compartment from the back seat is a simple matter of pushing a button and folding the seat forward. Once that's done, I lean into the tight compartment and recover my backpack, which contains food, water, clothing, and a bottle of Ambien.

I open the side hatch, search for the jaguar, and then I toss the pack to the ground. I return to the storage compartment and find a satchel bag, a first aid kit and a machete. I take it all and toss it out the door with the same abandon that I'd flung the pilot's insides. A third trip to the compartment reveals nothing more of interest.

I'm about to vacate the plane, when I spot Matheus's belt. A knife is sheathed on the side, covered in gore. The blade could be useful, but I've already got the machete. I recall him also having a canteen, but I can't bring myself to search his body for it.

Better to leave with what I have, and my life, than stick around any longer and risk it.

I slide out of the Cessna, trying to be quiet, wary of the big cat. I scan the low-lying foliage and see nothing. Breath held, I hear nothing. The jaguar is either waiting to pounce, or has taken its meal someplace private.

Confident I'm not about to be torn apart, I collect the bags and gear. My bruised and worn out body groans from the weight of it all, but I resist the urge to lighten my load. I'm alone out here, with no way to resupply. I need everything I carry, and since I don't yet know which direction to walk, I just want to put as much distance between myself and the open jaguar buffet as I can.

Making note of the location from which the jaguar attacked yesterday, I round the plane and head in the opposite direction. A downward slope helps me along, the earth squelching under my boots.

I pause every few minutes, to listen. Other than buzzing insects and bird songs, I hear nothing. No sounds of pursuit. No signs of civilization. No people. Of course, out here, the only one of the three I'm likely to hear is the first. So I keep my pace steady, and never stop long enough for my muscles to grow tight.

By noon, or what I think is noon, my body protests.

Why am I trying to tell the time by the sun? I wonder. *I can just check on—*

My phone!

Heart pounding again, I reach into my pants pocket and all but tear the phone free. Despair takes root when I see a shattered screen, but Gwen's screen has been broken for the past year. It's ugly, but still works. I push the power button and nearly whoop when the screen glows to life. My thumb print grants me access, and then I look at the bars.

None.

What were you expecting?

There could be hundreds of miles between me and the nearest cell tower. A satellite phone might have reached the outside world, or even the plane's radio, but the former might as well not exist, and the latter was destroyed in the crash.

Tears fill my eyes as Gwen and Juniper smile at me from the background image. I rub my fingers over them, inadvertently pulling down a menu. The sudden departure of their faces snuffs out my source of sorrow. If I'm going to see them again, it's not going to be because I stood around doing nothing.

So I keep moving.

Heading nowhere in particular.

And I don't stop until I have no choice, which is far too late. As the jungle begins to darken, my vision fades faster. I drop to a knee, confused and dizzy.

I should have drunk more water, I think, and then pass out.

4

I wake beneath a waterfall, the cool torrent peppering my face. I gag and spit and shield my face, providing my eyes with a momentary reprieve. Just long enough to realize that the water is not falling from a river, it's falling from the sky. And it awakens my thirst.

I open my mouth and swallow gulps of the only water in the Amazon that doesn't need to be boiled or filtered before safely drinking. When my stomach is full nearly to bursting, I push myself up. Mushroom clouds of pain expand and contract inside my head. Dehydration headaches are relentless. Ask anyone who has had a hangover. They're the body's way of saying, 'Keep this up and you're going to die.'

Now that I've had my fill, all I really need to do is wait for my cells to rehydrate. Which is fine, because I can barely see ten feet through the rain. Aside from the hiss of falling water, the jungle is silent. Well, maybe not silent, but at least drowned out.

Not feeling endangered by anything beyond a severe case of pruning, I move to the crook of a twisting, four-foot-tall root curved like a flag caught by the wind. The tree above diminishes the amount of rainwater pouring atop me and my gear, but it doesn't stop the deluge. I have a poncho in my backpack, but I don't bother retrieving it. I'd only soak the bag's contents, and it's too late. I'm already soaked through.

Alone with myself in a jungle of white noise, my thoughts drift to home.

Do they even know yet?

I'm not sure what time it is, but I sense the sun somewhere above the thick clouds, which are mostly hidden by the jungle. The night has come and gone. I missed last night's scheduled call. And someone must be missing the plane. And the pilots.

My heart aches for Gwen. She's a strong woman, fully capable of doing anything and everything without me. But she also loves me. Adores me. I've felt lucky since the day she agreed to marry me. The possibility of my being missing, or worse, will leave her feeling lost.

I can see her, pacing the kitchen last night, dressed in a long T-shirt and panties—what I consider to be the world's best lingerie—calling my number over and over. She'd be worried. And then angry. And then worried again. By now she's probably desperate. She had my itinerary. Knows who my trip was organized through, knows where I was flying from and landing. If anyone can track me down, it's her.

But I'm not the only one she has to worry about.

Juni is three. And as the daughter of an attachment-parenting mother, she can't be ignored for long. She's not in pre-school, either. Homeschooling was the plan. It's intensive and hard, but Juni is worth it, and on top of traditional schooling, we can teach her to be a compass-ionate human being.

But how can Gwen do any of that while worrying about me?

She can't.

I should have never come.

The thought repeats like a mantra, coupled with, *why am I here? What was I thinking? Can I survive this?*

My vision of Gwen shifts. She's calling me. Worried at first. Then angry. Then Juniper needs her. To eat. For comfort. And while Gwen continues to worry, she doesn't call again. She writes it off. This morning, when I still haven't called, she's got enough time to make one call, probably to me, but then her own duties become the priority. I might be her love, but Juni is too, *and* her responsibility.

Gwen will eventually realize something has gone wrong, and will find a way to make those calls and spur people to action. Of that, there is no doubt. But the timeframe will not be as quick as I'd first imagined.

Tonight? I wonder. Will she decide to take action after I've missed two calls? If so, she won't be able to reach anyone until the following morning. And then how long to mount a rescue?

Best case scenario, two days.

And even then, how will they find me?

They won't.

I can't pin my hope of survival on Gwen. It's unfair to her, and there's really not much she could do.

I turn my thoughts to Juni, and have to steer them quickly away. While my imaginings of Gwen were fueled by the woman's strength, Juni is a child. A sensitive child. She'd be shielded from my disappearance for a time. But eventually, she'll ask. She's young, but smart. She'll note that I haven't talked to her on the phone. She'll sense Gwen's distress. Any time I think of her, my thoughts invariably turn to the moment she's told that Daddy's gone and he's not coming back.

I see her small face, twisting up in pain. I see her childhood robbed. I see her innocence shattered. As a father, I want to protect her from pain, not become the source of it.

"Damnit," I say, barely able to hear my own voice over the rain. So I shout, "Damnit!" and it does nothing to help me feel better.

The rain keeps me motionless for two hours, and then, all at once, it disappears. The transition from dark gray clouds to bright sun is seconds, and the temperature rises as quickly, turning the jungle into a sauna.

I stand to strike out again, heading nowhere in particular, and my feet squelch with water.

I close my eyes, take a deep breath and let it out slowly.

Being saturated is uncomfortable, but not dangerous. Walking with soaked feet is another story. Macerated skin, which has absorbed water and become more fragile as a result, is prone to blistering. Even a thirty-minute walk could result in a bevy of painful blisters. But when macerated skin dries, it's robbed of natural oils and often cracks open. In both scenarios, the resulting wounds can become infected. And if that happens, it's not just my feet that will be affected.

Self-recommendation: dry my feet. Dry my shoes. Put on fresh socks. If the comforts of civilization were an option, I'd suggest salve to restore oils. But that's not going to happen. In my case, I just need to make sure my boots and feet stay dry from here on out.

Dry feet in the rainforest...

I sigh and feel thankful that the boots aren't waterproof. Contrary to shoe-seller marketing, there's no such thing as a completely waterproof shoe or boot. Water will find its way in, whether it be through the sock, or via the skin's pores. Non-waterproof shoes allow water, and air, to flow. While this might mean wet feet sooner, it also means dry feet sooner. Time is the key factor in avoiding blisters and cracks.

Unable to move, I retrieve my poncho and lay it out on the sodden earth, using it as a thin, nylon rug. I remove my shoes and socks, confirming that my toes are both exceptionally pale and wrinkled. I lay the shoes and socks out, and then remove my clothes to drape over the tall root system. Drying in the humid air will take time. It might not even be possible. But somewhat dry is better than feeling like a sponge.

Being nude feels liberating for a moment, but shame drives me to don my spare pair of black boxers. Just in case rescue comes sooner than expected. I sit on the poncho and survey my gear. I know what the backpack holds, but the satchel is a mystery. I'm not even sure which pilot it belonged to.

The leather, like me, is swollen and soft. But the buckle and strap holding the top down is tight, and the zipper beneath is still sealed. *Sorry,* I think to the dead and eaten pilots, and then I pry the satchel open.

"Huh," I say.

The contents at the top—a foil-wrapped meal and a water bottle—are not what I expected, but they're certainly welcome. I place the food and water aside and dig down further. There's a notebook, its pages partially full of Portuguese writing that I can't read. It could be notes about flights or a novel, for all I know. But the pages are dry and will make good kindling in a place where everything else is wet.

I pluck a Zippo lighter from the satchel next. Its brushed metal has been etched with a pot leaf. I open the cap, give it a flick and feel a touch of relief upon seeing a strong flame. I close it quickly, nervous about using its fuel.

A flannel shirt lines the satchel's bottom. It's dry and at least two sizes too small for me, so I pull it out, intending to use it as towel.

But when the orange, brown, and white plaid fabric emerges and reveals what was hidden beneath, I forget all about my wet feet.

There are four objects lying at the bottom of the bag. The first is a brick of what can only be marijuana. I pull out the plastic-wrapped bundle and smell it to confirm my theory. Definitely marijuana, which some doctors are still opposed to, but I think it provides an opportunity to heal, stop pain, and free people from opioid addictions the medical community created. I haven't actually smoked it myself, and this amount is likely illegal in most parts of the world, but I have no moral objections to it...on its own.

The rest of the satchel's contents put it in a different light. The first is a smaller pack of white powder, which I assume is cocaine. Enough of it to sell for a significant profit. I can't think of a way to test it without getting high, so I open the bag and discard its contents into the soil. I would hate to be rescued only to be arrested.

A bundle of cash—American dollars—is next. I flip through the bills and guess there's at least $5000 in hundreds. I put the money beside the brick of marijuana and remove the last two items—a handgun and a spare magazine. I have no idea what kind of weapon it is, or what caliber bullets it fires. I know very little about weapons, and am generally opposed to people carrying them like we live in the Wild West, but out here...it brings a smile to my face.

In a land where more than a few of the denizens would be happy to make a meal of me, the ability to kill from a distance will keep me alive and out of digestive tracts. It could also help feed me. I count thirteen bullets in the magazine. Assuming the magazine already in the weapon is loaded, that's twenty six bullets.

Feeling a bit safer thanks to the satchel's contents, I feel bad judging my pilots, but can't help myself. When they're not ferrying doctors or tourists, they could be running drugs, or weapons. Or both. They were both kind men, to me at least, but I'm sure the company they kept was questionable at best.

What if there were more drugs on the plane?

The question comes from the recesses of my mind, but quickly moves to the forefront. What if there is a hidden compartment? Or drugs in the tires? Or in the seat cushions. If that's the case, then maybe someone will come looking for the plane.

I glance down at the dumped cocaine. *Crap.* Then I look to the bundle of cash. That should cover it.

And it changes my plan, at least for now. I'm not going to walk aimlessly, I'm going to wait, near the plane, and hope someone comes looking. Of course, that means I have to find the plane again and with my footprints erased by the storm, that's easier said than done. But for now...I'm going to rest, and relax. I look at the brick of marijuana, the notebook full of paper, and then the lighter.

I even have munchies...and my body is aching.

Screw it, I decide, and I set about rolling a joint for the first time, hoping it will do as much for my emotional turmoil as for my physical pain. Like any good doctor, I know the solution to any malady isn't found in symptom treatment, but in diagnosing and eradicating the cause. Anything else is just a temporary solution. But right now, it's better than drowning in the knowledge that, walk or stay, I'm likely never leaving this place.

5

I've never been high. Never been drunk. The idea of losing control didn't sit well with me.

Didn't. Past tense.

Lost in the Amazon rainforest, I'm feeling pretty good. Not about my chances of rescue, or even my survival, but just life in general. You know, like, life. It's all around me, like never before. The birds calling out. The monkeys. I think they're monkeys. I saw some of them high above a few minutes ago. And they had tails. So, I think they were monkeys, because monkeys are primates with tails.

Anywho, wait. Do apes have tails? Are there even apes in the rain forest? Yeah, there are, but not this rain forest. Not in South America. Not unless someone brought them here.

I gasp and cover my mouth. That's how the gorillas can be saved. Why hasn't anyone thought of that? Bring the gorillas here, let them do their thing, bingo-bango, the population recovers in a jungle so big that poachers don't matter.

Of course, there are hunters here. And even worse, logging companies slashing and burning the world's most important landscape, but still, gorillas could make a comeback here. I'm sure of it.

But maybe the monkeys wouldn't like that?

They didn't seem to like me, especially when I joined in with their hooting. They all kind of stopped and craned their heads toward me. They didn't say anything, because, you know, they're monkeys, but I got a strong sense of 'Who the hell do you think you are?' from them before they high-tailed it out of here.

Can monkeys 'high-tail' it? I think that phrase stems from deer. Because they raise their white tails when they run, confusing predators.

But the monkeys here have prehensile tails.

That's a funny word. "Prehensile." I laugh. "Pre-hen-sile... Prensile. Pretzel. Pretzel tail!" I snort as I polish off the cold pork sandwich from that satchel.

Oh man, I am high.

A laugh bubbles up from deep down. I don't curse. Not even in my head. Not much, anyway. I'm not really sure why. I think I just never wanted to slip up and offend anyone, especially on the job, or at the pantry, or at home, which pretty much covers the majority of my time on planet Earth.

"But not now!" I say with a grin. "Now it's just me and the monkeys, and maybe the gorillas someday. So, shit, shit, shit, shit, shit, and a happy fuck-a-doodle-do."

I'm not sure how long I've been here, in my little alcove, and I don't really care. I'm fed and comfortable, laid out on my poncho, surrounded by curtains of clothing hanging from the tall roots that remind me of that wall in Game of Thrones, but made of wood instead of ice.

"Winter is coming," I say with a chuckle before having an imaginary sword fight with The Mountain.

Gwen hates *Game of Thrones*. Honestly, I'm not sure why I enjoy it. All the swearing, and gore, and nudity, and general focus on the depravity of people, usually isn't my thing. I think I'm hoping that, in the end, good will win out even though the odds of that happening seem insurmountable.

"Oh, shit. Oh, damn." My hands squeeze the sides of my head. "What if I miss it? What if I'm here when it ends? I can stream it." My heartrate slows. "Oh, thank God, I can stream it. No spoilers, though." I point to the low hanging branches above me, from where the small monkeys scrutinized me. They're gone. I know that. But I can still see them, like a residue on reality. "No spoilers!"

I'm not just high, I'm *really* high.

This was a bad idea. The thought comes and goes like the breeze. I *know* it's a bad idea, to be out of my head in such a dangerous place. I just don't care.

Because the pain is dulled.

My body feels good.

And the agonizing thoughts about Gwen and Juni, and the imag-inings of my fate have faded into a psychedelic background, replaced by profound realizations about the universe, and for the first time ever, a questioning of my place in it.

"What if," I think aloud, "someone traveled beyond the edge of everything? What would be there? Just nothing? Would the vacuum of space end? Or reverse? Maybe God is there? Or, ohh, maybe you'd just end up on the far side of the universe, and have to make the whole trip over again. Or maybe there is no end to the universe. What does that say about the Big Bang? If the universe is expanding, there has to be an end, right? But maybe it's expanding faster than anyone can ever travel, and if you could travel that fast, by the time you reached the end, the Earth probably wouldn't exist anymore, because of Einstein, and then what would be the point, right?"

The monkey that arrived during the middle of my monologue, chewing on something that's crunchy on the outside and gooey on the inside—a bug, or fruit—critiques my theory by releasing a streaming fecal stew.

"Well, what do *you* think is beyond the universe's edge?"

The monkey goes rigid, its head whipping toward a series of high-pitched squeaks.

"If you're going to shit on my ideas, you could at least—"

The monkey leaps away.

"Fine," I shout. "We'll see how you like it when the gorillas move in! They know sign language, you know!" An image of signing gorillas getting frustrated with stupid monkeys sets me laughing.

Those were warning calls.

"Pfft. They're just afraid of thinking for a change."

Something is coming.

A predator.

"I ain't got time to bleed," I say, laughing. "Because I'm a sexual Tyrannosaurus."

My smile falters when the head of a snake slips around the root wall, and flicks its forked tongue in my direction.

"Did I say you could taste me?"

The snake slithers further out, its body tapering out to the width of a candlepin bowling ball. How much further can constrictors expand? I've seen photos of snakes that have swallowed farm animals, and on occasion, people. But I think those are anacondas. "My anaconda don't want none, unless you got buns, hon."

The snake turns toward me, not because of my poorly sung Sir Mix-a-Lot, but because that flicking tongue smells something tasty. I don't think it's me. I'm pretty sure all the blood was washed away in the deluge. And if it was following the scent of blood, it would be more interested in my clothing.

My eyes widen. It's after my pork sandwich. I look down at the foil wrapping and the few nuggets of pork it still holds. I pick up a piece and toss it toward the boa. "Here you go, buddy."

The chunks of meat sail past the snake. The third biffs its forehead and bounces away. The snake flinches back, as the rest of its body slides into view. At least twenty feet long.

I start singing Hall & Oates' *Maneater*, and realize that I like movies, TV, and music a lot more when I'm stoned. What other parts of my personality have I been suppressing? "I'm kind of a goody two shoes, old fuddy duddy," I tell the snake. It's unimpressed and unmoved by my words. Its long body coils up, jaw flexing.

Even high, I can tell its warming up for a strike.

"Really, man? I'm too big to eat."

I *think.*

But I'm not too big to kill.

Maybe I should let it? There're worse ways to go than asphyxiation. Dehydration. Starvation. Infection. They're all slow and painful. This would be quick, and I'd be dead by the time it tried and failed to eat me. Its bite would hurt, but how long would it take to die? A few minutes?

"I can't let you do that," I say. "I have to at least try to get home. You understand?"

It doesn't. The snake inches closer, nearly within range.

I pull my bare feet back. "Really? Not cool, man. Not cool."

I reach out for my backpack, loop my fingers around the strap and start dragging it toward me. The snake redirects its attention to the orange pack, flicking its tongue.

The handgun is within reach.

The machete, too.

But once I've got the backpack shield between me and the snake, I reach for the smoldering remains of my notebook-paper joint. What are they called when they're this short? A roach?

I don't really think getting higher will help, though it could make death a little less unpleasant. I just pick it up, wondering why anyone would name it a 'roach,' and suck in a lungful of mind-altering smoke. "Weed gets a bad rap," I tell the snake, coughing out the smoke while deciding to recommend it to all my patients, which could just be monkeys. "I blame Reagan."

The serpent doesn't care.

Sensing the snake's building tension, I slide my cross-legged shins in behind the backpack and try to make myself small behind it. I feel like a kid again, hiding from my friends, the king of manhunt once more. I was a master of stealth and concealment. Not that I can hide from the snake. It might not have the best eyes, but it can smell-taste me, and sense my every movement as a vibration in the ground.

My next inhalation polishes off the roach. Ashes fall to the ground while non-cancer causing—maybe even anti-cancer causing—smoke swirls in my lungs.

A hiss is followed by an impact that feels a little bit like Rocky just slugged the backpack. I peek over the backpack's top, eyeing the snake, whose head is three times the size of my fist. Its hooked, needle-sharp teeth are snagged in the pack's fabric, top and bottom.

The wide-jawed snake senses it hasn't struck anything living. It thrashes back and forth, trying to dislodge itself. A closed-mouth snort launches twin, upside down geysers of smoke onto the snake. It flails harder, more panicked than pissed.

Doesn't like the smoke, I decide, and I unleash a long stream of pot fumes into its face and open mouth.

"Embrace the high," I say, when the last of the smoke has left my lungs. I follow the sentence with a string of coughs that shakes my body and the backpack, jostling the snake loose.

The boa snaps back, twists away, and hauls non-ass back into the forest.

I chase it away with a lazy, "Don't do drugs!"

I spend the next two hours talking to myself, and the monkeys, and the snake that left and never came back. About everything and nothing. I can't remember most of it, which is fine with me, because as it starts to wear off, reality descends.

I'm still lost.

Still separated from my family.

On the plus side, my clothing, socks, and shoes are relatively dry, and the humidity has tapered off a little. I don't regret turning to marijuana for help. It kept me out of the slough of despond, and its lingering effects are helping keep my thoughts centered on hope and action rather than despair.

For now.

By the time I'm dressed and packed up, reality is a little clearer and a lot more depressing.

"You've only been here for a day," I tell myself, disappointed in my weakness, and already hankering for another mental escape. "Man up and move."

I turn in the direction from which I think I fled the airplane, take two steps, and then remember the jaguar. Why was I going back to the plane? Because Matheus might have been in cahoots with drug dealers who would move Heaven and Earth to retrieve their drug plane, which might be laden with a million dollars' worth of cocaine...or a jaguar.

Feeling certain the big cat wouldn't simply abandon a plane full of meat, I shift plans again and head in the opposite direction.

Destination: who knows where.

6

Humming a tune reminds me that I'm still in a world where technology exists. I *could* listen to music on my phone. I've got a wide assortment of tunes downloaded. But that would use up the battery and prevent me from calling for help in the future—doubtful, but maybe—and looking at photos of Gwen and Juni, which I'm going to try to do as little as possible. Because seeing their faces hurts. A lot.

To protect the phone and save the battery, I powered it down and sealed it in a Ziploc bag I used to carry vitamins. I then wrapped it in a shirt and packed it at the core of my backpack. I'm pretty sure it would survive a drop from a cliff, of which there are few. The terrain here is home to endless trees, some hills, and a network of rivers and streams, but nothing as dramatic as a mountain or cliff. Further west, where the Amazon crosses the Brazilian border into Peru—home of the tribal people I'd hoped to help—the Andes make the topography more dramatic.

When my humming repeats the same pop song to which I don't know the lyrics, I'm tempted to pull out the phone and play something— if only to reset my inner playlist. I've read that to get a song out of your head, you must mentally finish it. The problem is that I don't know this particular tune well enough to carry it through to the end. I'm just repeating the catchy chorus, again and again. It's enough to drive someone mad. Well, that and the blood-sucking insects, which have discovered my presence, but are currently being held at bay by a thick layer of bug spray and a large leaf I'm fanning through the air.

I decide to replace the song with something I know I can finish, and my mind leaps to Rudolph the Red-Nosed Reindeer. Halfway through, I regret the choice. In my mind, Bing Crosby is crooning out the tune, transporting my mind back to my childhood. I can smell the Christmas tree's pine scent. Feel the warmth of the Duraflame-fueled fireplace. Can feel the firmness of a gum drop chiseled from the roof of a gingerbread house. And then I'm home with Gwen, carving out our own holiday traditions—Bing Crosby on Pandora, Thai food, the Nutcracker in Boston, and sex. That Christmas Eve tradition led to Juni's birth the following September.

I clear my throat and mentally eradicate the painful memories conjured by the song. I turn my eyes skyward, but find only shades of luminous green. *I hate the jungle,* I decide. It's claustrophobic, like living in a covered pot of steamed broccoli.

I've been walking for hours, careful to rest, and drink, and listen to the animals and their warnings. I'd like to say I'm making good time, but I think that only makes sense if you have a direction and a destination in mind. I could be walking further from rescue for all I know.

If anyone is even looking for me.

"Don't go there," I tell myself, as I start to picture Gwen's current state of mind.

My next step transforms from a casual stride to a slow motion, Matrix-style bullet time, as my eyes drift back to the ground and I spot a trail of large ants. As much as I like animals, I'm not an expert on ants. When I was a kid, there were black ants, red ants, and their smaller, more peaceful cousins, the sugar ants. I spent enough time watching black and red ants battle to know their diminutive size belied savage tendencies. I've been bitten by both species and know both pack punches. But they're lightweights compared to the ants found in the Amazon. While not all species are dangerous, those that are, like bullet ants, whose bite feels akin to being shot, are best to be avoided.

I stretch my leg out, clearing the line and stepping onto the soft edge of a mound that looks like a root but is actually the outer edge of an ant hill. The jungle floor comes alive as thousands of ants charge the intruder.

Me.

I leap from foot to foot, shouting, the backpack and satchel slapping against me. Running like a gym teacher is shouting, 'Get your knees higher!' while prodding me with a taser, I prance away. Clear of the ants, I stop to brush away the few scaling my body, looking for flesh to bite. With my boots and belt cinched tight and my shirt tucked in, they'll have to reach my arms or neck to finish the job.

"Ack!" I swat the underside of my left arm and feel a small body crunch under my fingers. As a fiery pain mushrooms out from the bite, I shed my backpack, satchel, and shirt. I snap the shirt back and forth a few times and then brush my pants with it before snapping it back and forth again. Anyone watching me would likely think I'd lost my mind, but there's no one here to see my mania.

Confident I've defeated the enemy, I slip the sweat soaked T-shirt over my head again, tuck it in, and wonder for the hundredth time why I didn't bring a light, long-sleeved shirt.

Because I don't belong here.

Because I'm an idiot.

A stab of pain cuts my mental self-flagellation short. I twist the flesh of my arm for a few seconds. The skin is red, hot, and swollen, like a subdermal golf ball implant.

That's not good, but it could have been worse. Much worse.

No more humming, I decide. No more day-dreaming. No more looking for a sky that isn't there.

Depression settles on me along with the weight of my backpack. I want to lie down. In a bed. I'm tempted to settle down right here and wait for night, but I'm still too close to the ants. So I turn a hard ninety degrees and strike out once more, following the maze of trees, roots, and low-lying plant life, watching my step and damming my thoughts.

After twenty minutes, I have to hold my left arm out to keep the swollen bit from brushing against my shirt. Any contact hurts, but at least I haven't noted any other adverse effects. My shoulder starts to burn after just a few minutes, so I shorten the satchel's strap and position it under the arm, keeping it away from my side without any muscle work. The simple problem-solving encourages me. Makes me think that I can prevail, that I can overcome the challenges of this place.

Then I walk for hours, until my legs start to shake, and realize that if the immediate threats to my life don't get me, the jungle will still claim me in the long run. My water supply is exhausted. I've got food for a few days, if I ration it. But without H2O I'm going to be dead in three days. Granted, some people have lived longer without water, but not here, not where the heat sucks the water from your body and adds it to the undrinkable water that's heavy in the air. Best case scenario, I'll make it two days without water, and one of those will be spent immobilized and in pain.

It will start with extreme thirst—where I am now. Then I'll become irritable and confused. I'm pretty much there already. That'll be follow-ed by sunken eyes, low blood pressure, and a racing pulse as my heart tries to pump sludge through my veins. When I eventually break down into tears, there won't be any. A fever will stop me in my tracks, followed by delirium, hallucinations, unconsciousness, and then death.

So, as much as I'd like to stop, peel off my wet clothing, and fall asleep beneath the mosquito net I forgot that I'd packed, I need to keep moving. Need to find water, and then find a way to purify it.

Following the path of least resistance, I trudge down a slope. I'm pretty sure I've seen people hack Amazonian vines apart to find water, so I slice through every one I come across, dejected each time the severed vegetation fails to produce even a drop.

Twenty steps later, my boot slips over the top of a damp root. I twist as I fall, reaching for a handhold and finding nothing. My left side takes the brunt of the graceless landing. The satchel that had been protecting my arm now crushes the swollen bite. An unbidden scream erupts from my lungs, the sound of it absorbed by the lush foliage, but loud enough to silence the chorus of animals I only now notice when they fall silent.

My head and arm throb when I push myself up, wounded by the ant and dehydration. Anger swells.

I'm a calm person. I have excellent bedside manners. I've suffered injuries, personal setbacks, and a broken heart or two without ever losing my cool. But here, with no one to see, I go ballistic. Wielding the machete, I wage war against the root that dropped me faster than Mike Tyson could. Shards of wood fly through the air with each solid whack of the blade. It's not until the machete gets stuck in the root that I look away.

It's just a glance, and it takes two tugs of the machete for what I saw to sink in, but when it does, I forget all my anger. For the first time since crashing, I feel genuine hope.

Ignoring the pain in my head and arm, I push myself back onto unsteady feet and stare down the clear path.

People make paths.

And this one is clear enough to assume it's utilized fairly often.

After prying the machete loose, I follow the path, which mercifully leads downhill. I walk in silence, listening for any signs of habitation until the animal chorus returns, drowning out any chance that I'll hear signs of people before stumbling on them.

My pace quickens, becoming a jog.

My left arm hurts from my shoulder to my elbow, but I ignore it.

Ten minutes into the run, I tire. My vision fades until I stop to catch my breath.

How long could the path be?

Miles?

A hundred miles?

Despair hooks its claws into the upper layers of my skin, threatening to burrow deeper.

Maybe I can just sit and wait for someone else to come along? The path looks worn enough that people must come through here on a daily basis.

Just a little further, I think. The sun is starting to set, and the lower levels of the jungle grow dark long before the canopy. Walking during the day is dangerous enough. I'm not about to walk at night. But maybe I won't have to.

A hundred feet later, I find the trail's end.

At a stream.

It's a game trail, I realize, and I fall to my knees beside the gurgling creek.

My mind starts to drift back toward rage, but the sound and smell of water calls to me like a siren, filling me with lust that could end in death.

But what choice do I have?

I'm going to die if I don't drink.

And while the water itself might lead to my demise, it will be later than if I don't drink.

It goes against my medical instincts—I know my body has no defense against the bacteria in this water—but dehydration will kill me for sure. And while I might have to face dehydration from diarrhea at the hands of this water, it will come days after I would have already been dead. If I survive, and my body acclimates, I can drink with a little less concern, and stand a better chance at surviving long term.

I cup my hands into the water, bring the clear fluid to my face, and then splash it onto my skin. The cool water is refreshing, and resisting the urge to drink it is even harder, but it also wakes me up.

"Just hold off," I tell myself. "Wait until morning."

I spot a nearby tree, free of ants and surrounded by a veritable fortress of roots. I settle in for the night, clothes off and drying, protected by mosquito netting.

Sitting there, exhausted but kept from sleep by pain and worry, my thoughts turn to death.

What comes next, after this?

Will it be worse? Or better? I'm not sure how it could be worse. Even a forever of nothing would be better. Before I was born, I just wasn't. Would it be so horrible to return to that sweet nothing?

Gwen wouldn't be there. Nor would Juni. Nor any of the other people I've loved and who have loved me. If all those people simply cease to exist, what's the point? "What's the fucking point?" I say to no one.

Or am I talking to someone? If there's a God who's omnipotent and omniscient, is He here? Is He listening?

"If you are," I say. "You're an asshole. This is bullshit. You know that, right?"

Realizing I'm saying a prayer in my own, strange way, I dig through the satchel and remove the notebook. I feel a little disgusted by it. This is what I've come to? Praying to a creator that doesn't exist?

Screw it.

"Here's the deal. I'm not going to say anything nice about you, or this shitty world. I'm not going to God-damned lie, because what's the point, right? I am going to write down what I want…what I *fucking need*. When that happens, we'll talk. Until then, fuck you."

Lacking a pen, I dig my hand through the layers of leaves and into the damp earth. Using my soiled finger as a pencil, I scrawl four words—the fourth of which catches me a little off guard.

Why did I write that? I wonder. Lacking an eraser, I leave it be.

I don't think I'm asking for much. For God, my demands should be simple.

After putting the notebook away, sleep comes fast and hard. I never once stop to ponder what creatures might use the game trail, and which predators might hunt them.

7

I *think* I'm awake. The darkness of a dreamless sleep remains. So does the silence. *Where am I?* I wonder. My bed is hard and uneven. The air is thick. I open my mouth to call for Gwen when my memory catches up to my waking mind.

I'm in the jungle. Lost. On my own. And damn near dehydrated.

I can smell the water nearby. Can feel its coolness on my tongue. In my throat. I'm not generally a passionate person. Gwen has compared me to a Vulcan on more than one occasion. It's not that I'm unkind, or even cold, but I don't get fired up about much. But water …I'm lusting for it.

Did I take some water from the stream already? Or do I still need to?

I can't remember.

I think I still need to. I was resisting temptation before, but now the urge to drink is all I can think about. My cells are craving water. It won't be long before they stop functioning well, and soon after that, they'll stop functioning entirely. It's the unending heat, squeezing out what little moisture my body has left to spare.

If I don't drink tonight, I might very well die in the morning.

Just do it, I tell myself. Save yourself now and figure out how to save yourself from the negative effects of drinking Amazonian water later…when you're *still alive.*

I'm about to push myself up, crawl to the stream, and plunge my face into the water and drink. But something stops me. An instinct. Something is wrong. Other than my desperate thirst.

But I can't see anything. Can't hear anything. Despite being surrounded by strong scents, I can't seem to smell anything aside from water. But I should be surrounded by something else. Something that's missing. Being asleep, I didn't hear the change, didn't register the warning of complete silence. Hoping to not be discovered in the dark, the jungle's creatures have fallen silent.

My heart thumps a bit harder, and for a moment, it's all I can hear.

I nearly shout at the sudden sound of running.

It's followed by a thump, a moment of thrashing and grunting, and then silence again.

My imagination conjures images of a horrible beast, rending some wide-eyed jungle denizen's body limb from limb. It's inhuman. Dreadlock hair coats its body. Yellow eyes twitch back and forth. A hairless canine face is coated in blood. Crouching over its kill, a Disney cartoon in my mind's eye—not nearly enough to stave off the monster's hunger—how long before it discovers me, blind and defenseless?

I strain to hear the cracking of bones, the tearing of flesh, or the pop of joints. But there's none of that. It's just quiet. Peaceful.

A deep breath testing for blood in the air comes up negative. Was it killed in the water?

All at once, the jungle screams back to life.

I flinch, and scream, and twist around, seeing the monster reaching out hooked claws for my face.

But there's nothing there.

As the remnants of my shriek blend in with the calls of animals I can't identify, I try to stop my body from shaking. Drawing the gun from the satchel and holding it helps. A little. But the monster of my waking nightmare could be two feet from my face and I'd never see it.

I consider giving the lighter a flick—if I can find it. In the dense, dark jungle, it would shine like the sun. It would create a beacon for predators to follow. So I decide to let dehydration shrivel me up into an unappetizing human raisin.

The tactic works until the thirst in my throat becomes a pain in my gut. Eyes clenched shut, I do my best to endure it. It feels like there's an electric eel loose in my stomach, wriggling and launching electric assaults on my insides.

Think about Gwen, I tell myself. *Think about home.* The emotional pain of worrying about home will distract me. But I'm not even able to wallow. I see my wife for just a moment, dressed in sweatpants, head clasped in her hands, tired rings under her worried eyes. And then she's gone, replaced by the anguish of a dying body.

How long until daylight?

How long until I'm brave enough to approach the stream and drink?

And when I'm refreshed and rehydrated, how long will it take before bacteria assaults me? Will I have a day to recover? An hour? Will I recover at all? Despite all my medical knowledge, there aren't a lot of lessons in med school that apply to surviving in the wilderness.

I linger in an indecisive quagmire for what feels like an hour, but is probably closer to ten minutes. Pain has a way of stretching out time. It's the sound of feet on wet earth that pulls me back to the world beyond agony.

The first set of footfalls is followed by several more.

It's a pack. But of what?

Snuffling sounds fill the darkness, followed by slurping, gurgling, and greedy drinking.

It's too much. I can't stop myself.

After I slide from the mosquito netting, my hand acts autonomously, digging into my pocket, retrieving the lighter and flicking it to life. Several large creatures, their swine-like backsides pointed in my direction, stand by the stream's edge, heads lowered. Watching their throats constrict with each gulp, I nearly cry out.

One of them, probably sensing the light, lifts its head and cranes its long-snouted face around. The beast is huge. Probably a good five hundred pounds. In my current state, it could make short work of me. Lucky for me, it's a tapir, a pig-like herbivore with few natural predators aside from the jaguar, black caiman crocs, and man. Given the tapir's lack of panic at seeing me, I'm guessing they don't come across people often. Or perhaps it senses that I'm near death.

Whatever the case might be, the tapirs aren't about to eat me, and their calm presence suggests that whatever predator hunted here earlier has taken its prize and moved on.

Lighter in hand, I crawl from my alcove and work my way toward the stream. All five tapirs stop drinking and watch my slow progress, their dripping mouths turned up in grins, their dark eyes twinkling in the firelight. The earth bends beneath my hands and knees. I slip a few times, but catch myself on roots.

I place the lighter on the ground, nestling it in a cradle of mud. Then I lean down and stare at the flickering orange water flowing past. The tapirs watch, their attention unwavering, waiting to see if the pitiful creature will save itself.

Their grins turns up higher.

Forget what you know, I tell myself, *and live a little longer.* It's a sucky choice, but it's the only real option. I lower my face to the water, open my lips and suck in a mouth full of water. It's a little bitter. Grit tickles my tongue. But I can already feel my body absorbing the liquid, crying out for more. I swallow and lower my head again.

The tapirs accept me as just another mammal having a drink in the dark, hoping that something doesn't sneak up and eat me. One by one, they lower their heads and drink, having no fear about what the water might do to them. And then, one by one, they leave.

It's not until my belly slogs with each movement that I realize I've kept the lighter on this entire time. I close the Zippo with a quick snap and then flinch from a sudden pain brought on by the heated metal. The lighter falls from my hand. I hear it land with a thud, rather than a splash, which is a relief, but I can't see it.

I hold my hand over the ground in front of me and sweep it back and forth, a human metal detector. But instead of searching for magnetic fields, I'm feeling for heat. It doesn't take long to recover the still-warm lighter, but losing it even for a short amount of time fills me with a deep fear. Of darkness. Of being powerless. Of a primitive life.

Being born in the twentieth century suits me. I'm not sure I could have survived in a world without electricity, or toilets, or water filters.

But I'm going to have to, I think, clutching the lighter and crawling my way back to the alcove. At some point in my genetic history, my ancestors hunted, and killed, and lived by firelight. Or not. The only real difference between them and me is state of mind. Given my First-World upbringing,

I'm probably taller, stronger, and in far better physical condition than any of them. I just need to change the way I think, and stop being so afraid.

Then again, my ancient ancestors probably had an average lifespan of thirty-something years and never ventured into the depths of the wilderness alone.

I crawl into my alcove once more, slip beneath my netting, and fall asleep before I can wonder if I'm going to need an Ambien.

When I wake in the morning, I do so with a string of curses, some of which I've never used before in my life. Not because I'm in immediate danger, but because it's raining.

8

The fever starts ten hours later.

After waiting out the rain, dressed only in boxers and mosquito netting, I spent the day hiking, this time following the stream on the not-very-straight, but fairly narrow path to nowhere in particular.

Trying to apply logic to my course, I decide that the stream will eventually lead to a larger stream, and then a river, and another river, and eventually to some proper portion of the Amazon that's been settled by people who have already emerged from the jungle and are attempting to join the modern world. The winding path isn't exactly efficient, but I'm pretty confident that it's my best chance of finding people.

I trudge downstream until the jungle grows darker once again, and the fever makes itself known with a chill.

Exhausted from carrying my gear over many miles of uneven, saturated terrain, I settle down beside a lump of earth that hints at some-thing solid buried beneath. A tangle of roots snakes through the soil, holding it in place and creating a partial ceiling above me. In the jungle, it's as good a place as any to ride out a fever.

The heaviest part of my gear is also the most recent addition. During this morning's storm, I put my poncho to a very different kind of use. After tying the open hood shut with a tight knot, I inverted it and collected at least three gallons of water. Had I thought to do this on my first day in the jungle, my blooming fever wouldn't be a concern.

I'm not a fan of hindsight, so I try not to dwell on what could have been. The clean water held in the poncho improves my odds of surviving the next few days—if I'm not eaten.

I passed a few game trails during the day's hike, but I see no evidence of recent visitors here.

There's just the endless jungle, the stream, the creatures living in the world above, and me.

As my body quivers from chills that are growing in frequency and severity, I hang the mosquito netting from the earthen mound and attach it to the jungle floor, creating a small pocket of insect-free air. With all my gear stowed inside, I won't have to worry about having my blood sucked.

Lining the dirt floor with large leaves takes just ten more minutes, but it nearly undoes me. By the time I'm done, my body is shaking. I slip inside my temporary home—not fit even for the First Little Pig—and I lie down. Thirty seconds later, my bowels prod me back to my feet and outside.

Stark naked, I clutch a tree, squat down, and unleash a torrent to rival the morning's rain. After a quick wash in the stream, I return to the tent, hoping that's the worst of it.

It's not.

As night falls, the routine is so ingrained that I'm able to do it in the dark. Shit, rinse, rest, repeat. In between attempts at sleep, and hydrating, I venture out to expel bacteria I invited into my body. During my sixth excursion, I add vomiting to the mix. It's so violent that anything nearby with ears knows I'm here.

With morning not far off—*how do I know that?*—I move from station to station on my hands and knees, shaking, delirious, and too tired to be afraid.

As desperate as I was to drink a day ago, I'm now tempted to stop drinking entirely. Dry things up. But I know that won't stop my body from leaching the fluid it needs from my organs. As horrible as being a human lawn sprinkler is, the faster I expel everything from my body, the faster this will be over.

It's a nice theory. Maybe even true with access to modern medicine, but out here, it's a fantasy.

Shit, rinse, rest, repeat.

For three God damn days.

Days without wind.

Without rain.

Without food.

The air is moist and heavy with the scent of my own waste. I haven't seen another living thing on the jungle floor during my time here. I suspect even the curious jaguar would find the odor of my personal sewer to be repellant. A troop of monkeys ventured into view, scrabbling over the branches above. I watched them until the pack leader stopped as though slapped, and slowly backtracked and leapt away.

In a jungle filled with deadly creatures and plants, I'm currently the most abhorrent thing in town.

On the morning of the fourth day, when my stomach hurts from hunger, rather than from nausea, I know the worst of it is over. As the sun rises above the canopy, I nibble at my last energy bar. When I've eaten a quarter of it, I resist the urge to down the whole thing, and save it for later. With nothing else to eat, I'm going to have to ration the bar until I figure out an alternative. Best case scenario, with all the calories I've burned while sick, and will burn while hiking, the bar will last me two days, tops.

I assess the water situation and find myself with a half-gallon, which will also last me two days. It's not enough to stave off dehydration, but it will keep me alive.

Health returns in a matter of hours, and by the time I sense the sun is directly overhead, I'm feeling vigorous compared to the past few days. After packing up and striking out along the stream, fueled by a renewed hope and a desire to escape my own stench, I learn that 'vigorous' is a gross exaggeration. Relief is not the same as rejuvenation.

Lightheadedness stumbles me to a stop.

I need calories. Today. Right now. So I eat the rest of the energy bar. It's enough to stave off my growing weakness, but it's not going to sustain me for long. Not if I keep burning calories.

But I can't stop, either.

The jungle here looks no different than it did days ago. I've seen no signs of human habitation, and few animals since I shared a drink with the tapirs…if they were real. It's occurred to me that the smiling beasts could have been a hallucination.

Do what you have to, I tell myself. *One day at a time.*

I drink half the water, and feel almost normal when I'm done. I'll try to ration the rest, but I'm not sure I'll make it through the night without finishing it. And then what? Wait for more rain? Drink from the stream in which I've spent the past three days rinsing diarrhea off myself? Hope that my body can handle the bacterial soup better the second time around?

"One day at a time."

I make good time, maintaining as straight a path as possible while the stream twists and turns. The path of least resistance that formed the stream's course was a chaotic, coiling route with more turns than the Ebola virus.

After another hour, I notice that the jungle's sounds no longer startle me. Where living in the city leaves you immune to the sound of horns, sirens, and engines, a few days in the Amazon has left me acclimated to the sounds and smells of another world. What I'm not yet used to is the heat and humidity. They're relentless, leaving me slick and itchy.

Of course, the itchy could also be mosquito bites.

A memory makes me smile. I've known Gwen since I was seven, when her family moved to town and she joined my school. In the latter years of junior high, and the early years of high school, when other girls were...developing, Gwen had the physique of a boy. As a result, her nickname was 'mosquito bites.' The name's use ended on the first day of our junior year, after a summer of late...growth. My smile fades when I realize this is the first time I've thought about Gwen in nearly four days.

The jungle goes quiet.

I react by calmly crouching and listening.

My heartbeat remains steady.

This happens on occasion. Sometimes I hear distant struggles, but most of the time, the danger passes without me ever being aware of what triggered the silent alarm. Of course, the worst alarms are the non-silent variety, when the monkeys erupt into spasmatic wailing. I generally assume that means there's a jaguar or some kind of deadly snake nearby. When that happens, I draw my gun and wait. For silent alarms, I just pause, knowing that it's possible that *I* could be the cause.

But this time, it's not me.

Or a jaguar.

Or a snake.

The monkeys don't scream, but something does.

The sound is high-pitched, but nothing close to a monkey. The cry lasts just a second. I try to picture the kind of creature that could have made it, but struggle to picture it.

Doesn't matter, I decide. *Just keep moving.* The sound came from my left. With the stream on my right, continuing forward will take me away from the creature being killed, and whatever is killing it.

I make it five steps before pausing again.

My stomach aches with hunger.

I need to eat.

If something has made a kill, what's to stop me from taking it? I dig the gun out of my pocket and feel its deadly potential. There are meals all around me if I'm willing to kill them. Being far from a vegetarian, and on a path toward starvation, I decide to be proactive. Machete in my left hand, gun in my right, I take a step toward the sound's origin.

Then it cuts through the air, this time warbling with what sounds like syllables.

What kind of animal can—

I gasp.

It's a *person.*

A *woman!*

Without any thought, I sprint toward what I now recognize as a cry for help, crashing through brush with the same disregard for what lies ahead displayed by a silverback gorilla, but with a fraction of the size, strength, and speed.

9

The jungle conspires against me. Has been for days, but never so obviously. Every branch or low-lying plant I pass clings, slaps, and scratches me, turning what is meant to be a direct route into a chaotic, tumbling path. I'm pummeled by my backpack and satchel. The poncho-wrapped water cinched to my belt slaps against my thigh, throwing off my balance. A large leaf resists my passage like a backhanded slap from a giant. I nearly lose my grip on the gun and machete, but my white-knuckle grip doesn't relent.

I'm tempted to shed my gear, but I'm certain I'd never find it again.

And without it, out here...

Then again, maybe I won't need it at all. If there's a woman in danger, and I can help her, I might be free of this green hell before the sun sets.

Unless she dies before I can reach her.

If that happens, I'll need everything I have.

But what if my being slowed down by my gear is what prevents me from helping the woman?

Assaulted by the jungle and indecision, I charge onward, unable to alter my plans, for better or worse.

The next scream I hear is a string of words. Angry words. And I can't understand a single one of them. I can speak a few words and phrases in Portuguese—enough to get food, find a bathroom, or greet someone. It's not much, yet I have no trouble recognizing the language. Whoever lies ahead, she's *not* speaking Portuguese.

That she's speaking at all means there is at least one other person with her. But are they hostile, or also in danger?

Doesn't matter, I decide, and when the terrain slopes downward, I let the weight of my gear turn me into a cannon ball.

Just as I start to feel my weakened body cramping up, the ground cover thins, revealing a sight that makes me sick, and triggers some kind of deep rage that makes me forget about my physical condition.

There are two men. Naked aside from colorful arm bands. Tribal people. Light brown skin free of tan lines. Short black hair. Their backs are to me, one of them standing, the other face down...on top of the woman.

She's slapping and clawing at the man atop her, who's indifferent to her struggle as he attempts to position himself between her forced open legs.

The woman's screaming, and the standing man's laugh, conceals the sound of my approach.

I catch sight of fabric lying on the ground beside two discarded long bows and a wad of arrows. The woman's meager clothing lies strewn on the trunk of a nearby tree.

The standing man hears me a moment before I strike. He whirls around, surprise in his younger-than-expected eyes, framed by red paint. The top of his head is shaved, half way back. Sticks poke out from the sides of his nose, like a jaguar's whiskers. A pattern of red paint covers the front of his hairless body, covering arms, torso, and legs, but not his erect penis.

I throw myself at the man, and when he yelps in surprise, I unleash my anger as a loud roar. As I sail through the air, I finally realize that I have no idea what I'm doing. I've never been in a fight. MMA fights— even the commercials for them—make me sick to my stomach. I've never thrown a punch, never wrestled a friend, never fended off a bully. My attack is guided by instinct alone, and part of that instinct is to protect myself.

Just before impact, I curl in on myself, arms raised over my head, body coiled into a ball.

My target, easily fifty pounds lighter and a foot shorter than me, takes the full kinetic force of my airborne body and discovers Newton's first law of motion when my forward momentum comes to an abrupt stop against his body. He careens away with an anguished shout. Given the force of our collision, and the part of his body I struck, it's a safe bet that he's got a broken rib or two.

And I hope he does, because that should take the fight out of him.

I land atop a carpet of damp, rotting leaves. Then I push myself up, fighting tired muscles and the weight of my gear.

The man lying atop the woman is frozen in place, as is the woman beneath him, whose face I see for the first time. She's young. Maybe early twenties. A red-painted forehead hangs over her dark brown eyes like sunset through smoke. Her eyebrows are pinched up, and her lips frozen in a grimace, but in her eyes, I see hope.

Because of me.

"Let her go!" I shout, my voice raspy and loud.

The man can't understand a word I'm saying, but he understands my intent. He leaps off the woman, who is naked and makes no move to cover herself, and he faces me.

He's older than the man I knocked to the ground, but their similar faces, haircuts, and red-painted bodies speak of a tribal relationship, if not a familial one. I glance at the young man, still on the ground, clutching his side. The men have the same eyes, cheeks, and body types. *A father training his son in the ways of debauchery,* I decide. Both men, and the woman, are hairless from the eyebrows down to their wide feet. I'm not sure if that's from shaving, or from genetics, but it makes all of them, even the older man, look younger than they probably are.

The father, body low, arms spread wide, starts to walk around me. He's calm. A hunter. I see confusion in his eyes as he looks me over, though. He lingers on my facial hair, a few days thick, and then on the machete in my hand. He doesn't even glance at the gun.

These are uncontacted people.

Nothing about them hints at previous contact with the outside world. No trinkets. No T-shirts. No plastic doo-dads. And no recognition.

The man stalks around me, not closing the distance, but working his way around toward the bow while also putting his son directly behind me.

While I have no experience fighting, these two men are clearly hunters—killers—who I've managed to catch off guard. Despite what I might look like to them, they're not going to back down or run away in fear.

"Chema don richo," the woman says, eyes locked on me. It sounds like a warning.

In a knock-down drag out fight, I'm going to lose. Armed or not, my body is weak, and I'm as coordinated as a drunk squirrel.

I need to scare them, I decide.

Machete raised, I step toward the man, shouting. I meant it to sound like a roar, but to me it sounds silly.

The father jumps back, but doesn't retreat. His eyes linger on the blade, understanding its deadly potential, but like a hyena harassing a lion, he remains just out of reach and keeps circling.

"Shazi!" the woman shouts, just as the sound of running bare feet reaches my ears.

I swing out with the machete, feel the subtlest of resistance, and then hear a shout.

I've struck the boy.

Before I can assess the damage, the woman shouts again, and I swing in the other direction, this time striking nothing. The father leaps out of the way, no trace of fear in his eyes.

I stab the machete at him and shout, "I don't want to hurt you!" I point the gun toward a random patch of forest. "Go... Go!"

The circling continues.

I manage a glance back at the son. A thin red line, dripping wet, cuts across his stomach. It's hardly a scratch. Nothing a few band-aids couldn't handle. But another inch closer and he'd have been eviscerated.

When the father starts speaking harshly to the younger man, I'm pretty sure this is the message being relayed.

While the moment is a life lesson for the boy, I find it profoundly disturbing. I nearly killed a man. I've spent the majority of my life avoiding violence and preventing death and suffering. And now, to save one life, I might need to take another, or two.

But that's not right either. This isn't choosing one life over two. It's an even split. Either the woman and I will live, or the father and his boy. Unless they never intended to kill the woman. I have no idea what is considered normal social behavior by these people. But I know what's right, and that their sexual assault was unwanted.

I have to stop them, even if it means killing them.

The gun shakes in my hand as I raise it toward the father's chest. He watches it rise, but shows no fear.

"Leave," I growl, and the sound of my desperate voice seems to unnerve him for just a moment. Then he's moving again, and so is his son.

"Damn you," I whisper, and pull the trigger.

Nothing happens.

Had these two men been from the modern world, they'd understand what I just attempted and would have already rushed me. But the man doesn't even register my attempted murder. He just remains calm and steady, now just ten feet from their scant clothing and bows and arrows. I hear the boy moving again, and catch movement out of my left side peripheral vision.

They're both heading for the bows.

Let them go, I think, maneuvering to face them both, putting the woman at my back.

They pick up the pace once they're around me. When they dash for the bows, taking their eyes off me, I look over the gun, find the safety switch, and flick it off.

They're both lifting bows and nocking arrows when I point the gun forward. I could kill them. Both of them. And the woman behind me, now pleading, would like me to do it.

Kill or be killed.

That's the way of the jungle.

But it's not my way.

I raise the gun above their heads and shout again. "Leave! Now!"

As arrows are turned in my direction, I pull the trigger.

The boom drops both men to the ground, their arrows fired wild, disappearing into the trees. They shout back and forth at each other, eyes wide and searching for the sound's source.

I shout again, drawing their attention back toward me. Then I pull the trigger again.

The men snap back, eyeing me, understanding that I am the source of a sound so loud it hurts their ears.

I grit my teeth at them and hiss. I don't really put any thought into the action, but it feels right. Like a warning.

"Leave!" I shout, and then I fire the weapon again.

The men scramble away from me, twisting and fumbling in the dirt. Then they bolt for the trees, loincloths and weapons left behind. I watch them go, making sure they don't stop, slow, or change course. When I can no longer see them, I flip the safety back on, slip the hand gun into my pocket, and turn around.

The woman stands before me, stark naked, horrified, and wielding a small blowgun that's pointed at my chest.

10

"Whoa," I say, hoping the tone of my voice communicates my apprehension. I take a slow step back, lowering myself and my weapons. "Whoa..."

I crouch slowly, watching the blowgun track my every motion. On the outside, it's not a very intimidating weapon, but most Amazonian tribes use poisoned darts for hunting. A puff of air is all it would take for her to kill me.

"It's okay." I keep my voice soothing, like I'm helping Juni come down from a tantrum. "I'm not going to hurt you."

I place the machete on the ground. The gun, too, even though she doesn't know what it is. I have no intention of hurting this woman, even to save my own life.

I'm not sure the same can be said for her. Free of the men assaulting her, she has the steady gaze of a hunter. The father and son must have caught her off guard, preventing her from using the blowgun in self-defense.

Hands empty, I extend my open palms and take a few more lowered steps back. We can't speak the same language, but some things, like smiles, laughs, and open palms are understood by all cultures around the world. They're behaviors developed by our earliest ancestors and hardwired into the DNA of every human being since.

The woman watches me with confused eyes. Perhaps she thought I was claiming her for myself. Maybe she's rattled by my appearance, gear, and the thunderous report of a modern weapon. She's still afraid, but not enough to kill me.

I stop beside her discarded clothing. There's not much to it. Some fabric and twine. I'm not even sure how it would be worn. But it's hers.

So I crouch down, pick it up, and offer the bundle to her.

The blowgun angles downward. The woman squints at me, suspicious, but she also turns her lips aside and lets out the breath she'd been holding.

I inch toward her, my posture submissive, bundle extended.

"Chut," she says, her voice forceful.

I'm pretty sure she's told me to 'stop,' so I do, and I wait for further instructions. She eyes me up and down, perplexed, but still fearful. A moment ago, I wielded a power the likes of which she'd never seen nor heard, and now I am submitting to her authority. I'm not sure if all Amazonian tribes are patriarchal, but global history suggests that would be the case. If so, she's probably never seen a man act like this.

If she even sees me as a man.

My hair, clothing, gear, and the gun's boom are probably as alien to her as a UFO to the civilized world. My submission to her is probably even stranger. I'm powerful enough to frighten away two skilled hunters, but I cringe before a lone woman. I realize that's a sexist point of view, especially given the blowgun pointed in my direction, but they are primitive tribal people. Then again, maybe the stereotypes about indigenous peoples are as rife with errors as they were when the Europeans slaughtered millions of 'savages' in the Americas. For all I know, this woman's tribe of actual Amazons is as matriarchal as Wonder Woman's fictional Amazonians.

The woman makes a "ffft" sound with her lips, motions to the clothing and then waves her hand toward herself. She wants what I'm offering, but doesn't want me coming any closer.

I toss the garment to her feet and take a step back.

Her unwavering gaze locked on me, she bends down, picks up the cloth, and then with the suddenness of a surprised deer, springs into motion.

She bounds away, leaping foliage and disappearing before I can shout a desperate, "No! Wait!"

A few seconds later, I can't even hear her.

"Shit," I grumble. "God damnit!"

That woman...even the two men...

They were my best chance of escaping the jungle. They might still live in tribes, but they must have encountered civilization at some point, or know people who have.

My eyes linger on the spot where the woman had stood naked before me. Two things leap out—her footprints, and a splash of bright red.

After retrieving the machete and the gun, I crouch by her footprints and move aside the detritus covering the red object. It's an arm band, I think, like the ones the men were wearing. It's made from tightly woven feathers. Bright red, green, yellow, and blue. The work is intricate and beautiful. I suspect the woman would have worn it on her upper arm. It just barely fits onto my wrist.

My attention shifts to the woman's footprints. There's a trail of them, leading into the brush and the jungle beyond. I'm by no means a tracker. I have trouble finding my keys most days. But the woman's footprints are easy to follow. And if I can follow her tracks, the two hunters I sent running will have no trouble finding her either.

If she doesn't kill me, I might even be able to communicate my need to escape the jungle.

Before heading out, I collect the hunters' long arrows, wrapping their black tips—what I assume is poison—in a shirt, and then inserting the bundle in my backpack, feathered end protruding three feet from the top. I take both bows, strapping one around my chest and keeping the other in my hand.

Unlike the gun, I have used a bow in the past, but it's been a long time since wielding a compound bow at Camp Keswick in the Berkshires. Curiosity drives me to pull an arrow from my oversized, makeshift quiver. I nock it, draw the string back and take aim at a nearby tree. The bow feels sturdy, and the string is taut. Its potential power strains against my weary muscles.

With a *thwip*, the arrow flies, strikes the tree, and shatters. The firm, dry wood would make short work of an animal's—or a human's—soft flesh, but it doesn't stand any more chance against the thick tree than the doomed Cessna. I'm tempted to nock an arrow and keep it at the ready during my travels, but if the woman spots me coming, and I'm sure she will, I don't want to look like I'm hunting her.

I leave the men's meager garments on the ground and set out after the woman. It's a risky move. She could kill me on sight. Could send a hunting party after me. But she's still my best chance of survival. I did save her. Maybe not her life. I have no idea if the two men would have killed her. But I'm sure rape is as abhorrent to victims in the depths of the jungle as it is to those in the rest of the world. I'm hoping gratitude will transform into mercy.

Following the trail of footprints is easy for the first mile. She ran the entire distance. Each print left a deep impression, visible even where the leaf litter is thickest.

I lose her trail in a stand of trees with a wide-reaching network of roots. She used the natural formation to depart the ground and erase her trail. It's possible I could traverse the border of the root-laden land, but it covers a lot of terrain, and her passage through it seems like an intentional attempt at leaving no trail. If that's the case, I doubt I'll find any trace of her.

But her disappearance isn't my only problem. The search for her has left me exhausted once more. My muscles, pumping with adrenaline for the past thirty minutes, now ache and twitch with every step. I'm going to need to rest soon. And as easy as the woman's path was to follow, the tracks left by my boots might as well be neon signs reading, "The white man you want to kill went this way."

I've never really had a nemesis or an enemy. I get along with most people. But now, two out of the three people I've encountered in the rainforest probably want me dead. And I'm not sure about the third.

What are my options?

Reverse course back to the scene of the crime and then follow my tracks back to the stream and continue to follow it. That's probably doable, but I have no idea where the stream will lead, and my path will be easy to track. How long before the hunters return with friends?

Will they even come back at all?

I made an impression. Of that there is no doubt. But was it enough to keep them from coming after me? From seeking revenge? If they tell anyone their story, they might seek me out just to prove that I exist. And when they *do* find me, how long will it be before one of the men decides to prove his strength by killing me?

It's all fiction at this point, but I can see it happening. It doesn't feel like a stretch. Human nature is the same the world around, especially when it comes to men with injured pride.

My other option is to continue forward, use the woman's root-crossing technique to hide my own path and hope I find her again. There's no way to know if she continued straight on or diverted in another direction. Even if I don't find her, not leaving a trail is probably a good thing.

I set out across the roots and have a hard time not touching the ground. The solid boots roll over each root, leave patterned divots in the ground, and mud smeared on the bark. Ten feet in, I'm leaving as obvious a trail as I was before.

"Damnit..." I lean against a tall, winding root and look down at my mud-covered boots. They're damp, and heavy, turning my feet into blistery raisins, and now, leaving a trail. Going against what every hiking guide says, I untie my boots and pry them off. If bare feet works for the natives, why not for me?

The socks peel away slowly. I flinch as skin from popped blisters go with them, peeling away in neat strips like frayed skin around fingernails—except more painful.

After tying the boots to my back and stuffing the socks inside, I take a tentative step. I flinch in pain as my unprotected foot compresses on a solid, narrow root. But when I take a step, I don't slip, and my feet stay free from the ground. It takes a good ten minutes to find a rhythm, but then I'm moving over the roots at a normal pace, hands extended for balance, and leaving no trail in my wake. A half mile further, the tangle of roots come to an end. I step gingerly onto the leaf-covered ground on the far side and then another, looking back to see if there's a path.

If there is, I can't see it. But then, I'm not a hunter.

A true hunter might see what I don't.

Might not need to see anything.

At close range, I could probably be tracked by scent.

From a distance, even if I'm silent, the jungle's song might give me away.

What has become a constant background noise to me, might tell native hunters a complete story about who or what is where.

But I can do that, too, can't I?

I stop, close my eyes, and listen, straining my ears for the sound of monkeys. Or silence. I'm familiar with the cries issued at my approach. Wouldn't they do the same if tribal hunters were nearby?

And that's when I hear it.

The warning.

But it's not the sound of monkeys, or birds, or silence that tips me off.

It's the sound of men.

A lot of men.

11

They're still far away, and though I can't understand the language, the sound of arguing is universal. They're not sure which way to go, I think. Confounded by the roots and the disappearing tracks. But who are they chasing? Me, or the woman?

Doesn't matter. If they find a trail to follow, it will be mine.

I step as carefully as possible, using roots when I can and avoiding any brush that might be disturbed by my passing. But this is the rainforest. Aside from the towering trees with their matching tangles of roots and branches, everything is mobile. Leaves bend and sway as I pass. Dead leaves fold and stick beneath my feet. The soft earth, free of rocks, grass, and a firm bedrock below, compresses under my weight. With my pack and gear, I'm at least twice the weight of the men I encountered. A behemoth in a world where those who tread lightly survive the longest.

I'm also deep in their territory. The father and son didn't take long to return with help, so they're either part of a larger hunting party, or we're not far from their village. Whatever the case, I'm sure that they know this land. They'll be able to spot changes easily and move through the terrain with calm efficiency.

How many people live in the average Amazon tribal village?

I have no idea, and I'm not sure it matters. I couldn't kill two men intent on raping a woman. Slaughtering all the men and women capable of hunting me from their village isn't remotely possible. I'm either going to escape, or die trying. As melodramatic as that sounds—like the description of some thriller novel—it's a pretty good summary of the past week. Life and death hang in the balance with every decision I make. That I'm still alive has little to do with me and everything to do with a fortuitous page turn of the *Choose Your Own Adventure* into which my life has devolved. One bad decision, or unlucky turn of the page, and my story will come to an end.

I start to relax when the voices fade behind me, but is that because I'm distancing myself from them, or because they're back on the hunt, quiet and stealthy?

My gut and my nerves say it's the latter, that any second now, a poison-tipped arrow will pierce my back, and I'll die a horrible slow death, watched by a red-painted hunting party. They'll be pleased. They'll feel powerful. And after they pillage my belongings, they'll have had their first contact with the modern world. Despite all this, I feel bad in advance for the man who plunders the gun and pulls the trigger. If he's lucky, it will fire into the air and simply terrify him. But it seems just as likely that he'll shoot a friend, or himself.

A swell of nervous energy puts my bladder into overdrive. I have a near unbearable urge to urinate, but I'm certain any good hunter will have little trouble spotting the wetness. It might be even easier to smell. In my dehydrated state, my pee is going to be potent.

I make it another fifty feet before I have no choice but to stop, drop trou, and relieve myself. Another few seconds and I'm pretty sure I would have pissed my pants, making me easy to find, if not to the human hunters, then to the other predators stalking the jungle. Then again, it's been days since I last showered, and I'm constantly bathed in sweat. I've grown accustomed to my own stench, but I have little doubt my scent would be hard to miss for anyone nearby.

My aim is shoddy at best. The target, a crevasse between two long roots, is elusive. With my weak legs, heavy gear, and a mad rush to not soak myself, I do a decent impression of a loose fire hose.

Maybe they'll interpret my lack of concealment as brazen confidence? After all, I did chase them off with the sound of thunder.

Doubting that will be the case, I put myself back together and continue on my way to nowhere.

An hour later, I'm numb.

To the fear.

To my life.

I just want to stop.

"I want a cheeseburger," I tell the monkeys in the trees above me. "In and Out. Double, double. Animal style. Fries. Chocolate shake. Prisa!"

I'm not sure why I'm speaking Spanish to the monkeys. Probably because I can't speak Portuguese. Is that mildly offensive? Is it racist? To think two South American languages can be used in place of the other? Shit. Neither of them are truly South American. No more than English is North American, or Canadian.

Who gives a shit?

Why am I even thinking about this?

A monkey glares at me.

I flip it the bird.

For some reason unknown to me and likely unknown to the monkey, it takes offense at my gesture. The bared teeth come first, and then the shriek. I'm not sure what kind of monkey it is, but if it's a new species and I get to name it, I'm going to go with, Piece of Shit Sonuvabitch Monkey.

"Shut-up," I whisper-shout at the small mammal.

It carries on despite my protest, and soon the whole troop joins in.

"Shut-up!" I say, louder now, and point my gun at the little bastard who sounded the initial alarm. But shooting the monkey will be louder, and will carry farther than the monkey's cries.

So I run.

Well, run is a generous word.

I hobble quickly. The soupy air and the jungle slow me down further.

There's no attempt at being quiet, or not leaving a trail. I'm just hoping I can put a little more distance between me and the hunters. That they haven't caught me already seems like a small miracle. But if I can go far enough, perhaps they'll give up?

How far would that be? Ten miles? Twenty? What's the range of the average Amazonian tribe? I doubt there is an answer. Especially if they're nomadic. For the hunters, a twenty mile hike might just be all in a day's work.

I put the water poncho to my lips and tip it back. I feel a few drops of water tickle my bottom lip, and then nothing. There is more water dripping from my body than from the water source that has sustained me. I know what comes next. Remember the desperation that thirst can create. And if I come across another stream, I will probably drink again.

Survive today, and worry about what's going to kill me tomorrow, tomorrow.

But there is no stream. No hint of rain in the air.

And the monkeys...those little assholes...are following me, continuing their wordless rant. They're putting me at risk. Used needles of the jungle.

I stagger to a stop, leaning against a tree, breathing hard enough to see stars. Thick blood is hard to oxygenate.

How long do I have before walking is impossible?

Minutes.

Ten at the most.

Less if I'm caught and killed before then.

A tickling on my arm draws my attention. Ants carrying leaves four times their size march down the tree trunk, climbing up and over my arm, continuing their path without missing a beat. How long can they go without water? Probably longer than me. My eyes drift from the ants to a series of red welts.

The mosquitoes have been drinking my thick blood dry, feasting while I've been too preoccupied to fend them off or apply what remains of my insect repellant. Not that I would bother using it. The smell would be easier to track than my body odor or piss.

Sucking in deep breaths, I take a moment to listen and realize the monkeys have gone silent. *I must have left their territory,* I think, and I glance back. The monkeys are above, crouched low on branches, eyes focused on the jungle behind me, motionless and silent.

They're here.

Unlike the monkeys, I have no hope of blending in and going unnoticed. So I move, focusing on putting one foot in front of the other. I'm not sure how far I make it before leaning against another tree trunk, feeling unconsciousness scratching at my mind, looking for a way in.

At least I won't feel the arrow.

Hell, maybe they won't kill me if I'm already dying.

Would that even be better? Maybe a quick death would be better? Should I be running the other way, rushing into battle like Leonidas and then the story of my death will be told to generations of tribal children?

If I sit down behind the trees' tall roots, and position myself behind some arrow-repellant cover, maybe I could shoot them all.

I've fired three shots. There are ten in the gun and another thirteen in the second magazine still in my pocket. I'm not sure how good my aim is, but maybe killing one of them will be enough? The sound and appearance of a magical wound might be enough to turn them away for good.

And then what?

Crawl until I pass out and die?

And can I really kill a man? Can I take one of the lives I had hoped to help by coming to this steaming hellhole? Just to survive?

For Juni.

The thought is quiet, almost easy to miss, but it churns my insides. Could I kill a man to save Juni's father? To spare her that pain?

She won't remember you, a louder voice says. *She's already forgotten you're gone.*

What about Gwen?

She'll recover. She's young. Beautiful. Intelligent. Funny. There isn't anything about her another man wouldn't want. It won't be long before another man becomes the salve for her emotional wounds. I'm like Tom Hanks in that movie...*Cast Away.* Even if I survive this mess, the only package I have to deliver is a partially used brick of Mary Jane. I don't think I'd have much in common with the intended recipient.

I'm drifting. Thoughts come and go like rapid fire tides, sliding in and out with waves of weariness.

And then, I can't breathe through my mouth. My lips are sealed, held together by something now tightening around my throat and chest.

A constrictor, I think, and I slide toward the ground, the pressure tightening. Consciousness slips away as I reach the ground. *It's a merciful way to go,* I decide, closing my eyes, suddenly comfortable and ready for a permanent sleep.

As the last of my life slips away, I hear a voice whispering to me in a language I can't understand. Silly snake, I don't speak your language. I can't even—

12

"Hey, baby," I say with a cheeky grin. I'm speaking to Steph, Gwen's best friend. While my tone of voice suggests I'm flirting, the indiscretion is revealed to be a joke when I sit down beside Steph's actual baby, Mel. She's a year younger than Juni, but twice the work. She also adores me.

Gwen and Steph can't seem to comprehend why. She doesn't like most men, including her grandfather. But the secret is simple: act like a kid. Some children are incapable of simply walking up to another child and saying, 'Hey, let's be pals,' and just start playing. Most adults can't do that either.

Step one is to act indifferent. A kind smile is enough attention. It says, 'I'm nice,' but doesn't smother with attention, which makes most kids uncomfortable. Step two is to get down on their level and play. Alone. There's probably a psychological term for it. Like co-play. But the message is, 'I'm here to play and have fun, not to be entertained by you.' Step three, after several minutes of co-play, offer a toy. No strings attached. Just reach out and hand over one of the toys you've been having fun with.

Step four is on the kid. There's an unwritten rule in all people, but it's nearly impossible for kids to disobey. When someone gives you something, you return the favor. Once that toy is offered, received, and returned, friendship is born.

"So when is Gwen going to get here?" Steph asks.

I look back from my spot on the living room floor, expecting to see Gwen standing behind me, holding Juni.

Weren't they there?

I remember them being there.

"Soon. I think."

Steph seems indifferent to the answer, turns her head and looks out the sun-drenched window. I turn my attention back to Mel. She hands me a folded piece of paper, which I promptly pretend to eat. There's no better way to break the ice with a kid than pretending to eat something unexpectedly. You just have to be careful that the object you're 'eating' isn't a choking hazard, because as soon as you hand it back—and you better hand it back—the kid is going to either pretend to eat it, too, or *actually* try to eat it.

Mel laughs as I munch the paper. "Don't eat paper," she says, her small voice scratchy. Despite her warning, when I hand the page back, she promptly pops it into her mouth and giggles. When she looks to her mother, she stops.

Steph is still looking out the window.

What's out there?

What is she looking at?

"Steph..." She doesn't turn at her name. Doesn't blink. At all. "Steph?"

She's frozen in place. I turn to Mel, expecting the young girl to have picked up on the wrongness of her mother's behavior, but she's just staring at her mother, unmoving. Devoid of emotion. They've been turned into statues.

I reach out for Mel's arm and give her a poke. Nothing.

"What are you looking at?" I ask Mel, and then to her mother, "What are you looking at!"

I stand and approach the bright window. The backyard at this time of year is a wash of green. There's a four-foot-tall fence, walled in by lush maple trees I think I'll tap for syrup when I'm retired.

But that's not what I see.

Bright light forces my eyes shut.

Hands raised, fingers layered in a waffle pattern shield, I look again.

It's the sun. In my yard. The light flickers into my eyes from behind glowing green leaves.

Mel says something, her voice strained, but the words are indecipherable. She's standing now, glaring at me. A string of words flows from her small lips, the sound of her voice older now.

"What?" I say. "I don't—"

Steph lunges at me, knocking me back, pinning me to the couch, hand over my mouth. Through bared teeth, she growls, "Shut the fuck up, Greg. They're coming!"

I'm locked in painful rigor, my body a plank.

The light becomes a blurry haze, like a watercolor wash that's suddenly pixelated and digitized. My eyes' resolution increases with each breath. My view out the window clarifies. I see the leaves again, bending in the breeze, and then the sky above.

The sky…

How long has it been since I gazed at its blue?

Wait…

Above?

I'm looking out the window, aren't I?

My periphery grows dark. Steph fades away. The living room becomes a memory…or a dream. The window was never there.

I'm on my back, looking up.

At the jungle canopy.

Shit.

I was home. Just for a moment, but I smelled it. Felt it. Believed it.

But like here, Gwen and Juni were gone. How long has it been since I last thought of them? Dreamt of them? Survival leaves little room for pining. It weakens the soul, and while they remain my motivation, dwelling on them breaks me down.

So I leave the dream, or perhaps the hallucination, and focus on the here and now.

I'm not alone.

Someone is behind me, their strong hand wrapped around my mouth.

Whoever it is, they're not here to hurt me. I'd be dead already if that was the case. The gentle shushing in my ear and the hand over my mouth communicate that I should be silent. Steph's warning replays.

They're coming.

While I can't understand the languages spoken in this part of the world, it seems my dream self is capable of understanding enough to deliver a message.

They—the hunters—are coming.

I relax my body despite the intense pain in my stomach and my head. Dehydration has become my bedfellow once more. I raise my empty hands and gently motion them to the dirt floor.

The message is understood. The hand slips away from my mouth, and I remain silent.

Where are we? Above, I see trees and sky, but little else. Is this a cave?

Can't be. There aren't any caves in the Amazon, because there aren't any rocks.

A pit, then.

I'm lowered back on to the damp floor, moisture saturating my shirt, cooling my back. I flinch when I realize that my backpack is missing. A firm grip on my shoulder keeps me from exploring any further.

It's the woman. The one I rescued. She's staring at me with dark, intense eyes. The kind that say life and death hang in the balance and that things like backpacks are best forgotten. When I relax again, she stands naked and shameless above me. For a moment, I see her, bathed in light, her body covered in mud—nature's readily available camouflage. She reaches out of the pit just as I hear shouting voices.

She takes hold of a branch and pulls. A framework of branches, covered in earth and plants slides overhead, carving into the circle of daylight like a solar eclipse. Darkness swallows us up. The cover is a perfect fit.

How long has this been here? And who built it?

The woman's people, I guess.

How else could she know it was here? And the system of roots? We're in *her* territory, not the hunters'.

She slides down beside me, bumping into me several times.

Our breathing feels loud in the dark, mine quivering, hers even and smooth.

When the voices are close enough to hear through the makeshift hatch, we hold our breath. The men sound angry, and then all at once, they cheer. They've discovered something that pleases them, and it's not us.

My backpack. She left it outside as an offering, or a distraction, knowing its contents might satiate the hunters' curiosity for a time. That's my guess anyway. The shouting becomes excited, morphing into a celebratory chant. And then, it fades.

The woman lies down beside me, her body against mine. She shushes in my ear and then seems to disappear as she goes motionless. What is she doing? If the men have gone, then—

The hatch shakes. Grit falls on my face, peppering my open eyes. I turn my head, blinking, and the woman shushes again. My eyes try to tear up, but there's not enough water left in my body.

Another shake and whoever was above has moved on, unaware that they've just stalked over our heads. While many of the hunters moved on, it seems that at least one of them is still on the prowl. How could she have known he would stay?

Probably the same reason this hideaway exists: this isn't the first time she, or her people, have encountered these men.

Rival tribes, I think.

Part of me wants to look down on them. They have all this space. All this land. And yet, they fight each other for it, divided by who-knows-what. But then I remember that I live in a time when leaders of powerful nations, with more resources than these simple people could comprehend, wage Twitter wars, along with actual wars, for no better reason than the acquisition of *More.* Like the silly Garfield poster I had on my wall when I was thirteen: *He who has the most toys wins.*

People are the same the world around, no matter how technologically advanced.

Beside me, the woman pushes herself up. I can't see what she's doing, but she's moving fast. When I feel a thump on my right side, and then pressure on my chest, I realize she's straddled me. If I could see, I'm pretty sure I'd have a close-up view of her butt.

My breath catches when the hatch shifts.

The hunter has returned...and he knows we're here.

13

There's a moment of total silence, from below and above, everyone tensing for a moment of confrontation. The best I can manage is to lie still and wait. I don't like being helpless, but all the medical knowledge in the world isn't going to keep me alive. Right now, my life is in the hands of a stranger, who is, like me, trapped in a pit.

Light stings my eyes. A sliver at first, and then a broad circle.

The hunter stands above, bow drawn back and aimed down, toward me. He's naked and young. The son. He must have stayed behind to prove himself to the others. To his father. The older men were satisfied with recovering my backpack, but this man is driven by ambition.

The young woman is revealed, crouched over me, head turned up, blowgun aimed. Before the hatch is fully removed, her lungs compress. There's a puff of air and a blur of motion.

The young man grunts and the arrow flies.

There's a wet slap as the projectile embeds itself in something soft, but I feel no pain. I lift my head, which takes all of my strength, and find the arrow stabbed into the earth an inch to the right of my thigh.

The hunter gasps for air, eyes wide, hand on his neck. He plucks the wooden dart free, looks at it with wide eyes that then twist up in fear. He knows as well as I do that he's been poisoned, that the injury, small as it might be, has sealed his fate.

The young man staggers back a step. How far could he make it?

Too far is the answer, apparently.

The woman scales the walls using a network of roots worn down by previous use.

How many times has she taken refuge here?

She catches the man's wrist. He tries to pull back, and nearly manages to break free, but the woman is relentless. She grasps his wrist with both hands, plants her feet against the pit's edge, and pushes with her legs. The man topples forward, falling into the pit.

I grunt in pain, as instinct forces me to roll out of the way. My whole body groans, but I manage to stay quiet.

Mud splashes against me as the man belly flops into the pit. The woman drops down behind him, using his body to cushion her fall. Then she's back on her feet, retrieving the hatch and putting it back in place.

Darkness descends again, transporting me through the Earth and straight to hell.

The young man lying beside me is not dead.

Not yet.

The poison in his body has locked him down, making him as immobile as me. But his involuntary muscles—heart and lungs—are resisting the poison's effects. His breaths are short and shallow. He'll be unconscious soon, if he's not already.

I could save him.

I *want* to save him.

Not letting people die is in my nature. But I'm not capable of saving myself at the moment. And if I'm honest, there is no universe in which this man and I both survive.

He needs to die.

He would have killed me. Would have raped the woman.

If he survived, I'm sure he'd do it all again.

I listen to his breathing slow. If he's conscious and panicking as the end nears, he's incapable of showing it.

When what's left of the air in his chest is expelled by relaxed lungs, escaping his mouth as a death groan, his life comes to an end. A moment later, the scent of piss and shit fills the pit.

Oh God...

I try to lift a hand to my face, but lack the strength.

The woman doesn't move. Doesn't react to the man's death, or the smell of his released bowels.

What has she experienced to become so hardened?

Hours pass. Maybe longer. It's hard to keep track as consciousness comes and goes. When the temperature drops, I'm pretty sure night has fallen. As slippery things slide against my body, emerging from the soil, attracted by body heat, I fall asleep.

There are no dreams, which is a mercy in a way. Dreaming of home again might make my mind as broken as my body.

I don't realize I'm awake until the woman moves and bumps against my leg. I try to speak, but all that comes out is a hiss. The woman scolds me with whispered words, and then lifts the hatch a few inches.

The light hurts my eyes, but doesn't bother me nearly as much as the dead man's face staring at me, eyes bulged open, tongue lolling out, skin pale.

The hatch opens further as the woman rises, taking her time to see if enemies are about. Judging by the casual monkey and bird calls so common in the morning, I think the coast is clear. The woman lifts the hatch and climbs out. She glances down at me, eyes sad, and then slides the hatch back in place.

Wait, I try to say, but I can't manage the single word. *Don't leave me!*

Plunged into darkness once more, I realize this hole is actually my grave. I'm going to lie here, beside the corpse of a stranger.

Unless I can move.

I'm not dead yet.

So move, damnit! Get up!

I try, with everything left in me, I try.

And fail.

How long until I join the young man in death?

The answer is: more than two hours. That's how long it feels between the time the woman left me, and her return.

She climbs into the pit, leaving the hatch open. The hunters have left. I'd sigh with relief if I could move.

My eyes lock on a large folded leaf, bound together with twine to create a kind of pouch. A bundle of fabric hangs from the sash now wrapped around her waist. Its beige color would have made her stick out in the jungle. *That's why she wasn't wearing it while still fleeing from the hunters.*

She's washed the mud off, too, and despite wearing at least a little clothing, her clean body seems even more naked.

She speaks to me in a calm voice. "Dun delay foos."

When I fail to respond, she opens her mouth and taps her lip.

I mimic her movement, opening my mouth. She leans in close, holding the folded leaf. She pulls out the large, curved stem. It looks like a tea kettle. And that's when I realize what she's got.

I try to lean closer, desperate, but immobile. She trickles the water into my mouth, just for a moment. I swallow and then open my mouth for more. It's fresh and clean. Almost sweet. Hopefully free of bacteria. She speaks gentle words, waits a moment, and then gives me some more.

She's doing it right, I think, despite my desperation. Giving me too much too fast would just result in my puking everything up. She needs to ease me back to health, letting my body recover without giving it more than it can handle.

An hour later, and I'm starting to feel better. The pain in my gut is gone, replaced by a desperate hunger. But the rest of my body still aches, my muscles seized by a strange kind of rigidity. I try to lift an arm, but a stab of pain stops me.

"Shoov," she says, and gently lifts my arm. A red rash with fractal edges covers my forearm. "Shoov."

An infection. That explains why the effects of dehydration were so quick and profound.

After another half hour, she lets me polish off the remaining water, which is enough to wake up my cells, but I'll need more soon.

"Thank you," I say.

She doesn't know what I've said, but understands my appreciation. She smiles, and reaches into the fabric pouch hanging on her side. When she withdraws three purple fruits, I nearly shout for joy.

Her hand on my chest calms me. When I lean back beside my dead bedfellow, she sets to work on the fruit, which I recognize. It's passion fruit. The Amazonian super fruit contains significant amounts of vitamins

C and A, as well as potassium, and magnesium, copper, iron, and phos-phorus—all of which my body desperately needs. It's also a great source of water, and the alkaloids it contains reduce anxiety and depression.

She splits the fruit in two, revealing the squishy, seed-laden insides. The fruit's smell mingles with the stench of death, making it less appe-tizing, but I don't care. Driven by hunger and sickness, I take half the fruit and devour its insides.

She eats one fruit, and then doles out the remaining fruit to me in halves, giving me time to digest between each. When she's done, the signs of dehydration have dwindled, but the infection is still hit-ting me hard. No longer close to death, I can feel the fever running its course.

Were we anywhere else, I might be content to lie still and allow this woman to care for me. But I can't stay beside the corpse any longer. Not only is it vile, but as it decays, it's going to become even more of a health risk to both of us. And the odor wafting up and out of the pit will likely draw predators.

I'm guessing she already knows all this, because when I try to push myself up again, she helps.

Weak muscles quiver as I stand, infirm but not entirely incapable.

The woman motions to the pit's open top, and says, "Fet," which might be a word, or perhaps just a sound, but the message is clear. *You first.*

I make it halfway up, using the same roots I watched the woman use, before my muscles can no longer lift my weight. I flinch when two hands shove on my buttocks, but the woman is stronger than her size suggests. With her shoving from behind, I manage to reach the top and pull myself part way out. Before I'm fully freed, the woman climbs up and over me. Grasping my wrists, she drags me the rest of the way out.

We lie in the open air, catching our breath.

I feel horrible, head to toe, but I'm happy to be alive.

And to no longer be alone.

I turn to offer a thankful smile to the woman, but I frown instead. Not because of her, but because of the two men standing behind her, arrows nocked and drawn. One man is a stranger. The second is the boy's father, no doubt searching for his errant son...who's lying just ten feet away and six feet underground.

The elder rapist's nose twitches. He's caught the scent of death.

It won't be long until he realizes the smell is coming from his son. And when that happens...

14

A rapid-fire conversation takes place between the woman and the man I haven't seen before. She's pleading her case, I think, explaining her side of things. My stomach churns when she motions to me and the man looks me over, unimpressed.

All the while, the father inches his way toward the pit, eyes and arrow locked on me. When he finds his dead son, I'm going to die in the same way, gasping for air while my body slowly shuts down.

And then the woman who saved me is going to die.

I can't let that happen now, any more than I could when she was a total stranger. I don't really know her. We haven't shared a single word, but I know she risked herself to save me. And I get the sense that she will continue to help me. Our survival is linked.

I lower my right hand behind the satchel, which remains hung over my head, and reach into my pocket. The gun feels heavy in my hand and on my heart. I draw it slowly, keeping the muzzle pointed to the ground.

What will it take? A single shot into the dirt? Should I try to wing one of them? Or will the surprise make them release the arrows?

I don't want to hurt anyone. A bullet wound in the rainforest would probably be a death sentence.

"Chua sans," the father says, silencing the conversation. He's close enough to the pit to see his son's wide feet. His face pinches up with hurt and anger, but he needs to see it. Needs to know for sure.

The woman whispers to the second man. She knows what's about to happen.

But her pleading falls on deaf ears. The man gives an indifferent shrug and adjusts his aim toward her head, waiting for the signal to fire.

The father inches toward the pit, eyes still on me.

"Wait," I say. "You don't need to do this."

I know it's useless, but I think I'm speaking to myself as much as I am to the father.

"Stop," I warn. "I don't want to—"

The father turns his head to the pit. His eyes widen while his forehead crushes down. His teeth grind and his lungs fill, preparing to shout the order.

Fuck.

Damn it.

I look for another solution, but there isn't any. The way of the jungle, at least right now, with these people, is merciless.

To survive, I'll need to become like them.

I dive toward the new man, raising the gun.

An arrow cuts through the air behind me, embedding itself in the ground. The new man adjusts his aim toward me, but he's not fast enough.

I pull the trigger once, unleashing a boom that hurts my ears.

With just a few feet between us, it's impossible to miss.

The man jolts and lets out a kind of squeal that breaks my heart. His arms go slack, the arrow unfired. Wide eyes turn down to the center of his chest where a neat hole leaks blood.

The wound is just to the left of center. Even in the world's most advanced hospital, with the best surgeons, there would be no saving him.

As horrified as I am, I'm also not done.

Lying on my stomach, I roll over and aim the gun at the father. He's got a fresh arrow nocked, but his eyes are on his friend, who falls to his knees, and then lands face down in the mud with a slap.

His attention shifts back to me, and then the gun.

He gets it. Understands the power I wield. That his simple arrow is no match.

But he's lost in rage, craving vengeance for the death of his son, and for whatever the dead man was to him—friend, brother, cousin? The bow string goes taut, the arrow drawn back.

"Stop," I tell him. The gun shakes in my hand. Tears blur my vision. But he's too close to miss. "Please."

I pull the trigger before the arrow is even aimed toward me.

The sound of it surprises me as much as it does the father. We yelp in unison.

The gun falls from my hand as the bow drops to the ground. While my only wounds are to my psyche, the man grips his bloody arm.

I've winged him.

He's going to survive—for now.

The woman screams an unintelligible sentence. When I look back at her, I realize she's speaking to me.

She wants me to finish the job.

I can't, but the father doesn't know that. He turns and runs, disappearing around a tree.

The woman crouches in front of me, reaming me out with a flurry of hand gestures at my head, and then in the direction the father retreated. I don't need to speak her language to understand. I should have shot him again. Should have killed him. That's the man who was going to rape her. He was going to kill us both. Killing him was justified. He's going to get reinforcements.

My eyes widen with that final realization.

Shit.

She's right.

I grasp the gun, slip it back in my pocket and stand. To my relief, the woman, despite her anger with me, helps me stand. We might not be on the best terms right now, but we're still partners.

While she gathers the dead man's meager belongings—a pouch full of plants I can't identify, and five black-tipped arrows—I check his pulse. I'm sure he's dead, but the doctor in me wants to confirm it. To mark the time of the first death at my hands.

I look at my wrist, but there's no watch. I haven't worn one in years. Not since smartphones became prevalent.

My hand snaps down to my cargo pants pocket, slapping against the hard rectangle wrapped in a Ziploc bag. My heart pounds from the moment of panic. If the phone had been lost, my only connection to my family would have gone with it. I haven't looked at their photos for a long time, but I still could if I wanted to, and that's enough.

I take stock of what I have. Machete. Gun with eight rounds. Spare magazine with thirteen rounds. The Zippo lighter. And the satchel holding a brick of marijuana, a notebook, five thousand dollars, and my mosquito netting—thank God.

But I have lost much more, including all my clothes, the poncho, my water bottle, insect repellant, first aid kit, wallet, and passport. I look down, wiggling my bare toes in the sodden earth. I've also lost my boots.

The woman pats her hand in my face, snapping my attention back to her. She speaks, but I don't understand anything other than her tone.

She's worried. Nervous. Explaining the importance of leaving, maybe. Then she stands and motions for me to follow.

"I'm sorry," I tell the dead man. "I wish it could have been different."

Had I never crashed, this man would still be alive. So would the young man in the pit. I look to the woman, my rescuer. Without me, she might be dead. That's something, at least. My existence can still be about saving people. Just not everyone. It's an identity shift I'm not comfortable making today, and one I hope I'll never need to.

I rise to shaking legs and motion for the woman to lead the way. She sets a pace I can't maintain after the first fifty feet. She slows for me, motioning for me to follow, constantly spurring me on. When I stumble, she catches me. When I slow too much, she prods me from behind with one of the bows. She speaks gentle words of encouragement that mean nothing to my intellect, but keep me upright. I don't want to disappoint her. Don't want to let her down. We've come this far. I can't be the reason we're caught.

The hunters will come for us again, led by a vengeful father. Our only hope, once again, is to escape and hide, to evade them until they give up, or we've traveled beyond their range.

But in my current state, I don't see us outrunning or outdistancing the hunting party.

She steps on roots whenever possible, and I do my best to follow, matching her steps with far less grace. She's a short woman, but petite and lithe, strong, and graceful.

When I'm too weak to move, she motions for me to lean against a tree and rest, not lie down. I'm not sure if that's because my body will leave an impression on the ground or because she's afraid I won't get back up once I'm down. Both concerns make sense, so I stay on my feet and wait.

In her absence, the jungle becomes a dark and foreboding place once more. Despite being chased by human predators, I hadn't noticed that I had stopped fearing the jungle itself. The woman, so capable and confident, tames the jungle with her presence.

She returns ten minutes later with a handful of berries. I don't recognize the green and red orbs, but they have a thick skin similar to cranberries. She thrusts the berries at my face, insistent. When I notice that she's already munching on some, I take her offering and try a single berry.

It's crisp. And tart. When my face pinches up, the woman laughs.

The sound of her amusement is like spotting a flower in a field of decay. I smile back at her, and nod in thanks. After the tart blast, the berry tastes a bit like an orange. It's not very sweet, but given the circumstances, it's delicious.

I eat the handful, a few berries at a time. I'm not feeling much better when I'm done, but the woman motions for me to come with her, and when I struggle, she throws my arm around her shoulder and points ahead, to a hanging vine. "Ishee popo." When she then points to her mouth, I understand.

Water.

As we approach the heavy vine, I try to take note of its features. It's beige and hangs straight down from the canopy high above. In some ways, it resembles a giant tape worm and looks like it could wriggle away. Its twists and coils make it look flimsy, but upon reaching it, I find a surprisingly solid and thick vine. Depending on how it's connected to the canopy, I'm pretty sure it could be climbed.

Visions of Tarzan fill my thoughts when I give the vine a tug.

The woman taps my hip, striking the machete. She holds out her hand and motions to the vine. She doesn't have a blade. I'm certain none of the tribes this deep in the Amazon do, but she knows what it is. Perhaps her people have had encounters with the outside world, if not now then during the time of the Portuguese Conquistadors, with stories being passed down by oral tradition.

I slide the weapon out from my belt and hand it to her. She wields it like I've just given her Excalibur, examining the blade with a look of innocent wonder in her eyes. Then she's in motion, scaling a nearby tree with nothing but her hands and feet. After just a few lunges, she's twenty feet up. Locked in place, she swings with the machete and severs the vine.

I hobble to the side to avoid the toppling cord, which thumps to the ground beside me. The woman lands beside me and sets to work on the vine, cutting it into two-foot sections. When she's done, she hands one to me.

I don't need to be told what to do next. Water pours from the severed end when I tip it over my mouth. It's just a trickle, but it continues for a full minute. When I'm done, I pick up another length and repeat the process. We stand still for several minutes, drinking the vine dry.

When we're done, we share a smile. This is how people live in the Amazon. The jungle takes life, but also grants it.

The woman puts a hand on her breast. "Ashanika."

Having seen enough movies and TV series with this moment acted out, I'm pretty sure she is telling me her name.

"Ashanika," I say, and she smiles. Then I put a hand on my chest and say, "Greg Zekser."

"Greg...Zeksah... Zek-ser. Zekser." She smiles at me.

"How about just Greg?" I pat my chest. "Greg."

"Ahh." She smiles again, tapping herself. "Ashan."

Her shortened name, like mine, is easier to say. "Ashan."

"Greg," she says, and motions for me to follow her. We strike out again, and this time cover many miles, stopping only to drink and eat along the way. We never have a proper meal, but I'm never too hungry or thirsty. I'm slowed by weakness and fever, but my guide is merciful.

We travel without incident, building trust, until we reach our destination.

Three weeks later.

15

It takes three days for my fever to pass, but when it does, I feel better than I have since the plane crashed. Ashan takes care of me, keeping me hydrated and well fed. Where I see an inedible jungle full of poisons that would cripple or kill, she sees a bounty of food.

In the days since, I've become Ashan's student, learning everything I can about the jungle, about survival, and about her language. With nothing else to do but walk and learn, I've come a long way in a short amount of time. I've spent far more total hours immersed in her language than I ever did during several years of a foreign language class.

Ashan was quiet at first, until she figured out I was trying to learn. She's been talkative since, teaching me words for just about everything we come across. Some of what she says is hard to decipher, but context often helps make sense of it. When we're not on the move, I draw images in the earth, which entertains her and allows her to teach me words for things we haven't come across.

Weapons. Animals. Tribes.

All the while, we're on edge, waiting for the hunters to catch us. She tells me they're coming. She's insistent, describing them as jaguars. Tells me they have killed Dalandala, but isn't able to communicate who that is. When I pry for more, she closes down, haunted by something our lingering language barrier prevents me from understanding.

On several occasions she has mentioned Mapinguari while talking about the hunters. She describes it as both human and beast. Not like the other hunters. It's more like a monster. A boogeyman. Like a spirit of vengeance. While my language is still limited, I think she's described it as having two mouths, one eye, about my height, and hairier than me. I'm pretty sure it doesn't exist.

Real or not, she fears the man-thing more than the hunters she believes are still pursuing us. I have a hard time believing those men have spent the past three weeks tracking us, but maybe vengeance is part of the culture? Feuds in the civilized world, between entire nations, are common. Why not in the jungle?

People are people, whether they live in the wilds of a tropical rain-forest or in the penthouse of a Manhattan skyscraper. The vices that drag down mankind are universal. The realization feels almost racist, like I'm supposed to view all tribal people as noble and somehow in touch with a primitive lifestyle that's more spiritual than the modern world.

But they're no better.

No worse, either.

With little to do in the jungle aside from forage, hunt, and travel, I suppose vengeance could be entertaining for these men. It's also poss-ible they're tightknit enough that the young man's death has sent them into a frenzy. But three weeks is a long time. Their emotions should have settled. And they must have families. A village. Other responsibilities.

I nearly bump into, and trip over, Ashan when she suddenly crouches. Before I can ask why, she turns around and raises a finger to her lips, a gesture she learned from me. I've taught her a few words in the past weeks—machete, gun, satchel, paper—but she's also picked up some of my mannerisms, and me some of hers.

I squat down beside her, listening. I hear the jungle's background noise, but...

There it is.

In the distance. Monkeys are calling a warning. Predators are about. People. And not us.

I smile at the realization that, in a strange kind of way, I'm also learning to speak monkey. The smile fades when I realize what it means. The hunters haven't chased us. They've predicted our destination and beat us to it, probably because I was ill. Had they known, they might have just chased us and caught up weeks ago.

A series of hand signals from Ashan instruct me to stay low, stay quiet, and follow her. Before setting out, she readies a bow, keeping an arrow nocked, but not drawn back. I've been practicing with one of the bows taken from the hunters, but my aim is atrocious. I'm improving, but I'm nowhere near ready to shoot a moving target.

And I don't want to.

Most nights, I'm haunted by images of the boy slain by the dart, and the older man killed by my gun. Some mornings, I wake expecting to find their sunken, rotting eyes staring back at me. While trying to sleep, visions of their decomposing corpses would fill my thoughts. By now, with the heat, humidity, scavengers, and insects, they're likely just bones.

The terrain moves upward in a steady, but not steep grade. Ashan leads the way, each step silent. I make a little noise, but nothing loud enough to notice from a distance. I know I'm doing well when she doesn't turn around and scold me with a glare.

A wall of young vegetation—leafy plants, saplings, and ferns—blocks the path ahead. Between the trees and above the wall, I see swatches of bright blue.

A clearing, I think, almost salivating for a clear view of the sky.

Ashan lowers the bow as she creeps up to the wall.

Speaking simply in her language, she whispers. "Quiet. Hunters. Look." Then she points to the wall and starts easing leaves away.

I do the same, a few feet away, inching leaves back. For all I know, the hunters are ten feet beyond the wall and will notice me. When I move the last leaf blocking my view, my fear of immediate violence fades.

Ten men rummage through the remains of a village. The red paint framing their eyes and drawn in patterns over their bodies, coupled with the whisker-sticks protruding from their noses, identify them as members of the angry father's and dead son's tribe. They carry little—bows and arrows—and wear even less. There's a cord around their waists holding a minimal thong-like garment that covers their manhood. The clothing isn't designed to protect, just to keep things from being knocked about while moving.

What looks like building frames for a dozen large thatch huts, stand charred and useless. Ashes cover the ground where the primitive structures once stood. The clearing is two hundred feet across. Each structure would have been enough to house an entire family. How many people lived here? Fifty? More?

Ashan glares, the sides of her nose twitching up. I reach out and put a hand on her arm. She flinches, eyes flaring with anger. When she looks into my eyes, she calms.

"Who?" I ask.

"Hunters."

I shake my head.

"No. Who...live here?"

Her frown deepens. The red paint on her forehead was washed off two weeks ago. Her hair has grown out on the sides. She looks less and less like a warrior, but the look on her face leaves no doubt; she will kill these men if given the chance.

"Family," she says.

Oh my God...

This was *her* village. Her people. Her family.

I don't need to ask when. This destruction is many weeks old. Maybe months old.

Ashan's story fleshes out. She wasn't just found wandering the jungle. She was far from home, in enemy territory, armed with a blowgun and seeking vengeance of her own.

For this. For the destruction of her home and the killing of her family.

Were the hunters to spot us now, they'd see two pairs of glaring eyes. But the shade cast by the high sun keeps us hidden in shadows.

The ten men break into three groups, searching the ruins, probably for signs of our arrival. Bored with the chore, two of the younger men start kicking what looks like a ball. In that moment, they no longer look like dangerous hunters, painted red like demons. They're kids, playing with a ball, laughing in the sun, enjoying life.

Then I see the ball for what it is—a skull.

It could be Ashan's mother, or sister, or husband for all I know.

This is why she didn't hesitate to kill the young man. These men haven't just wronged her, they've committed genocide.

I've seen enough. After letting the leaves slip back into place, I whisper. "Sorry." I speak the word in English. I don't know her word for sorry, or even if there is one. But she's heard me say it enough, after every mistake I've made, that she understands its meaning.

She slides away from the wall, her face a torrent of emotion.

Part of her wants to rush right out and execute the men. She might take a few of them by surprise, but she'd eventually be slain. And what good is vengeance if it's incomplete?

She processes for several silent minutes, while we listen to the men make a sport of her peoples' remains.

A deep breath sighs from her lips like the ocean retreating over stones. Then she's clear. Focused. And pissed.

"Greg. Ashan. Kill."

"Kill hunters?"

She nods. "All."

My stomach sours.

"No kill." I try to think of a way to explain mercy, to communicate the sanctity of human life. But I can't. Not just because I lack the words, but because I have empathy. Without trying to, I've put myself in her position. If these men had killed Gwen and Juni, along with a vast number of my extended family, would I just let them leave? Could I live with myself if I knew monsters like that were left to murder, rape, and pillage?

"I kill alone," she growls and starts moving away.

She's going to leave me, I realize. After the past few weeks of nursing me back to health and keeping me alive when I'd have certainly died, I've betrayed her.

And I'm wrong to do it.

My modern-world morality makes no sense out here. There are no laws. No courts. No police. Right and wrong are determined by people willing to take matters into their own hands. I can't imagine a world in which genocide is justified, or in which men like this will someday be redeemed.

"Wait," I say. "I will help kill."

She stops, glaring at me, sizing me up.

"When?" I ask.

She starts moving away again, eyes still on me. "Tonight."

16

As the sun sets I come to the slow realization that I've made a horrible mistake. A lapse in judgement has brought me to the cusp of being a murderer. I'm already a killer. I've taken life, but that was, without a doubt, self-defense. Even in the civilized world, shooting that man was justified. But this...slaughtering a group of men in their sleep...that can't be right.

Or is it?

Had these men not come here to kill us, I wouldn't be in this position. Had they not attempted to rape Ashan, their lives wouldn't be at risk. But the cycle of violence started before her capture. It began here, in this village, where an untold number of people were slain, putting Ashan on a path of vengeance that led to her capture.

I've been sucked into a vortex of pre-existing violence that might have been spiraling for generations. Since I can swim—metaphorically— I have no choice but to go with the flow, or drown. Without Ashan, I'd be dead by now.

She's earned my help.

Had I killed the father and son when I first encountered them, we'd be safe. My lack of action put us in danger. I'm not going to make that mistake again. We can end this, here and now.

In the last lingering light of day, I slip the pistol from my pocket. It feels lighter in my hands now. I have enough bullets to kill each and every hunter. Just point and shoot until no one is moving. The darkness will help shield my psyche. The knowledge that I have killed several men will gnaw on my soul. The darkness will at least spare me from seeing the gore created by my actions. The less nightmare fuel, the better.

"No," Ashan says, motioning to the gun. "Gun loud."

She's squatting, digging a small hollow into the earth. Her eyes are both innocent, and full of deadly portent. She's a living duality. Yin and yang. Youthful beauty and experienced killer. Mercy and vengeance occupy equal portions of her heart.

"How?" I ask. "How kill?"

She points to herself, and then to the blowgun. Then she points to me and leans to the side, picking up one of the long, poison-tipped arrows we stole from the hunters. She breaks the rod a foot from the tip. After discarding the back end, she turns the tip around, angles her neck to the side and acts out jabbing her own throat. She then holds a hand over her mouth as she acts out dying from the poison's effects, her gasps muffled by her hand.

"Quiet," she says.

I had pictured a violent, loud, angry confrontation. Screams. Blood. A battlefield.

Ashan paints a different picture. We're to be assassins. Silent. Clean.

We won't propel the men into the afterlife, we'll ease them into it, one at a time, holding them still as their lives fade.

I'm not sure which version frightens me more.

"Quiet," she repeats and leans forward onto her hands, eyes locked on mine. She transforms into something predatory. I see the jaguar's eyes reflected in hers. She moves her right arm forward, placing it on the ground, slowly putting her weight down. Low to the ground, she lifts her left leg and brings it forward. Then her left arm, and right leg. Each limb moves with fluid ease, compressing the earth slowly, never making a sound. "See? Quiet. Now you."

I've marveled at the way Ashan moves through the forest, making little sound and leaving even fewer traces. Thinking I can duplicate her second-nature abilities feels akin to Michael Jordan trying to play baseball...if Michael Jordan was an unathletic doctor who needed to take vitamin D on account of how little time he spent in the sun. But I'll oblige her. Her lessons keep me alive. And tonight, I'm going to need all the help I can get.

I mimic her pose on the ground, hands and feet. The tight pull on the bottom of my foot stings as the still-healing sores from weeks of barefoot travel stretch and tear. The pain is minor compared to what I endured during our first week of travel, so I barely acknowledge it before taking my first step.

I reach out with my hand, and slowly transfer my weight to it without making a sound. I smile at Ashan, who is amused by my childlike need for approval, but still dubious. When I move my leg forward and catch my toes on a root that snaps back to the ground, she shakes her head.

"Slow," she says. "Quiet."

Our language barrier keeps her from verbalizing any more than that, but she doesn't need to. I understand. If we're quiet, we'll have all night. The men's deaths will be drawn out. Unrushed, I will have time to contemplate and debate my actions.

The debate is over, I think. *Right and wrong have already been defined. I'm doing what needs to be done. It's as simple as that.*

I stalk around the jungle, hands and feet, imitating the careful gait of a chameleon. It's all about weight dispersal. Lethal delicacy.

My progress is impressive until Ashan redirects my path toward some low-lying foliage. "Through. Quiet." She watches my progress while digging her small hole.

Slipping through the brush without making a sound is impossible. It doesn't matter how slowly I move. Branches and leaves catch on my clothing, stretching out and snapping back into place. I try three times without success. By the time I give up, I'm ready to draw the machete and decapitate the stalks. My fury toward the plants eclipses how I feel about the hunters.

Ashan's hand on my shoulder makes me flinch. She's silent, even on two feet. "Nuvi," she says. Realizing I don't understand, she tugs on my shirt and repeats it. "Nuvi."

"I know," I say in English. "It's getting caught."

She sighs at my frustration, and steps back. "Nuvi." She undoes the tie holding the sash around her waist. It falls away and I divert my eyes. Ashan is basically naked all the time. The sash around her waist conceals about seven inches of her abdomen, just below her belly button. But it does nothing to conceal what's below, or the rest of her body.

At times, I'm accustomed to her perpetual nakedness, but I am, at times, distracted by it. She is...beautiful, and strong. She is hard to ignore. Seeing her without the sash, despite the skin beneath being nothing taboo to the outside world, still feels wrong. Intimate.

She hisses to get my attention. When I resist, she snaps her fingers, a trick I taught her. "Look. See."

When I give in and look, she motions to her body. "Nuvi."

Nuvi means naked.

She steps up to the brush, drops to her hands and knees and then moves through the brush without a sound. The leaves slide over her body with little more than a hiss. Then she's through and back on her feet.

Ashan points at me. "You. Nuvi."

"Oh," I say, looking down at myself. "Oh..."

While Ashan is shameless, I have maintained my modern world sensibilities when it comes to my own nudity. If Ashan has to relieve herself, she stops, drops, and takes care of business. I still find a private place behind a tree. It took me shouting for her to realize she wasn't welcome while I was defecating. It amused her, but she's respected my boundaries since.

And now...she wants me to take off all my clothes.

I'm not a total prude. I've been with a couple of women in my life, but other than the three of them—including Gwen—and my own parents, I haven't been naked in front of anyone. When I go to the gym, I change in a stall. Other guys don't mind letting it all hang out, literally, but I've always been wired to conceal my business.

Not only does Ashan want me to get naked in front of her, she wants me to sneak around through the jungle, with all its bitey things, and kill a bunch of men.

I've agreed to perform a reprehensible act, and now I need to do it fully exposed. As awkward as that feels, out here, it's normal. The naked-ness at least. The vengeful killings... Hopefully they're less common.

"Nu-vi," Ashan says, enunciating her impatience.

"Fine," I mutter and yank off my shirt. I'm about to just go for it and shed the rest of my clothes in one pull, when I note Ashan's attention. She's looking at me, eyeing my chest with a different sort of interest.

With a rising sense of shame, I look down at myself. "Huh…" I'm more muscular than before. It's hard to say how much I've transformed and how much is new muscle versus a leaner body, but I'm pretty ripped. Days spent working hard and eating no refined or processed food has done good things for me. It hurt like hell, and nearly killed me in the process, but the rainforest has made me a new man.

A stronger man.

And a killer.

Ashan's hand on my chest snaps me from my thoughts before they turn dark again.

My stomach clenches as her fingers slide up my torso, but I don't move. It feels…nice.

She smiles up at me and my stomach lurches again.

This is wrong, I think. *You're still married. You've only been gone for—* How long have I been missing? Five weeks? More? Days blur without a schedule. Without a calendar.

"Mapinguari," Ashan says, and with a shriveling embarrassment, I realize her interest has nothing to do with lust. She balls her fists, grasping the hair on my chest and tugging. It hurts, but I say nothing.

Her fingers explore my growing beard and hair.

I've never been told my hairiness was admirable. Gwen mostly tolerated it. Had she not found hairless man-boys even more repulsive, I might have subjected myself to laser hair removal.

Ashan, on the other hand, grins with delight. She looks up at me with renewed interest.

"No Mapinguari." My argument falls on deaf ears.

Ashan takes a step back and motions to my remaining clothes. "Nuvi!"

Having a woman all but beg to get me naked while having zero sexual intentions is a surreal experience. It also puts me at ease. In Ashan's mind, my hairy body and height resembles that of a mythical creature. She knows I'm human. She's had to coddle me like a baby for weeks. I'm no more a savage man-killer than I am a jaguar. But for her, having a partner that resembles the infamous Mapinguari could be beneficial. Like a kind of psychological warfare.

Men are easier to kill when they're running away. I think.

"Greg," she says, voice stern. "Nuvi."

Resigned to my fate, I strip and stand before her, totally exposed.

At first, she's thrilled. I'm hairy everywhere, in a way that Amazonian men just aren't. And then, in a flash, she becomes just as uncomfortable as me. She heads back to her small pit that looks like the impact site of a bowling ball.

I don't bother redressing. Being naked isn't just part of the culture out here, it's a necessity for what we're about to do. For me to perform, I'm going to have to be comfortable in my own skin first.

While Ashan and I avoid each other's gazes, I return to the brush, drop to my hands and feet and slip through. There're a few whispers of leaf over skin, but nothing catches. I nearly laugh a few times when the stalks tickle my skin. Otherwise, my performance is good enough to put Ashan at ease.

"See?" she says. "Nuvi good. Quiet."

I join her by the small hole, sitting in a way that hides my nether region. "Nuvi good." Desiring to move onto more comfortable subjects, like murder, I motion to the hole. "What?"

Her response to my simple question is a simple answer. She squat-walks over the hole and demonstrates her complete lack of shame by urinating into it. While I watch with raised eyebrows, she slides some of the soil she removed back inside, thrusts her hands inside and churns it into a thin mud.

As realization blooms, my body sags. "God damnit."

17

The potent smell of earth manages to mute the aroma of Ashan's urine, which is good for two reasons. First, it helps me forget that my naked body is now slathered in a thin layer of mud made from piss. Second, it will keep the hunters from smelling our approach. Granted, we're going to wait until they're asleep, but strong smells have been known to rouse people from even the deepest slumber. When eyes and ears fail to detect danger, the nose is up to the task. Gas leaks, rotten food, and death itself can all be detected by the nose.

Then again, maybe smelling urine is nothing new for these people. Coming from the sterilized world beyond the Amazon basin, the scent of urine is out of place. It means something is wrong. Someone's had an accident. Out here, where there are no bathrooms, and no sanitation, pissing ten feet from your slumbering friend isn't taboo.

Ashan has taught me that on many occasions since our meeting.

We crouch at the clearing's periphery hidden by a comingling of darkness and mud. The hunters have started a fire, cooking a monkey. Seeing the bipedal body stretched out over the flames made me queasy at first. Then I smelled it, and my stomach awoke. After weeks of eating a raw vegan diet, my body is craving animal fat. With the hunters on our trail, Ashan thought it best to avoid cooking. I wasn't sure that starting a fire in the Amazon was even possible. Everything seems so wet to me, all the time, but it has been a few days since the last heavy rain. Honestly, I know nothing about starting a fire without a Duraflame log. Even then, my success rate is spotty at best.

A lesson for another day.

If we survive the night.

The men eat and drink around the fire for hours. I'm not sure what they're drinking, but it's definitely not water. As the moon rises above the clearing, their voices grow louder. They take turns telling stories. I catch bits and pieces. Hunters killing prey. Jungle monsters. Conquests. While most of the tales sound ominous, they all get laughs, too.

Seeing the men like this, just being regular guys around a fire, softens my heart. Just a little. But not enough to change things. I have not forgotten what they've done or what they've traveled here to do.

As the night wears on, my eyes drift to the sky. While I've been hankering for a clear view of the daytime sky, and to feel the sun's direct warmth on my skin, I haven't thought much about the night sky. Living just outside of Boston means the night sky has more light pollution than stars. The big dipper. Orion's belt. Venus, Mars, the North Star. Those are the stars I'm used to seeing.

The view tonight makes me feel like a child again, when everything was new, and colors were vibrant, and each experience was visceral. I've heard that childhood seems to move more slowly because new experiences shift our perception of time, and every experience for a child is new. When we grow up, life becomes routine. We work the same job. Repeat the same habits. Visit the same places. Eat the same food.

Since crashing in the rainforest, time has slowed to a crawl. Every day is something new. The world is potent again. Flavors are powerful. And things like the night sky, revealed without a curtain of light, fills me with a spiritual sense of wonder.

This is why people believe in God.

Uproarious laughter draws my eyes back toward the men. One of them is urinating into the fire, filling the air with putrid steam. The drunken men all stand, shouting a chant I can't understand, dancing around the flames, all of them pissing now.

This is why people believe in the Devil.

It's several hours before the men either pass out or fall asleep.

Waiting in the dark, under a blanket of stars, surrounded by the fragrance of cooked meat and flowers I can't see, *I* nearly fall asleep. Back home, with an expensive bed full of springs and foam and down feathers, I can't sleep without an Ambien. During the past few weeks, I've had no trouble falling asleep. I close my eyes and the next time I open them, the sun is up.

I've often wondered how people about to engage in battle stay calm. How they keep themselves from simply walking away. Why fight when there is so much to live for? Obviously, there are some good reasons for fighting—freedom from oppression, from tyranny, from terror. But not crumpling into a fetal position from fright at the knowledge that the moment you engage the enemy, your life could end with the crack of a bullet? That's always eluded me.

I thought it was because I was a coward. Sure, I can help people. That's pretty much what I've dedicated my life to. But fight? *Kill?*

The truth, I now know, is that I never had a reason to fight before now. I lived in a safe neighborhood, in a house with deadbolts, window locks, and ADT security. I drove an SUV with the highest safety rating, surrounded by airbags. And even though the soup kitchen operates in a part of town usually avoided by folks in my neighborhood, the people there know me, and what I give to their community. If anything, I'm safer there than in my own home.

Ashan puts her hand on mine. She's been low to the ground, eyes never leaving our target. The silver-moon's light and the Milky Way's dull glow illuminate her eyes and little else. She leans in close, her breath warm on my piss-mud caked ear.

"Now," she whispers and then lowers to her hands and feet.

I lower myself down and begin the sloth-like four-legged walk into the field. A weight lifts as I exit the jungle, like I can breathe again. Despite the fact that we're about to take several lives, I feel invigorated.

Or is it *because* I'm about to kill people that I feel invigorated?

I don't know the answer. And right now, I don't care. This has to be done. Like a tumor that needs removing. What's that make me?

A scalpel, I decide, as my hands and feet slip over the packed dirt in which Ashan's people once lived. Skeletal remains frame our path, guiding us toward the village's center, where the fire glows and men sleep. How many memories is she reliving? Where was her hut?

As hard as this might be for me, it must taste like shit in her mouth. Killing these men, avenging her family, it might help keep us safe, but I doubt it will provide any kind of catharsis for her. Her family will still be dead.

And now, another tribe is about to lose its fathers.

I pause, my hand just an inch from the ground.

This won't be the end of it.

These men have sons. Wives. Daughters. If they're anything like Ashan, they're going to come looking for the woman who killed their husbands and fathers. I'm a stranger to them, but they must know of the white man who joined Ashan. In a jungle of tribal natives, I am an easy-to-spot aberration. There is no hiding who I am.

They already want to kill me. They are *here* to kill me.

Become part of the cycle, I tell myself. *Fight. Survive. The twisting current is too much to resist.*

This is who I am now.

The fire's dying light is just enough to see by. The hunters are lying about, within fifteen feet of the luminous embers. Those who passed out, lie sprawled, as if already dead. The others lie closer to the fire. All are asleep.

Approaching like a pair of jaguars, hugging the ground, homed in on our prey, Ashan and I stop beside the outlying pair. Both are passed out, their limbs in uncomfortable tangles. If they survived to morning and woke up, they'd no doubt be in serious pain.

We'll spare them that, at least.

Mimicking Ashan, who's now glowing a demonic hue of dull orange in the flickering light, I pluck one of the poison arrow tips from the pouch tied to my hip. She demonstrated how to do this, cupping a hand over my mouth at the precise time she jabbed a branch against the skin of my neck. I practiced the move on her until it became fluid.

But that was practice, and she survived every assault.

This man won't.

My hand quivers, threatening to throw off my aim. While the poison will still kill the man if I miss his jugular, it will take longer to work. The difference is just a few seconds, but in those moments, if the man wakes, adrenaline will allow him to fight—for just a moment, but long enough to rouse the others. For this to work as intended, I need the poison to enter the bloodstream rushing to his brain and his nervous system with every beat of his heart.

The effects will be almost instantaneous. Fighting, let alone screaming—or breathing—will be impossible.

I hover over my first target like the Grim Reaper, holding the man's life and death in my hands. It's kind of a strange power rush. I don't like it...but some part of me that's lain dormant since birth, looks forward to the more capable man I will become as a result.

A monster, I think. *I will be a monster.*

And alive.

Frozen by my dual competing nature, I look up at Ashan. She's poised over her target, calm and focused. She points at her eyes and then to the man. 'Watch,' she says without speaking. 'This is how you do it.'

It happens fast. While one hand slips over the man's mouth with a vice grip, the poisoned shard of wood penetrates his neck. His body jolts, just once, and then lies still. She remains frozen in place, waiting. After thirty seconds, she releases the man, whose head lolls to the side.

Dead.

She made it look easy. Like putting an exhausted child to sleep.

A hazy image of Juni slips into my thoughts. What would she think of me now?

She wouldn't, I think, growing angry. *She won't even know me.*

Unless I survive.

Unless I kill.

My hands move without thought, guided by practice and instinct. The man's greasy lips slide under one hand, which clamps down hard, while the other stabs the poison into his neck.

Easy.

18

The man's pulse slows under my finger, pressed to his throat, monitoring the irreparable damage I've done. The *thump-bump* of my heart slows in time with his. Despite having just performed a reprehensible act, I find myself calming. I've crossed the threshold, and I still feel like me and not at all like the monster I feared I would become.

Thump-bump...

Thump...bump...

Or maybe I'm just callous to death?

How could I be? That doesn't make sense. I've spent my life trying to save people from the conditions that lead to an untimely demise.

And yet, I'm unaffected by slaying this man, by holding his head as his life slips away. What does that say about me?

That what I'm doing is right, I decide. *It's not good, but it's not wrong, either.*

Thump...bump...

Ashan steps away from the man she killed and crab walks toward her next victim.

They're not victims. They're enemy combatants.

What the hell is wrong with me?

I'm a pacifist. I've protested wars. When my grandfather was drafted to fight the Germans in World War II—a more noble cause than mine—he took a stand against killing as a conscientious objector. As a result, he became a medic and was awarded with a Silver Star for saving hundreds of lives. I've always been proud of his character, and what he did. His service inspired me to become a doctor.

What would he think of me now?

Thump...

A lone tear slips from my eye, carves a clean trail down my cheek, and drops, now muddy, onto the slain man's face.

This is who I am now.

Who I must become.

Embrace it.

No more tears.

My grandfather's actions might have been noble, but so were those of all the men who fought in that war. Evil sometimes deserves mercy, a chance at redemption. But sometimes it needs to be snuffed out.

I lower the man to the ground and move to the next, taking my time, staying quiet. When I reach the man, lying on his side, more asleep than passed out, Ashan moves on to her third. She's an efficient killer, not slowed by the moral dilemmas plaguing me. I envy her for it.

I slip into position behind the man, hands like flared cobras, ready to strike. There's less hesitation this time, and a lot more fight.

The man's eyes flare open when the fresh arrow tip pierces his neck. His eyes twitch to the side, make contact with mine, and a shout builds in his chest. The poison will work in the next second, but his scream will escape before it does.

I react without thought, removing the arrow while twisting his head skyward. Then I plunge the arrow in again, piercing the center of his throat and the vocal cords within. The scream is nothing more than a raspy whisper, muffled by my hand.

The man goes still, the poison acting fast, pushed along through his system by a rapid heartbeat. I hold him still, feeling another pulse slow and stop beneath my fingers.

I shed no tears this time.

When I look up, Ashan gives me a nod of approval and moves on to her next target. Closer to the group, I can now see them all clearly. I count eleven.

How many were there before? Thirteen?

Shit.

They're not all here. When did they leave? Are they coming back?

I'm not sure how to communicate any of this to Ashan. Even if we could talk, I'd have trouble explaining my fears.

When she finishes her fourth kill and gives me a stare of disapproval from having failed to even start my third, I hold up an open palm. We've used this signal to silently communicate the word from our very first day together. I then point to my eyes, and then to the men. I point at each man in sequence, raising a finger with each to show I'm counting.

Her brows furrow.

I point to two locations where no one is, and then shrug.

She's not getting it.

Ashan mimics my gestures, going through the motions of pointing and counting and then stabbing her finger at two empty locations.

Her eyebrows reverse direction. She ducks lower and looks about. She's understood, but her effort to find the missing men is futile. Close to the fire now, seeing anything beyond the meager light's reach is impossible. Our eyes have adjusted to the light. Everything beyond it is invisible.

She points at the two men nearest me, putting a lot of force into the motion.

I give a nod and move on. She wants to do this quickly. My next target obliges. He's so drunk that he's probably halfway to being dead already. I cup a hand over his mouth and help him the rest of way into the afterlife. The only thought I give my action is to note how simple it is. I feel a strange sense of pride, knowing that I'm not the snowflake my Republican friends would have me believe I am. I can do what needs doing, and I don't even need a gun.

Upon reaching my final target, I look over his face. Like my previous kills, the man is a stranger to me. I look over the rest of the dead men, including the man over whom Ashan is crouched. I don't recognize any of them, which is to say, the only man I would recognize—the father—is one of the two missing men.

Ashan and I dispatch the final two hunters with equal ease, staying still and quiet as we monitor their lives coming to an end.

Eleven men dead in just a few minutes, four of them at my hands, one of them brutally so.

"Where hunters?" I whisper.

Ashan scans the darkness. "Tracks. Find."

The barren earth is covered with footprints left in the wake of the drunken hunters. But they haven't left the village since they arrived. All we need to do is locate the footprints headed away from the village.

We separate, crawling into the darkness. Personally, I hope we discover the men sleeping further from the fire. My gut says that's not going to happen. But where could they have gone? From a distance it looked like all the men were inebriated. Why would they leave?

I don't find answers to my questions, or any signs of the two men. What I do find, are more bodies, or what little remains of them. Given the size, the skeleton I've stumbled upon was a woman. The bundle in her arms contains a small collection of human bones. A baby. A newborn.

Did they kill the child? Did they let it starve to death in her slain mother's arms?

Emotions seep back into my psyche, powerful and mind-numbing. I'm not regretting my actions, or feeling guilty for being part of so much death and violence. On the contrary, I find myself hoping the missing men turn up, so I can help Ashan bring justice to the jungle.

These men deserve to die.

They *need* to die.

Allowing them to live would be like condoning genocide and the murder of children.

I nearly stab Ashan in the neck when she sneaks up beside me. I pull up short when I see her face, but her raised arm would have blocked the blow anyway. She looks ready to deliver a counter strike, but then notes the anger in my eyes and the bundle beneath me.

This is the first time I've seen anything close to despair from Ashan. She reaches for the bundle, opening it up to reveal the bones inside, picked clean by insects, some of which fall out and flee into the night.

She plucks the small head from the wrapped cloth and pets the smooth, white skull. "Chulo." She holds the hollow head up to me. Points at it. "Chulo."

"Sorry, Chulo," I say.

Ashan nods her thanks for my apology and returns the skull to its resting place. I'm not sure what the burial customs are, but there's no time for that now. Not with two men still on the loose.

"Good," Ashan says, patting my arm and pointing at the dead men. "Greg, good."

I appreciate her praise and show it with a simple nod. Looking over the men, I see the scene like she does, not as a massacre or a gut-wrenching mass murder, but as a job well done.

A dry *whack* noise followed by a spray of grit on my face snaps my eyes from the scene and down to the ground between us. A long arrow has punctured the earth, just inches from my foot.

Ashan and I turn in the direction from which the arrow flew. A wall of darkness greets us and is made more ominous when a chorus of hooting voices rises up.

That's more than two men.

"Hunters," Ashan says, a trace of fear in her voice. "Friends. Kill us."

"No shit," I say.

Our eyes linger on each other for a moment. Then we both look down at Chulo's small body, wrapped against its dead mother's ribcage. "No..." I grip Ashan's shoulder. "We kill hunters."

Her eyes flare with a thirst for blood.

"Machete," she growls. "Gun! Now!"

Then she dives away, rolling toward the fire. Arrows fly, chasing her as she moves, but they don't stop her from reaching the slain men, or from picking one of them up and tossing his body over the lingering flames, smothering the fire, and plunging us into darkness.

19

Close to the clearing's fringe, I trip. I'm not sure what my foot snagged on—branch, the remains of a hut, or the scavenged limb of a dead villager—but it takes me down all the same. There's a loud crack and a sharp pain in my leg. My first thought upon hitting the dusty ground is that my leg is broken. My second is, *I can't breathe.*

With the wind knocked out of me, I sit up gasping and reaching for my tibia. It's already swelling, but not nearly enough to suggest a break. To confirm the prognosis, I give my leg a squeeze. The pain is manageable. *Definitely not a break.*

The shouts of onrushing hunters spur me back into action.

Lungs half empty, leg throbbing, I throw myself through the foliage and into the dense jungle. My eyes are adjusting to the darkness again, but it's taking time I don't have.

Without my help, Ashan will not survive.

I have no way of knowing how many warriors have come to claim our lives, but the chorus of shouting says there are too many.

For Ashan.

For me.

But maybe not for the gun.

I need to find our supplies, wrapped together in a tight bundle, tucked into the nook of a tree, and covered by leaves the size of my torso. During the day, it would be hard to spot. Now...my gear could be a few feet in front of me and I might not see it.

Slow down. Think. Focus.

My eyes continue to adjust, irises opening to capture the meager amount of leaf-filtered moonlight and starlight.

Find the tree.

Most of the trees on the village's outskirts are tall and straight, topped with green clouds, but the tree cradling our only hope of survival is a shorter species adapted to low light conditions and full of twisting roots and limbs. Ashan seemed to have an affection for the tree. She sought it out. Accepted its comfort. I got the distinct impression that the branches, perfect for climbing, were not strangers to the weight of her body, now and as a child swinging, climbing, and practicing for a life in the wild.

I find the tree by careening into one of its lower branches, repeating the doomed Cessna's crash with my face.

I'm knocked backward, the air pushed from my lungs a moment after they'd been filled anew. I cough hard, and suck in mouthfuls of air, willing the squadron of Tinkerbells in my vision to either sprinkle their pixie dust and gift me with flight, or get the hell out of the way.

They retreat, slowly, and I'm able to find the tree's network of roots. I crawl around them, feeling the twisting, gnarled shapes, hoping to find something familiar.

"Damnit," I grumble.

A scream tears from the clearing. My body tenses until I realize it's a man. When the explosion of noise screeches to a stop, I see the man in my mind's eye, clutching his throat as Ashan's poison takes hold.

Being outnumbered, she'll eventually fall, but her body count will be higher in the end. While the hunters have one opponent to find in the dark, Ashan can fire blindly in the mass of men rushing toward her and is far more likely to strike a target.

It won't be enough.

"Damnit…"

I grip a cable of root and thrash it up and down, like an enraged wrestler from the 1980s. When I release the wood, I fall forward and reach out to catch myself. Roots and ribs collide, further battering my lungs, but my outstretched hands brush against something smooth and out of place.

I scramble through the roots, find the large flat leaves, and tear them away. My pants resist me like an angry anaconda, twisting in my hands as I search for the pocket in which the gun resides. I find the weapon, draw it free, and start to move away.

A scream flinches me to a stop—another man—and triggers my memory.

The machete!

I slip the blade out from between my pants and belt, and then, wielding two weapons, I find my way back out of the roots and start up the hill toward the clearing.

Halfway there, my thoughts clear again. I should have retrieved the spare magazine as well.

Too late, I decide. Finding the gear again will take too long.

Before I can resume my charge, the sound of feet sliding over leaves freezes me in place. Is the battle moving from the clearing to the forest? Is Ashan retreating?

A shadow moves through the night, small and graceful despite the darkness.

"Ashan!"

The figure alters course, heading directly toward me.

"Ashan?"

The runner doesn't slow down, reply, or adjust course.

It's not Ashan.

When he shouts a battle cry, there is no doubt. There is also no time to think. So I react.

Rather than aiming and shooting, I swing. It's more of a flinch. Bare-handed it would have been a failed attempt at a backhanded slap. Armed with the machete, it's a deadly slice, first through the air, and then through skin, muscle, and arteries.

I've struck the man's neck.

I don't see it happen, but the spray of hot blood against my face and torso, as the man tumbles into me, tells a story. He gurgles as I catch him, instinct guiding me to aid the man I've just slain. When I realize he's already dead, I leap back and let him fall.

My lungs fill for the first time since fleeing the clearing.

I feel...*alive.* Emboldened by the primal taking of a life.

A justified killing, I tell myself. Righteous. And it feels...*good.*

Is this blood lust? a small voice from deep inside ponders. The rest of me doesn't have an answer. Doesn't care to dwell on shifting moralities.

I'm done thinking.

Done caring.

The man I was—gentle, empathetic, compassionate—has no place in the Amazon. So I bury those things and decide to become something else.

My feet slip over slick earth like a cartoon character building up speed. Traction is delivered by a clump of leaves, and I'm propelled up the hillside. My breaths come as grunts, like an overworked horse galloping through the cold.

As I breach the clearing, I move the machete to my right hand and the gun to the left. I'm not sure why, it just feels right.

My steps come as leaps. I will not trip again.

The sound of shouting guides me.

It's not pained or angry. It's excited. The hunters have subdued Ashan.

"Greg!" she screams, revealing they've taken her alive, perhaps intent on finishing what the father and son started, driven by testosterone to kill and fuck, in the reverse order.

They sent one man after me, perhaps taking my exit as cowardice or retreat. That was their first mistake. The second was turning their backs to me. The solid wall of tan flesh glows dull orange in the fire's embers, still glowing beneath the fallen warrior's weight. Soon, the blaze will burn again, fueled by his flesh. Already, the scent of burnt meat fills the air.

Some part of me that understands strategy, and is still calculating the best way to handle things, says to sneak up on them. I project an image of myself, stabbing and slicing my way through three or four men before the group realizes they're under assault.

It's not a bad plan.

But it's not what I do.

An energy unlike anything I've felt before builds in my core and blossoms out through my limbs, building in my throat and expressing itself as an inhuman roar.

I've only heard something like it once.

At a zoo.

It was a lion.

A deep resounding, 'Arroo!' The intensity of it screamed, 'danger' in my mind despite being separated from the big cat by a moat, a wall, and a fence.

These men experience the sound from me in the same way.

Shock and fear greet me as they spin around, only a few of them thinking to reach for weapons. But there is no moat to hinder my leap. No wall to block my claws. No fence to slow my assault. There is just me and them.

I see the men's faces for the first time. Unlike the father's tribe, painted in red, the newcomers are covered in a black, maze-like pattern. It differentiates the two tribes, but as I descend on them, they are unified in their terror.

I catch sight of Ashan on the ground, bloodied, but not clutching her throat—not poisoned, not dying. For a flicker, she shares in the men's fear.

Then she sees me, coated in piss-mud and a dead man's blood— and smiles.

"Arroo!" I shout again, and I swing the machete.

20

The old me, that civilized man, would like to say I black out during what comes next, that I'm suffering from a psychotic break, but that wouldn't be true. I'm present in the moment, experiencing every hack. The weight of the machete in my hand. The resistance when blade meets flesh. The audible *ting* and vibration when metal strikes bone.

The hunters who scream in fear, cowering on the ground, survive the longest. They're the lesser threat. The few who overcome their shock get my full attention.

Machete cleaves bow in two as one of the three bravest men attempts to nock an arrow. The severed weapon falls apart, taking the man's hand with it. A shrill cry rises above the din as the hunter reels back, wide eyes on the wound that he knows will claim his life. Without doctors, surgeons, the means to cauterize the wound, or to treat the resulting infection, bleeding out is just a matter of time.

He stumbles away from the fight, defeated.

A second warrior rushes in, jabbing a long arrow-like a spear. The sharp tip nearly pierces my skin. The man is faster than me and guided by experience. If he kills me, mine won't be the first life he's taken. The machete alone might not give me enough advantage.

So I shoot him.

The bullet, fired at close range from the hip, strikes his torso at an upward angle, slipping beneath his ribcage and sliding through something vital enough that he collapses and doesn't move again.

The third brave man rushes in low to tackle me around the waist.

Head lowered, arms outstretched, he doesn't see me side-step.

Avoiding his strong arm and hooked fingers is impossible, but I'm not trying to avoid contact, not entirely. The machete resides where my body once stood. Instead of ramming his head into my gut, he strikes the lowered blade. The machete slips up over his forehead, over his skull and down his back, bouncing over vertebrae.

The man's grip on my waist slides away as he falls to the ground, opened up like unzipped fabric. He twitches in pain, unable to comprehend what's happened to him. Even in my current mindset, I can't help but feel empathy for the man. I step in close and bring the machete down on the back of his neck, ending his suffering.

A flurry of shouts rises into the night, drawing my attention back to the remaining hunters who have encountered something they had not bargained for. When I step toward them, drenched in blood, fury still building, they flee into the night.

"Arroo!" I scream before raising the gun and chasing the men with hot metal. I pull the trigger until the gun clicks empty. Two screams follow the fired rounds. The gun's report is followed by silence, save for the sound of men careening through the jungle in a variety of directions.

Chasing them all down is impossible. But maybe I can find one or two of them. I step toward the darkness, but am stopped by a hand on my shoulder.

I roar and spin, raising the machete.

The blade swings down, but stops just three inches short of Ashan's face.

She doesn't flinch. She just smiles up at me with wide eyes. Her hand rises to my bearded cheek, thick with wet earth and warm blood. It's like she's seeing me for the first time. If I had a mirror, I might see myself in the same way.

Who is this man who can emerge from the jungle with a roar? Who can dismember, stab, slice, and shoot men? Who can germinate in the jungle for a month and be reborn into something new?

Something different.

I look at my hands. In the darkness, they just look wet. But I can smell the blood. And Ashan's lingering piss.

Who is this man?

This is me. I feel no shame about what I've done. About the lives I've taken. And not just because they were righteous. This is life on Earth.

Outside the theater of war, mankind pretends that abject violence has no place in society, but it has always been the driving force that brings order.

American democracy with its lofty ideals maintains its dominion because it wields the biggest military in the history of the planet, with enough firepower to destroy all of humanity—even without the use of nuclear weapons. While most of the population sits at home, taking this for granted—myself included—warriors bearing the United States flag stalk the jungles, deserts, and dangerous places of the world, doing the exact same thing I've just done.

Vengeance.

Pre-emptive violence.

Justice through killing.

If anything, my actions tonight are patriotic.

I never saw it this way before. Judgement was my knee-jerk reaction when it came to taking lives for a cause. Holidays, like Thanksgiving, Columbus Day, and even the Fourth of July, always felt like a sham to me because they were made possible thanks to genocide.

But those long-dead colonizers, explorers, and rebels were just doing what people are hardwired to do. They can't be held accountable for what they've done any more than the lion who kills a competitor's spawn. It's instinctual. Modern man might pretend that life has evolved beyond such things, but it's all a ruse. I know that now.

People haven't become civilized, they've become controlled by the illusion of morality, imposed by governments and religions.

But out here, in the jungle, with Ashan, I've had the veil lifted. I now see myself for who I am.

For who I've always been.

An animal.

Just like everyone else.

A hiss warns of danger, but it comes too late and too fast to do anything about.

Thankfully for me, the hunter's aim is shit. As I turn toward the arrow's origin, ready to charge into the jungle, I hear a gasp from behind. Is Ashan surprised I still have some fight in me?

"I can do this," I say when she grasps my arm. I whip around, angry. "I said, I can—"

Ashan's eyes are nearly as wide as her mouth. She's trying to breathe, but her chest is frozen. That's when I see the arrow jutting out from her side. Without the power of a compound bow behind it, or a razor sharp modern tip, the arrow has only penetrated an inch. I pull it out and do nothing to stem the flow of blood. It's not what will kill her, and it could help remove some of the poison from her body.

Locked up, Ashan begins to topple. I catch her and lower her to the ground while scanning the area for danger. Seeing no lingering hunters looking to score a potshot, I turn all my attention to Ashan.

Without knowing what kind of poison was used, I'm not sure how to help her. I monitor her vitals, keeping two fingers on her carotid artery. Her pulse is racing, not slowing. Her heart is working overtime to pull oxygen from her non-functioning lungs.

She's not dead yet, but she will be soon.

I take a deep breath, tilt her head back, open her mouth and breathe into her lungs. Her chest rises and falls as I take another breath and repeat. Her pulse slows under my fingers—not because she's dying, but because it's working.

I flinch and miss a breath when the man lying on the fire finally catches, his body fat crackling as the flames rise toward the night sky. I deliver another breath and scan the area. The fire illuminates the village's remains, twelve lifeless bodies strewn about, and a face, watching me from the jungle.

It's the father. He's still alive, vengeance stolen from him again.

But he doesn't attack. Knows he can't win.

Instead, he watches, waiting for the poison to do its job, and no doubt wondering what I'm attempting to do. Perhaps he thinks Ashan is already dead. That I'm violating a corpse. He's brave for lingering. No one else has.

I struggle to ignore the man as I deliver breath after breath. I force myself to slow down when I become lightheaded. The last thing I need is to pass out and offer myself to the man.

After twenty minutes of the same, my patience wanes. How long will Ashan remain like this? Are the poison's effects permanent? Does surviving its effects require life support?

"Will the asshole watching me ever fucking leave?" The man ducks when I shout, but he doesn't retreat.

Five minutes later, Ashan's fingers start moving. Her pulse steadies. And her lungs begin to rise and fall on their own. I lean back and turn to the jungle, intent on facing the father and finishing this mess. He stares at me from the jungle's fringe. How far can he go before I catch him?

While I've embraced my primitive self, I'm not a skilled tracker. Even Ashan would have trouble following a trail in the dead of night.

Ashan's hand reaches up and clasps onto my arm.

The man's eyes flare, and I hear him suck in a deep, terrified breath. He's seen the dead rise.

"Ashan...Dead?"

I shake my head. "No dead."

"You save?" There is doubt in her voice. She knows what struck her. Knows that it kills, without exception—in her experience.

"Yes."

It's not the most eloquent dialogue. It never is with Ashan and me. But it is efficient, and not without its nuances and unspoken intentions.

When I glance back to the jungle, expecting to see the father returning my gaze with his dark eyes, I find nothing but leaves and tree trunks lit in flickering orange light.

After what these men have experienced tonight, I don't think any of them will be returning. I lie down beside Ashan, naked and filthy, and I place my palm on her sternum. I feel her chest rise and fall, each breath steadier than the last.

"Thank you..." Ashan says, her voice sleepy, "Mapinguari. *My* Mapinguari."

I accept the nickname, even if it is longwinded. Tonight, I found the animal in me, so it seems only appropriate that I accept the mantel of the mythic Mapinguari, the one-eyed, hairy beast with two mouths.

We fall asleep like that and rise in the morning to blue skies, dead bodies, and a months-long sojourn to nowhere in particular.

21

It's strange, being an outlaw in a land without law, but it's also enjoyable. There are four tribes in the region, all of them uncontacted. There had been a delicate balance of power between them for generations. Disagreements happened on occasion and were sometimes settled by combat, but often through peaceful means. But when Ashan's father, Hupda, chief of the Dalandala tribe, had refused to marry her off to the Guaruamo chief's now dead son, the insult was personal.

Father and son had gone to collect Ashan by force—a socially acceptable act—but Ashan was beloved by her people. Rather than let Ashan and Hupda fend off the men alone, the tribe stood beside them, and sent father and son away in shame.

The father, a man named Juma, is known for his ruthlessness. But no one could have predicted all-out war. The Guaruamo warriors struck at night, slaughtering the men first and then women and children.

Ashan believed it was possible that some of her people escaped into the night, or that other young women had been taken, but she had found no evidence for either. As far as she knew, she was the last of the Dalandala, meaning the territory we've been traveling through belongs to her...though none of the other tribes would agree to that claim.

Not only is she a woman, but her tribe no longer exists and the three remaining people-groups most likely already divvied up the territory.

The Jebubo people would certainly refute her claim. The men painted in black mazes had been Jebubo. They were closely aligned with the Guaruamo, and prone to violence. Hunters through and through.

The last of the tribes, the Arawanti, are agricultural and non-violent, but their chief tends to side with the majority when it comes to tribal disputes. We haven't seen any Arawanti hunters searching for us, but that doesn't mean we'd be welcome. The death toll from that night reached fifteen. Men from both violence-prone tribes lost their lives.

If we are found, we will be slain on sight.

I learned all of this today. I had figured out bits and pieces on my own, but the history of what I stumbled into was a mystery until I thought to ask Ashan about it. She wasn't keen on relaying the painful history—had she gone with the dead son, her people would still be alive—but she laid it out in sequential order, giving me cold facts without the emotion of a storyteller.

I had asked about it during the day following that nighttime slaughter, but we lacked a communal language to convey such things then.

In the months since, alone in the forest, with no one else to talk to, we've developed a unique comingling of English and her language, which I call Dalandan. I supposed you could call what we speak Dalanglish, but it's really a combination of Dalandan and English slang, which she enjoys learning.

We spend hours just talking as the sun sets, getting to know each other, learning what the other knows. When it comes to life in the jungle, I'm a perfect student. I don't like that Ashan often feels like a babysitter, keeping me alive because I'm incapable. At the same time, I revealed how to cheat death itself. I started by teaching her CPR, revealing how I prevented the poison from taking her life. I also explained that we'd been lucky. A poison that worked differently would have been impossible to stop without medicine, a concept that took time to explain. Once she understood, she was able to reveal a cadre of plants, herbs, and animals used to treat various ailments. Overall, I've learned far more from her than she has from me.

But I never feel less because of her. In her eyes I am...special. That's putting it lightly. For her, Mapinguari is more than a nickname. While I don't resemble the beast, I am different enough from any man she's ever seen that I'm...I don't know. A demi-god maybe. She knows I'm human. Knows I can die. But she still chooses to believe I'm also something more. Or could become something more.

I think it gives her hope. Our kinship does the same for me. I might be lost in the jungle, far from the reach of civilization and people who have no doubt given up on me by now, but my life is not over.

What was my funeral like? I wonder. *Was it a somber affair? Did people from the soup kitchen attend? Patients? How many of them forgot about me a day later?*

How long will it be before Gwen no longer thinks of me?

I look at the satchel bouncing on my hip as we trek through the forest. I'm tempted to power on the phone and look at her photo, to remember what I've lost, but I don't know how Ashan would handle it. I've explained technology, but it just sounds like magic to her. Showing her something like the phone would only solidify her belief that I'm a supernatural being. So, I don't look at my wife's photo, and part of me is glad that I don't.

With every passing day, my memory of the past clouds. I have a hard time picturing her face. And with this haze, the pain of what I've lost is numbed a little more.

I no longer think of Juni. I can't. I need to be fierce to survive. The Amazon basin is no place for a broken heart.

"Hey," Ashan says. "Where are you?"

She's stopped on the game trail, her body twisted around, her curves hard to ignore.

There has been an...attraction between us since the night I became an animal. I felt primal for several days, connected to the jungle and the creatures in it. That faded some as our dialogue became conversations, and I started to feel more human than beast.

But not everything awakened in me that night has gone dormant. I tell myself that desire and action are different things, and I attempt to maintain a physical distance. But that is not always possible. And the bond we've formed, running, hiding, hunting, and talking, is permanent. It's resolute.

I'd describe my bond with Gwen in the same terms, but under different, far less intense circumstances. I depended on her for affection, love, support, and companionship. All noble things. But I find myself comparing modern world notions of soulmates and romance against

Stone Age dependency that isn't necessarily deeper, but far more intense and necessary. At least in my case. Had we been living comfortably in a village, my experience would be different. But there isn't a tribe that would accept us without first running us through.

Gwen is my wife. She always will be, even if I grow old and die in this place. But Ashan...she is something, too. I'm just not sure what, yet.

"Right here." I motion to the leaf litter beneath my bare feet. "Duh."

She smiles at my use of 'Duh.' Of all the slang I've taught her, it is her favorite. Because it somehow sounds stupid. She's made creative use of the word, too, calling me a, 'duh-boy' and 'duh-face' on occasion, much to her own delight.

"Where are you, here?" She pats her head. "What are you thinking about?"

"You," I say, and I regret my honesty when she smiles and blushes. I have yet to decide how to handle our relationship. I don't want to hurt her. Don't want to make an enemy of her either. I have no idea how she'd react to being scorned. But to do so would be to lie as well. In my mind, she is without fault.

While my mind and body have acclimated to my new life, my heart is torn. How long have I been here? Six months? Longer? I've given up on tracking time. With no calendar, or appointments, or holidays to worry about, what's the point?

My wife is blameless and wonderful. Betraying her with Ashan reflects solely on my own weakness as a man.

My marriage is the only lingering trace of my modern sensibilities left. In all other ways, I am transformed. I've become the stereotype savage of the Amazon. I am a hunter. A killer. A warrior.

"Thoughts of me displease you?" Ashan is intuitive, reading my body language as easily as she does the monkeys' overhead.

I should just let Gwen go. Be done with my old self. I will not be happy until I do.

Can I be happy while being hunted?

Ashan raises an eyebrow, stepping closer. The look in her dark eyes is all mischief. My stomach clenches.

Yes. I can be happy here. But I won't allow it.

We've been here before, on the cusp, her closing the distance, me unsure. And as always, I raise my hands. That's all it takes. She knows what it means, knows what's stopping me. Her respect for it makes resisting her more difficult. Her permanent state of nakedness doesn't help, either. Not that I'm any different now. I wear the remains of my shorts, which is basically a loin cloth with cargo short pockets. The belt holds the machete and several pouches formed from my former clothing. The only things of mine still intact are the satchel and its contents.

"It's me, isn't it," she says with a grin. "I'm too much for you."

"You *are* covered in mud," I say, relieved that she's returning to our normal playful banter instead of challenging my resistance.

She looks down at her body, coated in a thin film of dirt that's caked a bit since we applied it in the morning. The wet earth provides natural camouflage, especially for me, and protects us from the barrage of insects looking to make a meal of our blood. "Maybe it will rain later."

When she smiles at me and struts away, I think, *God, I hope not.*

Then I look up to the sky glimmering through the leaves and am a little disappointed to not see clouds.

When I look back down, Ashan is crouched low to the ground, waving a hand back at me to do the same. She's seen something, or smelled something. I wasn't paying attention, which is another reason to put thoughts of infidelity out of my mind. The rainforest is a dangerous place for everyone, including people who grew up here.

I crouch low and crawl on all fours, sliding up beside Ashan.

With a hand gesture, I ask, 'What is it?'

She points to her eyes, and then straight ahead. I stare into the distance. The jungle is flat here, but thick with trees. The farthest I can see is a hundred feet. And that's where I find an aberration.

At first, I see what looks like an oversized porcupine. But the quills aren't rigid. They flow with the wind. Like hair. And the way it moves is all wrong. Unnatural, like a human being on all fours, just like I'd been doing a moment ago.

The creature lowers itself and all but disappears, blending in with the foliage just to the side of the game trail on which we're traveling.

I lean in close to Ashan and whisper. "What is it?"

"Mapinguari," she says, a quiver in her quiet voice. She looks me in the eyes, dead serious and afraid. "The real Mapinguari."

22

"I thought *I* was Mapinguari," I whisper through a half smile. I'm having trouble taking the legendary beast seriously. As steeped in jungle lore as I've become, I can still spot the difference between fact and fiction. The Mapinguari is a legend. A story meant to make people afraid of the dark, afraid of being alone. A parenting trick used to keep children from wandering off alone.

"Mapinguari is vengeance," she whispers. "But her wrath can be directed with the right tribute. The right sacrifice. The hunters might have given up, but they have paid Mapinguari's price. The beast will hunt us to the ends of the jungle. We cannot stay. Cannot fight."

It is surprising that Ashan, an adult, still believes the legend is true. But in a world without science, the great dispeller of myth and magic, monsters are real.

The thing on the trail ahead of us is probably a tapir tangled in brush. "I'll go. See what it is."

Ashan's hand latches on to my forearm, her grip like the jaws of a lion. If not for the dread in her eyes, I might have shouted in pain.

She motions for a silent retreat and grips a little harder, telling me debate is likely to get me killed, if not by Mapinguari, then by her.

A subtle nod frees me from her python grip.

Our flight is slow and quiet, low to the ground, like a pair of sloths.

This feels wrong. Running away from a fight. I've proved myself, haven't I? Ashan and I could stand against anything the jungle has to offer, man or beast. But I also respect Ashan's opinions, feelings, and beliefs. If turning tail puts her at ease, I'll do it. But I don't like it.

Ten minutes later, after covering just a few hundred feet, the creature waiting by the trail's edge loses its patience, and with a single roar of frustration, it tells me a few things, the first of which is that Ashan was right.

At least partially.

The animal *is* a predator—not a tapir.

It *had* set an ambush. And now...now it's hunting us.

Ashan rises into a squat, searching the jungle behind us. I do the same and find nothing but the same monotonous view of tree trunks, green foliage, and a brown forest floor. But I can hear it now, running without regard for the noise it's making.

The ambush suggests intelligence, or at least a keen hunting instinct, but the mad rush through the jungle is mindless. Crazed.

Its effect on us is immediate and simultaneous.

We run.

Like the thing rushing up behind us, our sprint is loud and tumultuous, the jungle's version of a screeching car chase. Ashan takes the lead, weaving a path through the maze of trees. I'm faster than her, but I'm not about to leave her behind, so I match her pace and put a portion of my mind on coming up with a backup plan. I can have the machete drawn in a second. The gun, now held in my satchel with thirteen rounds remaining, will take longer to retrieve, but will kill anything in the jungle, animal, human, or monster.

If my aim is good.

I've been lucky in the past, firing point blank or into a group. On the surface, my hit-to-miss ratio is probably better than average, but it's easy to hit a target that's close, standing still, and has no idea what a gun can do. To use the gun, I'll have to stop running and hope the thing behind us does, too.

Better to go with the machete, I decide.

Find my inner savage animal again.

That's hard to do while running away. Body and brain are locked in flight mode. Fight acts as a backseat driver, shouting at me to stop and stand my ground, but my allegiance to Ashan is stronger than either instinct. I go where she goes.

I'm in better shape than I've ever been. My body is lean and muscular. I can hike all day and wake the next morning ready to do it again. But long-distance running has always been a challenge for me, even as a kid. I could sprint faster than most, but I dropped out of most endurance races long before the finish line. Lungs tighten. Legs burn. The first aches of a cramp worm into my side. It won't be long before I'm forced to catch my breath.

"Ashan," I say, breathless.

My pained face and hand on my side says all that needs saying. I feel like I've failed her, that her personal Mapinguari has revealed himself to be fallible, but she already knows that. Still, I want to be superhuman for her. I want to stand and fight, even now. But I'm more likely to keel over and put up a fight comparable to a stuffed unicorn—mythical and then torn apart.

A roar spurs me past the pain. Thumping feet and crashing brush grow louder.

Where I had been slowing myself to maintain Ashan's pace, she's now slowing to match my dwindling stride. And the thing behind us is gaining.

"We have to fight," I say, hand on my satchel. She knows what I have. Understands the gun's power. But it's not enough to overcome her fear of the unknown.

She sniffs the air and says, "Not much further. This way!"

We course-correct to the right. I take a deep breath as I wince in pain, the cramp nearly crippling me. And that's when I smell it, too.

Water.

Is Mapinguari afraid of water? Is that part of the legend? Being a creature of the Amazon rainforest, that seems like the shittiest weakness imaginable. Whoever conjured the legend probably needed a way to control their children's fear of the monster. But water? Then it hits me. Mapinguari must be attracted to the stench of filth. Parents used the creature to con their children into staying clean.

Classic parenting from the stone age to the modern age.

Is that why we're headed to water? Does Ashan think washing will prevent the creature from attacking?

I hope not.

My breaths transform to wheezing as we start up a steady grade.

"Almost there!" Ashan grasps my arm, yanking me up the rise.

Ahead of us, the jungle thins. I can see the blue sky that signifies a clearing. It stretches far to the left and right. Whatever we're headed toward, it's larger than a stream.

I drop to my hands and knees. "I just...need a minute...to—"

My breathy pleading is cut short by the screaming of monkeys overhead. It's not the cry of fright, or even of warning. Whatever Mapinguari is, they're not afraid. This is the cry monkeys make when something else is about to meet its end. They're like spectators at a Roman coliseum, calling for blood, excited by the action. In the past, we've used the sound to avoid predators, and on one occasion, stole a python's kill. Today, it is a harbinger of my own demise.

The *huff, huff, huff,* of something approaching is coupled with the thumping of feet and the slap of leaves. It's nearly here.

Ashan slaps me in the face, hard.

"Leave!" I shout. "Go!"

She slaps me again, but her eyes are on the jungle behind me, wide with fright. She can see it.

"We will run together or die together," Ashan says.

I push myself with a growl, angry at her for not standing our ground when we had the chance, for using her life as a bargaining chip, and a little bit for slapping me in the face.

But it gets me moving.

She helps me along, shoving hard, pinching my skin so hard that it hurts more than the cramp, defeating pain with worse pain.

"Faster!" Ashan shouts, the alarm punctuated by a rising growl from behind us. It's unlike anything I've heard before, both deep and high-pitched, rumbling from the creature's chest to mine.

My foot snags and I topple forward, arms outstretched. *I'm sorry,* I think to Ashan. *I've failed you.*

And then my hands strike...nothing.

My torso folds forward as my gut takes the brunt of my fall. A wall of brown soil slaps against my hands, and then my face, transferring momentum from the top of my body to the bottom, curling me into a flip.

Ashan shouts as her legs tangle with mine. I can't see her, but I feel her topple over and past, landing with a splash.

My legs go vertical as I slide down a steep rise, face dragging through the dirt, neck bent at a dangerous angle. When my downward progress stops, my legs move forward again, sending me sprawling onto my back. My fall becomes a roll. Spirals of dirt fling up around me as I tumble over a drop and splash down.

Water envelops me. My feet search for a bottom, but I find nothing. With a few kicks of my feet, I breach the surface. Surrounded by smooth, flowing brown water, I turn my gaze upward. A twenty-foot earthy cliff topped with jungle and blue sky greets me. Up in the trees, monkeys squeal with delight, shaking branches and bouncing about.

Are they cheering for me? Or are they disappointed? It's hard to tell with monkeys.

I flinch when an explosion of dirt announces the arrival of the thing chasing us. While I'm expecting the thing to go airborne, diving into the river before dragging me under, it skids to a stop. I catch a glimpse of black on black-spotted skin, like a black panther's, and a tan mane of hair ...or brush.

It roars in frustration, scrambling back and forth. I can see its mane bouncing with frantic agitation, but little else comes into view. And it doesn't attack. Doesn't enter the water. Not because it's confounded by cleanliness, but because it can't swim.

I extend my middle finger, treading water with ease as the cramp fades. I've always been a good swimmer. Lessons at the YMCA. Summer camps. I attended one particularly brutal camp where to prove you could swim in the pool's deep end, you had to tread water while holding a brick in both hands. I managed it at age eight. Staying afloat in the river is the exact kind of respite I needed. "Fuck you, asshole."

The thing stops, turning its head in my direction, staring me down. At least, I think it is. The mane has flopped in front of it, concealing both body and face.

"That's right," I say, hoping the creature I'm pretty sure is a man in disguise understands the defiant tone of my voice, if not the English curse words. "Fuck. You."

When the thing turns away and bounds into the jungle, I laugh.

"It can't swim," I say to Ashan, but I get no reply. "Can you believe it? What kind of thing lives in the Amazon and can't swim?"

When I spin around to look Ashan in the face and share in the relief of our brush with Mapinguari, she's nowhere in sight.

"Ashan?"

I haven't seen her since falling on the ridge. I heard her hit the water, but...

"Oh shit. Ashan!" Mapinguari isn't the only denizen of the Amazon that can't swim. As I suck in three deep breaths, the sound of maniacal laughter filters out of the jungle, pursuing me deep into the muddy waters, where real monsters reside, and my only friend in the world might already be dead.

23

The hot chocolate water is impossible to see in. I keep my eyes open despite the grit, hoping to catch a glimpse of Ashan, but all I can see are shades of brown, lighter near the surface and almost black just a few feet down. I'll never find her with my eyes, so I probe the depths as I swim, hoping to feel her.

It's an impossible task, I know. The river is a good twenty feet across, who knows how deep, and is flowing.

My only real clue about her location is that she hit the water before me. Every time I surface for a breath, I turn and glance downstream, hoping to see her hand reaching out, her open mouth gasping for air— any indication of where she might be.

I dive deep, flailing about.

My leg strikes something solid, but pliable. I spin around in the water, still seeing nothing, and reach. There's nothing there. I try to swim against the river, but exhaustion is taking its toll. While swimming is less taxing for me than running, my anxiety and the extra effort hasten the cramp's return.

A second thump against my leg spins me around again, reaching, searching, finding nothing.

Burning lungs command me to surface, but I resist. She's down here. I'm sure of it.

A warning sounds from deep within, the small voice breaking through my panic for just a moment.

Something is down here.

That's when I feel them. Little things. Fish. Aquatic bugs. Baby turtles. Who's to say? They peck at my body, tickling my skin, picking off chunks of mud, caked with insects.

There's a simple rule of the jungle: where there are little animals, there are bigger animals who eat them.

I stop flailing. Stop searching for Ashan, in part because I know it's hopeless, but also because my frantic search could be interpreted as death throes, and nothing attracts predators more than an easy kill.

I swim to the surface, doing my best to not gasp for air, but I fail. With each throaty breath, the cramp flares. Even without the possibility of a predator sharing the water with me, I'm in real trouble. I'm fifteen feet from shore in moving water that's over my head. Then there's the shore itself. Right now, it's lumps of tall grass—the kind that capybara like to munch on and caiman like to hide in. Further ahead, the river is framed by tangles of roots ten feet tall. I might be able to catch myself on them, but climbing the slick limbs with weary muscles might be impossible.

And then there is Ashan, somewhere under the water, no doubt dead.

Maybe I'll just stay in the river. Let it have its way with me.

A thump against my foot tears me from my malaise, the danger reminding me that I want to live, even if it hurts.

I'm about to strike out toward the shore, when a pair of eyes slips up out of the water, staring at me. For a moment, I think it's a turtle. The casual nature of its arrival is non-threatening.

Then I feel another bump, this time against my waist.

Only one creature in the Amazon river can be both here and there. The forked tongue tasting me in the air confirms it.

This is why Mapinguari laughed.

That man-thing knows the jungle. Knows the river. Knows whose territory we leapt into.

I side-stroke toward the shore, eyes locked on the snake's head. For a moment, it appears I'm not moving at all, but the serpent is just matching my movement, locked in position. But why hasn't it struck? Is it going to attack, or does it realize I'm too big and is just escorting me from its territory?

Five feet from shore, I kick river bottom. Realizing I can stand, I plant my feet and rise a foot higher in the water.

The response is instant. The snake's jaws snap open, revealing four rows of sharp, hooked teeth designed to latch onto prey and not let go. Once those teeth find flesh, there's no prying them off.

I manage to catch the snake just below its head, the open jaws just inches from my face. But the anaconda doesn't need to bite me to kill me. It just needs a brace while it wraps itself around me and squeezes. Holding it in my hand does the same job.

Its long body coils around me, slipping over my right arm, each leg, and my torso.

"Fuck!" I growl, losing my footing as my legs are pried apart. My head dips toward the water. I'm going to be suffocated and drowned.

Standing on one foot, my chin just above water, the snake glares down at me, still fighting my arm for the privilege of biting my face. I let out a roar, the animal in me taking control once more. "No!"

The snake surges, pushing closer to my face. I resist with everything I have. "Fuck you!"

Pressure builds as the snake squeezes.

The machete's handle rests against my fingers. I had hoped to draw the blade, slicing the snake in the process, but my arm is immobilized.

A groan is forced from my compressing lungs. With its next big squeeze, my ribs will break. When that happens, I won't be able to fill my lungs.

A kind of raw hatred fills me, smothering my humanity, and spurring me into the only action of which I'm currently capable.

Instead of pushing the open jaws away, I pull.

As the snake rushes in, caught off guard by the sudden lack of resistance, I lean to the side.

Before the serpent can reel back, I turn and bite, applying all 150 psi of pressure available to me.

The snake doesn't flinch. Capable of holding its breath for long periods of time, I won't be suffocating it any time soon. Certainly not in the thirty seconds or so I've got left. Nor will I be drawing blood. I'm denting the thick, scaly skin, but not breaking through, and I probably couldn't without thrashing, and that's not possible.

My foot is wrapped and tugged, pulling it from the silty bottom.

Man and snake plunge into the moving depths together.

Water fills my mouth as the last of my air is squeezed out of me. Holding my breath isn't difficult—I couldn't breathe if I wanted to—

but the water in my mouth and the lack of air in my lungs is a pretty good approximation of what drowning feels like.

But the animal in me hasn't given up.

The snake, sensing victory, stops fighting against the combined grasp of my hand and teeth. It knows my grip will loosen in just a few moments. When I slide my hand up to its head, it doesn't react. It's a patient killer.

Fingers probe with the delicacy of a new lover, unsure of where to wander. Then I feel it, a slight bulge that shifts with pressure. Lover becomes monster as I stab my index finger into the eye as hard and fast as I can.

There's a moment of resistance, then a warm liquid pop.

The river turns into a frothing apocalypse of motion. I'm freed as every part of the snake reels back, trying to escape my wrath. Despite being desperate for air, I hold on with both hands, and my jaws.

Fully mobile again, I plant my feet and stand, pushing my head above the water and growling in the air around the snake's body. The giant creature twists in the water, frantic. Its twenty-five-foot body slides through the river with nothing to get traction on. I struggle to hold its weight against the current. This isn't a tug-o-war I can win.

But that's not the real contest.

When the snake tried to crush and drown me, it set the terms of this encounter. Kill or be killed. The snake might be backing down, but hell if I am.

I nearly lose the beast when I release my right hand, but it doesn't take long to draw my machete.

The blade rises from the water like a sinister Excalibur.

Snake skin bends under the weapon's tip, and then separates.

A quiver shakes through the snake's body, a last-ditch effort to free itself from my grasp.

But too late.

The machete punches through the anaconda's back, slick with its blood. Severely wounded, the now terrified serpent thrashes free and yanks itself back, finishing the job for me. The sharp blade slices through skull and brain.

Before the river can pull the limp body downstream, I snag its neck and trudge toward shore. When I reach the clumpy grass just before the wall of tangled roots, the water is just knee deep. I climb out onto wobbly legs, dragging the anaconda behind me.

I want to fall.

Want to cling to solid ground.

But I can't.

Mapinguari is watching. I'm sure of it.

So I haul the snake—the Amazon's most deadly killer—from the river and hold it up. With a quick strike, I sever the snake's head, hold it above mine and unleash a roar toward the river's far side. Then I throw it across the water, satisfied when it crashes through the leaves and into the darkness beyond.

Believing that's as clear of a 'fuck you' as I can manage without speaking, I take hold of the anaconda body and drag it into the jungle. When I'm sure Mapinguari can't see me, I fall to my knees, tears in my eyes. My victory over the now one-eyed, double-mouthed monster has cost me everything.

"I'm sorry," I say, and then collapse.

24

Thanksgiving.

Growing up, it was my favorite holiday. In part, because I liked to eat. I'd load my plate with turkey, cranberry sauce—homemade, not the gelatinous canned crap—mashed potatoes, yams with marshmallow, sweet rolls, green bean casserole covered with a thick bed of crispy onions, and stuffing. Much to my mother's dismay, I would mash it all together, experiencing the flavors all at once. But the real reason I enjoy-ed the day was seeing extended family.

There's something special about being with thirty-plus people who all, in one way or another, look, sound, and act alike. A literal kinship. That's not to say everyone thought alike. My family's beliefs covered the spectrum of political, religious, and economic Americana. But at the end of the day, no matter our differences, we were still family sharing a meal. In that way it was primal.

Why am I thinking about Thanksgiving? Lost in the haze between sleep and wakefulness, I search my memories.

A dream, fading in the periphery of my thoughts slips back into my conscious mind. I was in my parents' living room, laughing with family, headed for the kitchen. The décor was bright, orange and yellow and brown. Turkeys, red berries, fall leaves. A fire was lit, crackling as a rotisserie turkey rotated over a blue burning Duraflame log.

That's...different.

Then I'm in the kitchen, standing behind Gwen, hand-cranking cranberries in an old-fashioned counter-mounted meat grinder, the red mash dropping in clumps. The smell is tart and familiar. When I was ten, my mother taught me how to use the grinder to make cranberry sauce. It had been my Thanksgiving job until I met Gwen and she did it better. My mouth waters, but not for the sauce being made. My wife dances to music—tribal drums—shifting her hips back and forth.

I slip up behind her, hands reaching for her waist.

My fingers work their way beneath the apron, to the soft shirt hugging her slender midriff. She doesn't react to my presence until my arms are around her and I'm pressed against her back. That's when she pushes her ass into me and continues her dance.

I lean into her, slipping my head around her straight black hair.

Straight black hair?

I kiss her tan skin, following the line of her strong jaw, searching for her lips.

She turns to face me, deep brown eyes burrowing into mine, thick lips spreading to receive mine.

"Ashan..."

I wake with a start, having slipped fully into the dream again. This time, I open my eyes and try to push myself up. My body aches, everywhere. All I manage to move is my head.

Take it slow, I think. I'm lucky to be alive. Recovering is going to take a few days.

If I even have a few days. Mapinguari might know a way across. The jungle is dangerous enough on its own. I'm lucky something hungry didn't stumble across me while I laid unconscious on the ground.

My stomach growls as my nose flares. My hunger is being stoked by the smell of roasting meat, and it's not a lingering dream element. Smoke sifts through the air above me.

I reach for the machete. It's missing from my hip. The satchel is gone, too.

"Welcome back, snake killer."

The voice is feminine, tough, and not speaking English.

My body's pain isn't enough to keep me down. I rise with a grunt and find Ashan, alive and well, casually squatting by a fire, where a portion of the anaconda is being roasted.

She didn't drown. Given her unruffled demeanor, I don't think she was even close to drowning. She must have reached the far shore before I started looking for her. Feeling like a fool, I decide not to ask.

"Good dream?" she asks with a mischievous grin. I'm not sure what she finds funny until she glances down with unabashed interest. I follow her eyes and find myself in the throes of what modern man calls 'morning wood.' I'm not sure what Ashan's people call the phenomenon, and I'm not about to ask.

I shift my scant garment over myself, and cough-laugh my embarrassment away.

But she's not done with me. Not even close.

Lacking the shame that forces me to cover myself, Ashan waggles her body back and forth like she's riding me. "Ashan," she says, impersonating me. "Oh, Ashan."

The combination of her sultry movements and my abject horror keep my jaw from closing. "I didn't..."

She laughs and rotates the snake, wiping a finger through the juices dripping from its body and licking it off, all without breaking eye contact. "Ashan...more...yes, yes!"

When I feel like I'm about to pass out from embarrassment, she falls back laughing.

While Ashan enjoys herself at my expense, I take stock of my body. There's some bruising, pulled muscles, and the lingering tightness of day-old muscle strain, but everything moves. No bones are broken. I take a deep breath and feel no pain. As far as close encounters with an apex predator go, I fared pretty well.

The scent of cooking meat sets my stomach growling again. "Is it good?" The question is genuine, but I also hope it will redirect Ashan away from my dreams and their effect on the real world.

"You'll have to wait and see," she says, a wicked smile leaving me to wonder whether or not she's talking about the snake. My consternation deflates her amusement. "Why are you not happy?"

"What is there to be happy about?"

"You're serious?"

My silence says I am, but I'm already coming around to her point of view.

She stokes the fire, sending the flames higher to lick against the serpent's skin, charring it. Then she stands, with a fire of her own, burning in her eyes. "You survived Mapinguari. And stood defiant before him." She raises her middle finger as I did in the river. "Fuck you, asshole!"

I can't help but smile. She knows the words, understands their meaning, and enjoys using them, but her thick accent, unlike any I've heard before, makes them sound more adorable than offensive.

"You see?" she says at my smile. "You fought the snake and didn't just survive, you killed it! I have never seen such things. No one in all the tribes has witnessed such things."

"People don't defy Mapinguari?" I ask, my mood lifting.

"And live?" She lets the question answer mine.

"Well, it *is* an asshole."

Ashan covers her mouth, stifling uproarious laughter. I can't help but join her.

"And now it knows your strength," she says, and she grows suddenly serious. "Why did you remain in the water?"

I sit in silence, not wanting to answer.

"I heard you shout my name. By the time I arrived, you were severing the snake's head. Throwing it at Mapinguari was...foolish, but I enjoyed it. But why risk your life against the snake when you were already exhausted?"

She settles in to wait for an answer when it becomes clear I don't want to give her one.

"You will not eat until you tell me," she says.

"Can't we just enjoy the rest of today?"

"You will enjoy very little," she says, "unless you speak."

"For fuck's sake. Ugh. I...I thought you were drowning. I thought you were under the water. When I killed the snake, when I threw its head, I wasn't being defiant. I was enraged."

"Because I was dead."

I nod.

Her smile fades. Using my machete, she cuts off a strip of meat and carries it over to me. She squats down, steaming meat skin-side down on the dirty blade. "Scrape it over your teeth and the meat will come free."

I do as instructed, filling my mouth with warm meat. It has the consistency of dark chicken, slightly greasy, and tastes like very mild fish. Almost flavorless, which is far more pleasant than I was expecting. "Good," I say, pleasing her.

We spend the next half hour devouring the small portion of the snake that tried to make a meal of me. When our bellies are full, we lean back to enjoy what remains of the day.

"Mapinguari won't find us here?" I ask.

She shrugs. "Eventually. But not today. Not tomorrow."

"It can't swim?"

Another shrug. "It avoids water. That is all I know. The nearest crossing is several days travel."

"You don't seem afraid anymore," I note.

"I have you," she says, reaching her hand out. I take it without thought, squeezing my fingers around hers.

The motion makes me wince.

"You're in pain?" she says.

"Nothing some drugs couldn't take care of," I complain.

"What is drugs?"

"They're..." My eyes rise on my forehead. "Where is my satchel?"

Ashan reaches behind her, pulling out the satchel. I empty its contents, laying them near the fire to dry. I pause when I remove the bagged cellphone. The insides are still dry, but the device and the images it holds have little effect on me. I know what I'm after. The saturated notebook full of writing I can't read, and a single page scrawled with my desperate prayer comes next.

I open the book, tear out a blank page, and hand it to Ashan. "Dry this by the fire."

As she holds the sheet up, letting the heat wick the moisture away, I pull out the plastic-wrapped brick of marijuana and inspect it. The contents are dry.

I pry open the wrap, and scrape out a few ounces of dry buds.

"And now?" Ashan asks, holding up the dried page.

I take it from her, tear a rough rectangle and roll a joint so thick it looks like a slug. "Now," I say with a grin, recalling the expression my college roommate used, "we're going to get high as balls."

25

"I told him, you can't force monkeys to have sex." Ashan takes a long drag and holds the smoke in her lungs like a pro. She might be new to marijuana, but this isn't the first time she's smoked something. She lets it out slow, through smiling teeth. "But then he keeps cramming them together like things will just slip into place." She acts out the scene with her hands, holding invisible monkeys, letting loose with a deep belly laugh.

"The best part is that they were both males." Her laugh rises a few octaves and the creatures above us react with hoots of their own—a jungle laugh track.

Ashan is a lot of things: fierce, strong, mysterious. She's compelling, like a good novel. And she's not hard on the eyes. But chatty? I wouldn't have guessed it. But all it took to get her talking was three puffs of king joint, which we've whittled down to a roach the size of a cigar's width.

She's been telling me stories of her youth. Growing up among the Dalandala doesn't sound like it was easy from a modern world perspective, but she speaks fondly of even the most challenging events, and every member of her large, now-deceased family. Her younger brother is the central character in most of her stories. He was half her age, full of mischief and grand schemes.

The pot hits my tired body a bit differently than it does Ashan, easing my pain and loosening my mind. I'm slack on the ground, back propped up on a fallen tree, arms spread wide, head tilted back. The leaves above me look like spilled puzzle pieces, revealing gaps of blue table cloth. I reach for the pieces, hoping to rearrange them. But they're out of reach. Even if I could reach them, they look too similar. I could never finish the puzzle.

"I didn't know how to tell him," Ashan says. "He wanted to raise monkeys. Wanted to train them from birth. Everyone knows that to train a monkey, you need to capture it young. Pluck it from its dead mother's arms. If you're lucky enough to have given birth recently, you can suckle it yourself. That works best. Makes the bond permanent."

"Did you have one?" I ask. "A monkey?"

"Kaxuyana."

"Kaxuy-what-what?"

Something about her giggle fills me with affection. I adore this woman. Lacking any sense of shame, my eyes follow a lazy path around her body. The mud covering has been gone since our dip in the river, and as usual, she does little to cover herself.

How do the men here handle the constant nudity? How do the teenaged boys? A bumpy car ride was enough to set me off, never mind a tribe full of naked women.

"Kaxuyana," Ashan says again. "My monkey."

"How long did you have it?"

"Have *her*," she says. "I still do."

Has there been a monkey with us this whole time that I didn't see? Ho-lee shit! With wide eyes, I search the area looking for signs of a monkey. "Kaaaxu," I call with a sing-song voice that sets Ashan laughing even harder.

"She isn't with us," Ashan says. "I lost her when..." Her smile falters. "She was fast. Smart. She would have fled to the trees. She'll find me again. In time."

"What about your brother?" I ask. "What's his name?"

"Yabuti."

A snort of a laugh scratches from my nose.

Ashan's brow furrows. I love how it looks. That serious gaze.

"Your laugh mocks his name?"

I shake my head, sucking in another drag and laughing the smoke back out. Then I pass the roach to Ashan, who accepts it and fills her lungs.

"In my language, it sounds like 'Ya booty.' Booty is slang." I roll over and slap my ass cheek. "For ass."

Ashan coughs a series of staggering laughs. "Yabuti's name translates to 'your ass' in your language?" She's barely holding it together, struggling through the words.

When I nod, she unleashes a series of hiccup laughs that dwindle down to, "Ohh, ohh. He would have liked that."

"What kid wouldn't?"

"I would have hated it. I was…embarrassed. A lot. All the time."

Picturing Ashan as anything other than bold and confident is impossible.

"I was…" she pats her slender belly. "Fat." She puffs her cheeks out. "Lazy, too." A shrug. "I liked to eat. Didn't like to work."

I pluck the dwindling joint from Ashan's fingers and take a drag. "What changed? What made you into…this?" I motion to her body with both hands, making an hour glass shape. It's not a precise depiction of her body. Her hips aren't particularly wide, nor her breasts all that voluptuous, but she understands the motion, and the implication behind it—that I find her attractive.

"I met a jaguar," she says. "Who also liked to eat."

"What happened?" I ask, passing the meager joint back.

She turns around, showing me four two-inch-long scars. I'd noticed them before, but never asked where they'd come from. "The jaguar pinned me to the ground. It was casual. Slow. I couldn't fight. Couldn't move. An easy meal. I felt its breath on my neck. It was warm. Smelled like rotten monkey. All it had to do was bite."

"What happened?" I ask again, sitting up straighter.

"My father saved me." The remains of her smile fades away. Tears roll down her cheeks. The marijuana is opening her up, letting buried emotions surface. The roach flares orange as she sucks in all that remains. She doesn't flinch when the hot ash slips through her fingers. She just pinches it between her fingers, crumbling it up. She watches her exhaled smoke rise into the jungle.

"I have more." I pat the plastic-wrapped brick. "A lot more."

She wipes the tears from her eyes and stands. "Not strong enough." She retrieves her blowgun and steps away.

I struggle to stand, pain blossoming through the marijuana.

She puts a hand on my shoulder, holding me down. "You stay. I won't be long." Then she kisses my forehead, and slips away into the jungle without a sound.

After a few minutes alone with the unsolvable puzzle foliage, I decide that rolling and smoking another joint is a good idea. I set myself to the task with the gusto of a hungry pizza chef.

"Damn, I want a pizza."

The joint is smaller than the first, and sloppy. It's closer to a tilde than a straight line.

"Looks like you're all bent out of shape," I tell it, chuckling. "Looks like you could use a toke."

A few flicks of the lighter and I'm puffing on a fresh fatty, while saying, "Fatty," over and over. It's a funny word when you say it over and over. "Fatty. Ffffatty. Ffffatatay. Fatata. Fajita."

Damnit. I've got the munchies, which is also a funny word.

"Mmmmunchieees."

I take a fresh drag and am hit doubly hard by it, maybe because I'm a little more relaxed without Ashan and her nakedness here, or maybe because all that pot I already smoked is still working its way through my veins.

I smile at the image of little THC characters—they look like the letters—floating in a small boat, like the opening sequence of the old Land of the Lost TV series, except the river is blood flowing through my veins. A dinosaur rises from the red river. "Aww, shit!" I laugh long and hard.

Inspired by the T, H, and C now running for their lives through the arteries of my drug-fueled imagination, I belt out, "Run to the hills," doing a damn fine rendition of Iron Maiden's lead singer, Bruce Dickinson.

Air guitar follows, the chords hummed through my puckered lips, flinging notes and spittle into the air.

The music in my head and from my lips pauses while I hit the joint. Then I start at the beginning, singing all the stanzas, telling the story of white men crossing the sea, killing tribes, and pillaging the land. By the end, I'm no longer singing though.

The full weight of the song's meaning descends on me for the first time. I was something of a metalhead when I was a teenager. Had long hair for two years. Liked to thrash it around. Pretend I was awesome. Then I moved on. During that time, I never really thought about what any of the songs were about. I just liked that they made my parents angry.

Run to the Hills is about the invasion of white men from Europe, attacking the Cree Indians, taking their land, killing the men, raping the women. White men have murdered and stolen from Indians since their first encounters.

"Oh man," I say, slouching. "Oh damn. Is that what I'm doing?"

I've stolen.

I've killed.

I've...well, I haven't raped anyone, but maybe I'm stealing Ashan away from some young native.

I shake my head. They would kill her. They would have raped her.

But I'm still a white man changing the world around him, fucking with the status quo that has remained unaffected by the outside world for untold generations. What gives me the right?

"Hey," Ashan says, startling me. When I flinch out of my deep thoughts, she laughs at me. She says nothing else, but goes to work on some fresh-picked herbs, plucking the leaves away. I watch her through a stupor, Iron Maiden still running through my head and to the hills. There's a flash of orange in her hands, some furious rubbing, and then rolling between her fingers.

I take a long drag and let it out slowly, entranced by her work, and by her body, the way her back muscles dance when she's just moving her arms. Then she stops, turns to face me, and holds out a green nugget of rolled plant-stuff.

"What is it?" I ask, though I really don't care.

"Eat it," she says, plucking the joint from my fingers and putting it to her lips. "It's better than this."

"In that case." I take the rough green pill and pop it into my mouth. I chew twice before wincing and gagging.

She laughs hard at that. "Don't chew! Just swallow!"

I obey and when I see how much I've amused her, I forget all about how bad it tasted—like a tangy shit cooked in rancid grease.

And then...nothing.

My mind wanders back to the song. "I don't think I should be here."

"You're home." Her blunt and simple statement catches me off guard.

"We don't even have a place to live."

She squats down in front of me. "Home in the jungle has nothing to do with where, but with who. *You* are my home now." She squat-walks over my legs, her hands on my shoulder. "And I am yours."

Whatever she gave me hits me all at once. My heart rate goes from lackadaisical to angered gorilla. My senses sharpen. Beads of sweat roll down her skin. Her breath smells like fruit she must have eaten while she was foraging. I can smell every part of her—the scent fills me with uncontrollable desire.

"What's happening?" I ask, realizing for the first time that she did not partake in her concoction.

She moves in closer, pushing herself against me.

"What are you doing?" I already know the answer, but I'm struggling with the sudden shift.

"I am freeing you," she says. "From yourself."

I can feel it now. The animal inside me. Surfacing again, but this time, it's not enraged, or driven by need. It's raw desire, uncoupled from any notion of civilization and the trappings that come with it. All bonds to what once were are dissolved.

When I start to grunt, Ashan gyrates against me. "We're not monkeys," I say, smiling as the pot momentarily reasserts itself. "You can't just cram us together."

"Ahh, but we are not both males." She flashes a grin that stuns me and then lowers herself down, her aim impeccable.

What follows is as primal as anything I've experienced or seen in the jungle. I lose myself in the moment. In Ashan. The past melts away to nothing, leaving only the present. Free of guilt. Free of regret. Free of civilization's trappings, laws, guidelines, and social media shame. With each grunt, thrust, and howl, I transform into someone new.

Some*thing* new.

26

"I'm hungry," I say.

Ashan motions to the anaconda's twenty-foot-long remains. It lies in a thick coil, gathering flies. "There is plenty of snake remaining."

The twisted meat doesn't stink yet, but it will by the day's end. Cooked through, it would still be safe to eat, but I've had my fill of snake. "I want something warm-blooded."

When confusion flashes across her face, I realize the combination of cold and blooded in her language has no real meaning. Lacking biological study, living things are classified as predator, prey, and inedible—like the poison-dart frog. "An animal with fur."

"So go kill something. You were already thinking about it." She leans over me, face hovering above mine, breasts tickling my chest. "I can see it in your eyes."

I grasp her face beneath her chin, firm, but not enough to hurt. With a tug, I guide her lips to mine.

Ashan lingers in the kiss and then gives me a shove, sitting up beside me. "You're good enough with the bow now. So go hunt. You bring *me* something to eat for a change."

I push myself up, doing my best to hide the pain I'm feeling, now that the marijuana has worn off. I'm still not sure what Ashan gave me, but I think the effects are lingering.

I feel different.

No longer like myself.

I feel...better.

I gather the bow stolen from Juma, the poisoned-tipped arrows that accompany it, my machete, and my satchel. It's all I own in the world, and it's more than enough. "You stay here."

"Until I think you're lost," she says.

"I wasn't asking."

She grins at that. I've never been assertive. Feels good. And I think Ashan likes it.

I strike out on my own, hiking a good mile before stopping to evaluate potential game. The monkeys have sensed I'm not out for a stroll and are mostly quiet, hanging out in the uppermost branches. Even if my aim was perfect, the long arrows wouldn't reach that high, and couldn't pierce the layers of vegetation.

My fellow primates are off the menu.

Return to the river, I think. Find a game trail. Wandering in the jungle is not how to locate prey. You need to stalk the locations they're mostly likely to visit. Water is always a safe bet.

I adjust my course back toward the river, a good distance away from where Ashan awaits my return. Within fifteen minutes, I can smell the water. My belly grumbles at the thought of fresh food...and if I'm honest, the kill.

But what to kill?

Not another snake. That's for sure.

Like anywhere in the Amazon, the river teems with fish. My mouth waters at the memory of moist, flaky meat. But the river here is brown soup. Seeing the fish will be impossible, as will putting an arrow in one. Ashan will have to show me how to make a net, or make one for me. If I'm taking over hunting, she'll have to pull her weight in another way.

That's not fair, I think, and then tell myself to shut the hell up. Ashan helped forge the man I am now. Until she complains, I'll be who I've become.

What are my other options? Giant otter. A tapir, preferably young, both because it will be more tender, but also small enough to carry. Even disemboweled and full-grown, a tapir would be too heavy to lug back to the campsite. I suppose I could hack off its hind quarters. Butcher the prime cuts. Leave the rest to the scavengers and insects.

Speaking of which. I slap my arm, destroying a blood-filled mosquito. I crouch and dig my hands into the earth. Despite the heat and humidity, several days without rain have passed. It made for an easy fire, but the ground isn't very wet.

I dig past the layers of dead leaves, locating the rich soil that descends deep into the earth. When I've got a foot-wide hole dug, I piss into it. After mashing the dirt into a thin mud, I apply it to my whole body. To cover my back, I roll in it. When I'm done, I stand, hold out my arms and watch the mosquitoes come and go without ever settling on my skin.

"Screw off, little bastards."

I reach the river ten minutes later, sliding out of the trees above a cliff of tangled roots that descend into the muddy waters. Low to the ground, I survey the area. Lit by clear skies, the river's far side draws my eye. Slow-moving shallows have allowed tall grasses to grow. It's the perfect place for an anaconda to linger in wait of its preferred prey, but I'm close enough to where I killed the giant snake that I doubt there are any competitors hanging around. Which means the animal shifting the tall grass probably lacks pointed teeth.

It would be a thirty-foot shot. Difficult, but not impossible, especially if I remain unseen and my target remains still.

But I need to see it first.

Revealing myself will send the creature into retreat, so I linger in the forest's shade and wait.

Lying on the ground while crawling things make their way around, beneath, and over me, I think about nothing aside from the creature waiting below. What it has to offer me. How fast it will perish. What it will sound like. Smell like. Taste like.

An hour into my wait, I realize I'm smiling, relishing the hunt.

"It's time," I whisper to the hidden animal. "Show yourself."

Ten minutes later, it does. The brown, boxy head rises from the grass, its jaw working away on dripping plants. Its movements are slow. Had I not already been watching, I might have missed it. Despite a careful search of its surroundings, the creature doesn't see me.

Water ripples away from the reeds as the dog-sized rodent meanders toward shore. Capybara are the largest rodents on earth, so much so that they lack the stigma garnered by its smaller cousins. Instead of being exterminated, they're put on display in zoos. They're not much to look at, remaining immobile most of the time, but they're not reviled either.

The real question is: *what do they taste like?*

I stand slowly, nocking an arrow and drawing back the string. One shot is all I'll get. And no matter where I strike the Capybara, one is all I'll need.

The capybara steps toward shore, emerging from the grass, and pauses. An easy shot.

My fingers relax. Breathing slows. The drawn string rolls over my fingertips.

And then, the rodent squeals and leaps back. I flinch, loosing the arrow angled upward. It sails skyward and disappears in the jungle on the river's far side.

Did it spot me? I wonder, and quickly realize the truth. I'm not the only hunter with eyes on the capybara.

While the rodent backs away toward the river in which it can swim well, a jaguar slides out of the jungle, low to the ground, preparing to pounce. Both animals creep toward the water, each one waiting for the other to trigger the fast chase that will follow the crawl.

There's something familiar about the cat. Its right eye bares a familiar scar.

"*You*," I whisper, recognizing the cat that nearly made a meal of me at the crash site. The cat that I fed with my pilot's corpse. I step out of the jungle, irate. "Hey!"

Jaguar and capybara freeze in place. I can sense their combined desire to turn and look at the person shouting at them, but neither animal is willing to break the staring match.

"That asshole is mine," I shout, stepping to the root wall's edge, the river eight feet below.

The cat's yellow eye flicks toward me. It's just for a moment, but that's all it takes.

The capybara reels around and dashes toward the river. Jaguars are adept swimmers, but swimming is second nature to the rodent. If it reaches the cloudy depths, it will disappear.

I nock a fresh arrow, draw it back and lead my target.

As the cat lunges, arms outstretched, claws extended, I release the arrow.

There's a squeal as the arrow and the jaguar's talons pierce the capybara's skin simultaneously. Water and grass thrashes as the cat pounces, moving in to finish the kill. Unable to see either animal, I shout, "That's mine!" and I leap into the river.

Halfway across, my body reminds me that it's not impervious to harm or exhaustion. Adrenaline and anger drives me to ignore the pain and I make it across before the jaguar can finish the job.

I rise from the water, machete in hand, piss-mud dripping away. "Let. Him. Go." I follow the demand with a growl and a show of teeth. The cat's language and mine are even more disparate than Ashan's and mine once were, but it understands exactly what I'm communicating.

And it doesn't like it.

Pinning the capybara down, the cat bares its teeth and hisses at me.

I respond with a roar, raising the machete up and taking an aggressive step toward the cat.

However it saw me when I clambered out of the plane, that's not how it sees me now. It's pissed and defiant, but it's not looking at me with the same eyes it once did—the way it looked at the capybara.

The rodent tries to thrash free, but the movements are feeble, not because the jaguar has injured it, but because the poison is doing its work. This kill is mine.

The jaguar lunges and swipes its claws at my midsection. It misses by several feet—a warning. I reply by surging forward, screaming, and swinging the machete toward the cat's head.

If it didn't dive away, I would have struck and killed it. Instead, the blade chops into the capybara's neck, silencing its lingering struggle.

The cat paces at the jungle's fringe, watching me as I take the kill by the leg, drag it into the water, and start swimming toward the far side. Upon reaching the root wall, I scale my way up one-handed, holding the capybara in my right arm. Halfway up, I pause to catch my breath and rest my arms. The capybara could be a lot bigger, but it's easily a hundred plus pounds.

Feeling judged by the cat, I climb a little higher and then heave the capybara into the jungle above. Then I turn back to look the cat in the eyes. It returns my glare with one of its own.

"If you want it, come and get it." I heave myself up and over the edge, eager to tell Ashan my story and deliver her my first solo kill. After throwing the capybara over my shoulders, I head into the jungle, moving up river, where I'll find our camp.

I don't give the jaguar another thought.

27

The worst part of cooking a capybara over an open flame isn't the bloodletting or disemboweling that happens first; it's the stench of all that hair burning away. It's the most toxic scent I've encountered since my arrival, and it's only just begun.

The hair on its dangling legs catches first, striking me like a punch to the nose. I reel away as the growing flames light the young night. "I think we should have skinned it first."

"So much of you has changed," Ashan says with a grin. "But there is still some weakness in you."

"Hey." I stand, fists clenched.

Ashan's eyes move to my hands and the potential violence they project. Her smile widens. "False threats don't tell me I'm wrong. But don't worry, you're still changing."

"I killed all those men," I say. "For you. I defeated the anaconda. I defied Mapinguari. I...I brought you a capybara."

"A boy does such things for a woman," she says. "A man does them for himself."

The culture difference between life in the jungle and the modern world rears up between us, reminding me that, while I've acclimated to this life, I'm still an outsider, as much as I don't want to be. Taking her viewpoint to its logical end leads to disturbing conclusions. "Juma and his son. When I found you. Were they being men?"

She nods. "They were."

"And that is right?"

"If I am too weak to resist, then—"

"Bullshit."

She rolls her eyes.

She doesn't know what a bull is, but she understands the English expression. "We are surrounded by death. It waits for us." She motions to the dark jungle around us, full of nighttime sounds. "Out there. Man. Beast. Insect. All of it plots death against us. Only the strong survive. Those that aren't, don't."

She's just laid out the most basic, and accurate, understanding of Darwin's theory of natural selection. In the outside world, my job was to defy natural selection, to take the weak and sick, and free them from the laws of nature that have shaped all life on the planet. Out here, natural selection is still the rule of law that governs man and beast alike.

Kill or be killed.

That's not to say there aren't tribal rules, or laws imposed by the chiefs, but in the end, the uncontacted tribes of the Amazon haven't forgotten that life is governed by ancient laws that are still real and true, even if modern man tries hard to defy them.

"Survival of the fittest."

Ashan's eyes widen. "Yes. Exactly. That's what you're becoming."

"Becoming?"

"The fittest. Can't you feel it?"

I do feel different, but how could I not? I've gone from healer to hunter, pacifist to fighter, hopeless to self-reliant. But that's not what she's talking about. She's talking about the animal inside me. She's talking about real change.

"What did you give me?" I ask.

The rest of the capybara's body flares to life, becoming a rotisserie bonfire of unimaginable stench. When Ashan doesn't flinch away from the smell, I force myself to endure it, too.

"The scorched skin will hold in the juices," she says, and I'm annoyed that anything still needs to be explained to me. I've cooked enough in my life that I should have been able to figure that out.

A growl rises in my throat, catching me off guard.

What was that?

Ashan just smiles. "You are in process. You are becoming."

"Becoming what?"

"What I've always believed you could be."

Mapinguari.

"I wasn't sure until the river," she says.

In all the stories of Mapinguari I've heard, the creature is solitary. A lone hunter tracking down evil men and exacting a kind of jungle justice. In the Amazon, no other monster compares to its legendary penchant for violence, but as much as Ashan fears the Mapinguari, she also respects it, or at least what it stands for.

"There can be more than one?" I ask.

Ashan chuckles. "No."

"But...oh." Ashan has put me on a collision course with the current Mapinguari. "He's a man."

"Mapinguari is no man," Ashan says. "*She* is a *woman. Was* a woman. She is no more human than the beasts of the jungle."

"And this is what you would have me become? A monster?"

"You were already changing," she says. "I am only helping."

I want to take the news with the strong indifference Ashan expects of me, but the notion that I am becoming a real monster, rather than a metaphorical monster, leaves me shaken.

I gaze into the fire while Ashan tends to the roasting meat, rotating the charred body.

Is such a thing even possible? Can a person become something else? I search my dormant medical mind for possibilities. It doesn't take long. There's a list of conditions that can disfigure a person in ways that are historically considered monstrous: epidermodysplasia verruciformis, leprosy, proteus syndrome, elephantiasis, hypertrichosis. Hell, there are some conditions that lead to people growing bona fide horns, like the case of Madame Dimanche, who had a ten-inch horn growing from her forehead.

If the concoction Ashan gave me triggered conditions similar to any of them, I could become disfigured, covered with hair, and by most standards a mythical monster. Becoming a cyclops is unlikely—Cyclopia only happens at birth. I also don't think I can grow a second mouth—also only possible at birth in cases of severe conjoined twins. But like most legendary creatures based on something real, exaggeration is part of the equation. Though I've seen Mapinguari for myself, I couldn't give an accurate description of it. Of her. If I was standing around a campfire with friends, I might be tempted to embellish a bit.

But what about the psychological possibilities? To be a monster, you have to believe you're a monster, or maybe just lose your mind completely. The latter happens all the time. People snap. Cases of people trying to become animals or believing they've become animals aren't unheard of. Some of them made the conscious choice, but others just went insane, living, acting, and communicating like tigers, goats, parrots, and horses.

Perhaps most common and steeped in history is clinical lycanthropy—the belief that you are, or can become, a wolf—aka: a werewolf. It's a real psychiatric syndrome that's been affecting people for thousands of years. Psychosis combined with hallucinations leave the affected person with the unshakable belief that they're no longer human. Combined with physical deformations, I imagine the syndrome would be convincing to anyone encountering the afflicted.

Is that what Mapinguari is?

Is that what I will become?

Would that be so bad?

I shake my head. No. Surviving means adapting. The animal in me has kept me alive. I've been changing since I arrived in the Amazon. Whatever I become, I'll embrace it. That's the only way forward.

There's just one lingering doubt. "Will you be with me? After I change?"

Ashan cracks open the capybara's skin crust, digs a finger inside and hooks it around a strand of cooked muscle. She peels the steaming flesh from the body and offers it to me. "Mapinguari is not mindless. And its attention can be swayed."

"That's why it's hunting us?"

"Juma made a bargain," she says.

"For what?"

A shrug. "But when *you* are Mapinguari, bargains will not be necessary. None beyond those already made." Her grin leaves little doubt that she's referring to the recent evolution of our relationship.

She's turning me into a weapon, I realize. *Her weapon.*

If I didn't empathize with her so entirely, I might have a problem with all this. Mostly, I'm looking forward to finishing what Juma started, whatever it takes. Maybe that's the burgeoning Mapinguari in me, but I really don't care. About anything...other than Ashan.

I take the meat in dirty hands and eat. I moan. The warm, juicy meat tastes like smoked bacon, drawing a second moan from my lips.

"Can we eat this every day?" I ask, devouring the meat, letting the grease run down my chin and drip to my chest.

"When you are Mapinguari, you can do as you wish."

We've already eaten whatever we've come across, and haven't been bound by the laws of the modern world or even the local tribes. The implications of this revelation are far reaching. If I am Mapinguari, the uncontacted people of the Amazon will show me the same fear and respect as Ashan does the current Mapinguari.

She will be safe.

And I will be free...to do anything.

A darkness inside of me gurgles to life. *Anything.*

I smile.

"How do we finish?" I ask. "How do I become the real Mapinguari?"

"You have to kill her," she says. "You have to wear her."

Wear her?

I'm about to ask what that means when a deep growl rolls from somewhere in the dark jungle.

28

I'm not sure if it's exhaustion, the drugs, my ongoing transformation into Mapinguari, or the utter contentment delivered by eating really good meat, but my response to the threat is minimal. I could reach for the gun, or a poisoned arrow—both weapons deliver death without serious effort. Instead, I put a hand on the machete's handle, but don't draw it. I don't even grip it.

Ashan lunges away from the fire, loading a dart into her blowgun. "Get up," she hisses at me.

I lick the meaty grease from my left hand's fingers.

"It's a jaguar," she warns.

"I am Mapinguari," I say with a grin.

"Not yet." She points into the darkness. "And even Mapinguari respects the jaguar."

Movement catches my eye. The cat stalks just beyond the firelight, low to the ground.

"Here kitty, kitty, kitty."

I push myself to my feet, casual, unconcerned. I know who it is. My old friend come to claim his pilfered meal. As dangerous as the jaguar might be, it's still a cat, and fairly intelligent. If it's the same cat from the plane, and the river, it remembers me, too. I've earned its respect, and I've fed it. That combination might be why it hasn't pounced.

I take a risk and turn my back to the cat.

A growl makes me pause, but there's no roar, no sound of an attack, and Ashan remains locked in position, ready to act.

"What are you doing?" I see more doubt in Ashan's eyes than anything. She's probably wondering if pushing me to become Mapinguari was a mistake, that I'm losing my mind. But that's kind of the point, isn't it? To become a monster, I must no longer be human, and that means not fearing death.

I keep my back turned, draw my machete, and hack off one of the capybara's hind legs, making sure to include the meaty flank and rump.

"Greg..." Ashan hasn't used my name in a long time.

"Don't kill it," I tell her.

"Kill it? I can't even see it."

"You will."

I turn back to the jungle, my gaze drawing a fresh growl that stops when I hold up the cooked limb. I sit back down and cut away a chunk of meat. I take a bite of it and then toss the rest into the dark. There's a hiss, a rustle of brush, and then the sounds of chewing.

"What are you doing?" She sounds upset enough to turn the blow-gun on me.

"Making friends."

She huffs a laugh, aghast. "Friends? With a jaguar?"

"People do it all the time. Where I'm from." It's a gross exaggeration. Jaguars *can* be trained, but like Ashan's monkey, it's safest when done from birth. Even then, it's not without serious risks. I have no illusions about snuggling up with this cat, but it has earned my respect. And it's shown me mercy in the past. I don't want to kill it. "If you see a scar above its eye, let it be. If you don't..."

"You're crazy."

"I am who you're helping me become." The next chunk of meat falls short of the darkness. To get it, the cat will have to leave the shadows.

There's a long silence, and then movement.

The jaguar slides out of the jungle, low to the ground, poised to pounce.

Ashan whispers a string of curses I taught her, mixed with some of her own.

It's a beautiful creature, marred only by the scar. Yellow eyes remain locked on mine as it reaches out, tilts it head to the side, and grasps the meat.

"Good kitty." After carving another chunk, I toss it out, a little closer.

"It's close enough," Ashan says.

"Sit down. Eat. You're making him nervous."

"*Her* nervous," Ashan says. "Not everything dangerous is male."

I smile. Feminism is a different creature in the Amazon, but I'm glad to see it still exists to some extent.

Ashan tears away some meat and squats down, keeping her blowgun loaded and ready, and the fire between herself and the cat.

The jaguar gives me a snarl and a hiss. When I don't react, it inches forward and takes my offering. It's just fifteen feet away. If it decided to make a meal of me, I doubt Ashan or I would be fast enough to stop its inch-long canines from puncturing my skull.

After cutting a strip of meat for myself, I toss the entire leg to the ground. It's just ten feet away, forcing the cat to come closer, to break its mental boundaries and decide that we're safe. The process looks painful, as the jaguar hisses, crawls closer, snarls, and crawls again.

"Go on," I say, taking a bite. "I'm the guy that fed you before. We've done this already." I remember the cat's closeness, in the plane, just feet from me, yanking human remains through the window. It was nervous then, too. Perhaps it has always sensed the Mapinguari in me. I smile at the thought, and then wider when the jaguar plants a paw atop the limb and digs in.

I expected the cat to snag the meat and run, but that's not what happens. It settles in for a meal, content in the knowledge that there is more than enough meat to go around and we're willing to share.

Ashan's stunned expression makes me laugh, which gets a growl from the cat, but it never stops eating. "How... You..." Tears fill her eyes. "You will be the greatest Mapinguari to have ever lived."

Will be. Not yet. Not while she's still out there, hunting us on Juma's behalf.

We eat in silence for thirty minutes. I watch how the cat tears away chunks, chews twice and swallows the meat. The only time it really seems to be enjoying the flavor is when it pauses to lick the grease from its snout. I wonder how this compares to the raw meat it's accustomed to. Does it even notice the difference, or care? Is the cat enjoying this meal more than the first I gave it?

Part of me wants to imitate the way the cat eats—there's a lot I could learn from it—but the capybara tastes too good to not savor. The rest of me might go wild, but my palette will remain refined, especially when much of what I eat now doesn't taste spectacular.

When I've had my fill, I roll another joint, take several long drags, and pass it over to Ashan, who's been watching the jaguar with a mix of fascination and concern. After a few puffs, she relaxes. Perhaps sensing the reduction in tension, the cat relaxes, taking its eyes off us and gnawing on the thick femur.

Finished with its meal, the jaguar licks itself clean for a moment.

"It's cute, right?" I say.

Ashan passes the joint to me. "You're insane."

"I know you are, but what am I?"

Her faces fills with more wrinkled tributaries than there are in the Amazon. "What?"

"Something Pee-wee Herman said."

"Pee-wee Her...man?"

"A wise man," I tell her. "Who consulted with creatures and spirits."

"He could *speak* to them?"

I fill my lungs with smoke, my mind drifting through time and space, to Pee-wee's Playhouse. "There was Terry. He was a pterodactyl. A...bird. And Jambi. He was a genie."

"What is a genie?"

"It's like a spirit, but it grants wishes." I've used the English word for 'wish' because the concept hasn't come up before. "A wish is something you desire. Something you ask for that is then granted by a higher power. In this case, a genie in a box."

"It sounds like a prayer," she observes. Her people worship a pantheon of nature-derived gods, including some that smack of Incan myths, but I'm not certain. Ashan doesn't strike me as very devout, but when things get rough, she whispers to someone that isn't me.

"They're related, I suppose," I say. "But you can see a genie, and wishes are granted—or not—right away. There's no waiting or wondering where you stand."

"Have you ever made a wish to a genie?"

"I've never had the opportunity." I pass the joint back, feeling a bit like a genie myself. With my belly full, my mind loosened by the marijuana, the firelight dancing on the canopy's underside, and my strange and dangerous company, the otherworldly feeling that *Pee-wee's Playhouse* generated in my child-mind pales in comparison.

"Have you ever prayed?"

I glance at the satchel. "Just once."

"And?"

"No."

"No, what?"

"Just...no." I push myself up, drawing my machete. The cat eyes me, its lip twitching into a sneer, but it doesn't hiss or growl. It's just nervous. "I don't want what I asked for anyway."

"Perhaps you should do more than ask?" she says. "Gods like to be thanked. To be admired. For all that they have created and done."

"What has God ever done for me?"

Her eyebrows rise as her amused expression melts into a glower. "You're alive. You are becoming Mapinguari. The jaguar that spared your life now eats by your side. And..." Her expression lightens. "...you have me. Perhaps you simply asked for the wrong things? Perhaps you are not smart enough to see the answers, or not patient enough to wait for them? Does everyone in your tribe expect their desires to be met immediately?"

I sigh long and hard enough to get a hiss out of the jaguar. The cat is on edge again, ready to attack or bolt. I'm not sure which. "Calm down," I say, and when Ashan growls, I add, "I was talking to the jaguar."

"Oro," she says.

"What?"

"I'm naming her Oro. Your jaguar."

Oro stands and starts backing away. The conversation, my movement, and perhaps the pot smoke has unnerved her.

"Hey," I say, and I snap my fingers at Oro. She snaps to attention, eyes on me. "Wait."

With a hard swing, I sever the capybara's head from what remains of its picked apart body. The cat hisses, but remains locked in place.

I pick up the head, fingers in its empty eye sockets and mouth, like I'm about to go bowling. I approach the cat, crouching as I move. I reach the head out, offering it to Oro.

She glares at me, the intensity of her eyes similar to Ashan's. "Take it."

A growl is her only reply.

"You're not getting it unless you take it from my hand." I inch closer, letting her smell the cooked flesh and brain. "Go on."

The cat doesn't move any closer, but it doesn't retreat either. When the head is just a foot from her face, I see Oro's nose twitching. She licks her snout, eyes flicking between me and the offering.

When she steps closer, I hold still. In my peripheral vision I see Ashan locked in place, her breath held.

Oro licks the head once, opens her mouth, and grasps the skull. When teeth punch through bone, I withdraw my hand. "Good girl."

Like an arrow fired by a bow, she springs to life, retreating into the forest with her prize, disappearing into the dark.

Grinning like a piece of shit, I turn around to face Ashan. "How was tha—"

Ashan catches me off guard, shoving me to the ground. She stands above me, puffing on the joint. Then she holds up a familiar green nugget. Another animal pill. Time for my next dosage...and what comes with it.

Ashan tosses the herbal concoction down. I catch it and pop it in my mouth.

Swallowing, I say, "Tomorrow, we will no longer run. We will no longer be hunted. Instead, *we* will hunt."

I don't need to say what—or in this case, *who*—we will be hunting. Our goals for my future, for my becoming, are in concert. Tomorrow, Mapinguari becomes our prey.

My prey.

When I swallow, Ashan lingers above me, swaying back and forth until I can no longer take it. I pull her atop me, and the jungle fills with the sound of screaming once more.

29

Weeks of nothing follow.

Well, I shouldn't say nothing. There is hunting, and eating, and screwing, and living. For the first time, *really* living. I feel young again. Colors are brighter. Smells and tastes are stronger. Life is vivid now.

Things like fear, worry, and panic no longer have seats at the council of my thoughts. Running behind for a patient used to rattle me. Doctors are always late—not because they're unorganized or don't care, but because every patient wants more time, wants to talk about every ache and pain, every possible growth, and the stories related to discovering their ailments. As soon as one person goes overtime, the entire day is off. The real problem is that every patient goes over time. And it used to eat me up.

How many appointments have I missed?

I slip between two smooth-barked trees, careful to not rub against the fire ants marching up the surface.

Hundreds. All of my patients have been displaced. Not only are they missing appointments, but they're having to find another doctor. Another practice, maybe.

I only feel bad for them for being so weak. At least a quarter of my patients are fine. They experience the day-to-day pain of life as a reminder of their own mortality, living each day sure it will be their last. Another fifty percent come in with a common cold for which I can do nothing beyond give advice that will likely not be followed. Another twenty percent have bacterial infections, for which I can prescribe antibiotics they'll most likely use incorrectly. A smaller four percent have things like lice, bedbugs, and scabies. And then there's the one percent who have something more serious. Signs of cancer. A tick-borne disease. Something genetic. Those are the people who needed my help, whose lives could be radically alter-ed or even saved because of my intervention.

I pause.

How many of them were there? Of all my patients, twenty-one of them had serious ailments.

"What is it?" Ashan asks. She's crouched down beside me, wary of danger, hand on her blowgun.

"Nothing," I say.

"Why did you stop?"

"I was thinking."

"Think while you move." She pokes me in the back.

I push on, eyes on the ground, concentrating on not leaving a trail, while looking for one. We have been hunting for Mapinguari since our meal with the jaguar, but we've found no trace.

There have been other tracks along the way. Hunting parties, Ashan says, but their lack of concealment means they're hunting animals, not us. It seems the tribal peoples have given up on finding and killing us, leaving the task to Mapinguari alone.

After a few more minutes of silent stalking, Ashan asks, "What are you thinking about?"

Trying to explain would not only take a long time, it would also expose my lingering humanity. That's not me anymore. My patients will live and die without me, probably no differently than they would have if I'd come home. There are doctors to spare back in the States. Out here, I am unique. And when my becoming is complete, I will stand between life and death once more, though instead of always defying death, I will sometimes allow it...or speed it along.

"We're doing this wrong," I say. "Hunting Mapinguari is a mistake."

"You mean to give up?" Ashan's voice is heavy with disappoint-ment.

"I mean to alter our strategy," I say. "We are hunting a master hunter, who can conceal herself as a man, a beast, or a tree..." So the legends say. "She leaves no trail to follow. She is like a ghost."

"As are we," Ashan says, motioning behind us where there is no hint of our passing.

"Are you expecting us to bump into Mapinguari by chance? That one morning we will wake up to discover we have been sleeping beside her during the night, all of us unaware of the other?"

Ashan shoots blow darts at me with her eyes. My critique mocks her methods.

"We need to outsmart her," I say. "We need—"

"A trap." Ashan stands a little straighter.

"We feign weakness, leave ourselves exposed."

"Mapinguari will come for us," she says. "But we'll be waiting."

"*I'll* be waiting," I correct. "She is mine to kill."

Ashan grins. "How do we set such a trap?"

"We get sloppy," I say. "Slowly. Like we're struggling."

"Like wounded animals."

"Or sick ones."

"It could take weeks for Mapinguari to cross our trail," she says, "Even if she is still hunting us. The jungle is vast."

"Then we speed things up."

Ashan squints at me.

"We spread the word."

"Speaking with Mapinguari is not possible. She is a solitary creature. She—"

"Will I be a solitary creature when I am Mapinguari?" I ask.

Ashan starts to speak, but clamps her lips shut. "No."

"Animal, but still human, right?"

She nods.

"People are social. Even the wildest. So, who would Mapinguari talk to? Who was she before?"

Ashan's eyes widen. In all our talks about Mapinguari, even after I learned that the monster had once been a woman, we haven't talked about who she'd been before. "An adopted daughter of the Arawanti. Her parents were killed during her becoming, but her brother, Tikuna still lives."

"She killed her parents? Is that normal when becoming Mapinguari? Could I do that to you?"

Ashan puts a hand on my arm, touched by my concern.

"They tried to stop it. Being Mapinguari means leaving the past behind. Means becoming more than human. Her parents believed she was becoming less than human."

"More than, by becoming less than," I say. That's how I understand it. Mapinguari is a monster in appearance and action, but in a way, it's really just a devolution to pure humanity and pre-civilization, to a state of mind and body before people became tribal. Since arriving in the jungle, I've already gone through a long process of becoming, of moving away from the past, of being remade. I doubt my transition to Mapinguari will be much more dramatic.

"What was her name?"

"She is Mapinguari," Ashan says.

"That was the name her parents gave her?"

"When the change is complete, the person you were never was." The intensity with which Ashan speaks the words says even more. This is a tradition. A rule of law that cannot be broken. I'm sure that there is some superstition attached to it, maybe even a curse. But I'm not worried about those things. As primal as I might become, I still understand that science governs the world and that the supernatural is a hoax.

I lean in close, whispering, "When have we worried about customs or rules?"

"I was not always like this," Ashan says, a hint of shame in her voice.

I've never stopped to think about how Ashan had lived before our paths crossed. She was a hunter for sure, but the irreverent anger...that might be new. All along, I've believed that Ashan has been guiding me down this path of devolution, but we're traveling the spiral together. My destination is just lower than hers.

"Her name will undo her," I say, and I consider explaining how hearing one's name affects the brain, that the middle-frontal cortex, middle and superior temporal cortex, and the cuneus light up. The effects are even more profound when your name is spoken by a familiar voice. It's like smelling something from childhood. A mental transportation from the here and now, however brief. Short of a year-long science lesson featuring the past few millennia of medical breakthroughs, detailed anatomy and neuroscience, electricity, magnets, and ending with an explanation of MRIs, there's no way she will comprehend how I know this. So I simplify. "It will bring her back. Even if it's just for a moment. It could leave her vulnerable."

Ashan takes a step back. "I can't."

"You want me to defeat Mapinguari, but aren't willing to give me all the weapons I need?" It's a manipulative tactic, and it feels wrong—Ashan deserves better—but what do I care about right and wrong? My desire is all that matters.

"I said, I can't."

The force behind her words snaps me out of my flirtation with abject non-caring. The truth is, even if I become the most feared beast in the Amazon, I will still care for Ashan. Still want her to be safe. And happy.

If disrespecting Mapinguari in this way crosses a boundary, I'll respect it.

For now.

The seed is planted, though. She just needs time to mull it over. To let go of her own past, even if she isn't becoming Mapinguari.

"Which way to Arawanti?" I ask.

"West," Ashan says, and when I turn, I realize I've had my bearings in the jungle for a long time. Whether I can see the sky or not, I know which direction I'm facing. The Dalandala have different words for north, south, east, and west, and a simple understanding of how much territory they define. But I understand them well enough to know that traveling north or south won't get me anywhere fast, but if I traveled due east, I would eventually reach Brazilian civilization. And if I ventured far to the west, beyond Arawanti, I would reach the mountains of Peru, and beyond them, the modern world.

I could leave this place.

I could save myself.

I'm already saved, I think, and I strike out to the west, where a man named Tikuna will inadvertently lay a trap for the monster that is his sister.

The monster that I am to become.

30

"Someone is following us," Ashan says without showing any outward sign of concern.

"Uh-huh." My simple response gets more of a reaction from her than the revelation that we're not alone.

"What do you mean, 'uh-huh?'"

She understands the wordless expression. I've been using it since we first met, along with, 'yep, woot, huh, heh, hmm, and meh.' What she doesn't know is that we've been followed for the past three weeks since striking out for Arawanti, and that it's my fault.

"It's fine," I tell her.

"It could be Mapinguari."

"It's not," I say, feigning confidence. The truth is, I'm pretty sure it's not. It started one night when I woke from a dream in which I was a moray eel waiting for an octopus to knock crabs off the rocks above. The deep dark pressure of the ocean unnerved me, and while I sat in the dark contemplating the dream's meaning, I heard the sound of strong, chewing jaws.

In the jungle, only one land-predator can crunch through bones, so I knew it was a jaguar. That Ashan and I had not been attacked hinted that it had been Oro. In the morning, when the remains of our kill were missing, I said I had already buried them.

Since then, I have left food for Oro outside our camp and the cat—I think—has been following us since.

"Then who is it?"

"Oro," I say, and when she looks at me like I'm crazy, I explain. "I have been feeding her. Leaving food."

Ashan stalks toward me, anger flaring.

"You left *a trail?*" She shoves my chest. "We want to trap Mapinguari, not allow her to slaughter us in our sleep." Another shove, sending me into a tree's rough bark. In the past, being stared down by anyone, man or woman, with as much force as Ashan is able to muster, I would have deflated. I would have placated, open-palmed. Anything to maintain the peace. But I am not that man anymore.

So I smile, knowing it will be gas to the fire.

Ashan shoves me again, this time with both hands. I'm not angered or hurt by the violence. It is deserved. She might even be right. "All this time with me, and I thought you had learned. I thought you were more. That you could become." She shakes her head and scoffs. "But you're still just a stupid outsider with the survival abilities of a blind, tailless monkey with shriveled testicles."

My smile widens, this time unintentionally. That was honestly funny. The result is immediate and violent. Ashan draws one of her poison darts from the pouch on her hip and holds it against my neck, her body pressed against mine. Despite the threat to my life, I start to become aroused, and my smile does not fade.

It's not long before Ashan notices, her eyes flicking down for a moment. She's not sure what to think. Fearlessness is part of being Mapinguari. At the same time, it's preventing her from making her point, which angers her even further.

"Can you do it?" The words come like a growl, and are then followed up by an actual growl, but not from Ashan.

And not from me.

We turn our heads toward the sound.

Oro's head is partially concealed by a large leaf, but what we can see—her scarred eye and snarling snout—means business. She's close to pouncing.

Ashan removes the dart from my neck. "If she attacks…"

One good jab from the dart will do the job, but I'm pretty sure Oro would fillet at least one of us before the poison took effect.

"I don't think she will." I say. "Step back. Slowly." When she hesitates, I put my hand on her sternum and guide her away.

Oro's lips twitch. Her eyes are locked on Ashan. Not me.

"Easy," I tell the cat while opening my satchel.

"What are you doing?" Ashan asks, watching me with the same intensity Oro is broadcasting in her direction.

I ignore the question and remove a bundle of leaf-wrapped meat. I crouch with the bundle, unwrapping it. "Easy..."

When the meat is revealed, Oro's wide yellow eyes are drawn away from Ashan. The snarl is wiped away by a licking tongue.

I peel away a strip of monkey. The two-day old meat is dry and doesn't taste great, but I've seen Oro eat far worse. To a big cat, meat is meat. It means survival, and on more than one occasion, I have been the source of meat. Of survival. For the past few weeks, she's watched me from the shadows, leaving her food.

I reach out, hand steady.

Oro's nose twitches. She licks her snout, then looks from my eyes to the meat and back again, waiting for me to toss the food. That she approached during the day in full view of Ashan means she's hungry. But I'm not about to just hand it over.

"You're going to have to work for it," I tell the cat.

She hisses at me, but her ears aren't folded back, and her muscles are relaxed. She isn't happy with me, but she's not about to attack.

Ashan senses the shift as well, backing a few steps away and then squatting to watch.

I pinch the meat between my fingers and wiggle it around. "C'mon..."

Oro inches out from behind the leaf. I reward her progress by leaning in a bit and giving the meat another shake. "Go on, take it."

She hisses again, but this time just seems more frustrated with herself than with me. With the inexorable slowness of a tortoise orgasm, she eases herself closer. When the meat touches her nose, she opens her mouth and gingerly clamps her teeth down on the meat. After a quick swallow, her eyes grow eager once more.

I produce another chunk of monkey, but don't reach out for her. Instead, I slide down into a vulnerable seated position against the tree. Ashan and Oro both tense. In a world ruled by unwritten laws, I've confounded the pair by putting myself in a position of weakness, while still somehow maintaining my position of power. Oro could take the meat from me. She could kill me. And eat me. But she's smart enough to know that I provide a steady, danger-free flow of meat.

When I hold out another strip, Oro's mental confusion turns to simple-minded desire. She wants what I have and no longer fears me. So she steps closer with a suddenness that catches even me off guard.

It takes a level of discipline I didn't know I had to not flinch or draw back my hand. I manage it, but the sudden shift of nerves leaves me having to poop. Clenching my ass, I hold my ground and let Oro take the meat from my hand again. Her teeth scrape against my fingers, letting me feel her power.

"You are beautiful," I tell the jaguar.

She sits between my legs, chewing twice and then swallowing.

I tear away another strip. Oro could take it from me, but she waits, licking her lips. This time, when I offer the meat in my right hand, I raise my left toward her head. Her lip twitches, shifting from snarled warning to eager hunger.

"Don't," Ashan says. "She'll take your hand."

Oro focusses on the flesh when it reaches her nose. As she takes hold of it, I place my hand on the side of her neck. She flinches, and growls, but holds on to the meat. The monkey flesh is suspended between her teeth and my hand. As she tugs, I scratch. "Oro. Good, Oro."

Her short fur is soft on the surface and course underneath. The large, black-rimmed, yellow eyes look almost gentle now. It's an illusion, of course. Jaguars are almost impossible to keep as pets because they're somewhat volatile. But I'm not trying to make Oro a pet, just a friend, someone she'd rather not eat when there are other options.

With each bite, Oro allows me to pet her a little more. "Oro," I say again and again, withholding food until she makes eye contact upon hearing her name. When I feed her, I say, "Eat!" Then I scratch the side of her neck, behind her ears and the top of her head, positively reinforcing our contact with food. It's a trick that works with any intelligent animal species, and I can see an instinctual intelligence in Oro that I once feared, and now respect.

"Who's a good girl?" I say in adorable English. "Who's a good girl?"

Oro dips her head down, looking for the next nugget of flesh. I place my forehead against hers, eyes closed. "Good, Oro."

I place the last piece of meat on the ground between us. She glances at the food and starts moving to take it when I say, "Oro." She stops and looks at me. I pet her. "Good, Oro. Good."

"Eat!" She gobbles up the last nugget, and I rub her neck on both sides.

She lingers for a moment and then lifts her head, still hungry.

"All gone," I tell her, showing my palms. "All gone."

When I sense her gentle nature slipping away, I slide my hands from around her neck, scratching as I go. Then I move in for the kill, scratching under her chin. Her neck stretches out as she pushes down on my fingers, making my scratch harder. The more I scratch, the lower she gets.

When her head strikes my leg, she rolls onto her side, and then her back. I keep scratching, moving my hands down to her broad chest. And then I hear it, the rumbling purr of a man-eater. Food or not, Oro is content. After a few more minutes of rubbing, Oro swats her paws at me. If her claws weren't retracted, she's have sliced through my skin. Instead I feel the soft pads of her feet slapping my arms. I push her paws away, playing her game.

In the middle of my feline frolicking, I look to Ashan for the first time since our encounter began. Her cheeks are wet with tears, her eyes full of affection. She hasn't said the words, but I know she loves me.

And I love her.

"And you," I say to Oro, tugging on her cheeks as she swats at me.

I'm about to tell Ashan as much when Oro flips around, head raised, ears perked, eyes locked on the jungle to the east. Her nose twitches with the smell of something. She doesn't hiss or growl, but she doesn't linger either. Moving in complete silence, she walks low to the ground, heading west, away from whatever it is she's detected.

Ashan rubs her thumb and index finger together. It's her stealthy version of a snap, meant to get my attention. It could be a hunting party, or Mapinguari herself. One is a fight we don't want, and the other is one we're not yet prepared for, but neither of us like being followed, so we lay in wait.

Ten minutes later, we spot them in the distance. Ten men, each carrying a basket heavy with fruit and plants. We could tear through them in minutes. But we don't. Ashan motions in the direction Oro fled and we head out once more, hiking through the day, and into the night, stopping only when the scent of smoke and the sounds of celebration fill the night.

31

It's a party. I'm not sure what's being celebrated—could be a wedding, birthday, or any number of seasonal events or harvests. While I've been steeped in the culture of Ashan, I still know little about tribal customs.

Unlike the Guaruamo and Jebubo tribes, which are closer to hunter-gatherers, the Arawanti are agricultural. Orchards of fruit trees and edible plants grow all around the large village, sweetening the air. Ashan claims they have several more growing grounds throughout their territory, and that many of the people here eat only what grows from the earth.

Strange that Mapinguari would come from a place like this.

The people seem happy.

There are a few bows scattered about, but no one is currently armed.

What happened to make a woman from this tribe become a feared monster?

What happened to me?

The question slams into my gut, but is quickly smothered by indifference to who I once was. That man, and everything he cared about, is a stranger to me now, too pitiful to even think about.

Ashan and I lie beneath a mango tree on the village's outskirts. We're covered in her special homemade piss-mud blend, which no longer bothers me. The party is in full swing. People feast and drink, sing and dance. The Arawanti people, unlike the other Amazonian tribes, are relatively free of body paints and piercings. They're stocky people, accustomed to hard labor. Both men and women have the same, almost 1970s style, bowl haircuts. They wear thick sashes around their waists. The women's sashes are open on the bottom, while the men's look more like diapers.

There is nothing threatening about these people. If Ashan and I strolled out of the jungle, I suspect half of them would run upon seeing us, and the rest would follow after a double take.

"Do you see the brother?" I whisper.

She points to the village's far side, where a man sits alone inside a large hut with no walls. He's surrounded by baskets, some tame monkeys, and he's drinking from a clay bowl.

"He's alone."

She nods. "His sister is Mapinguari. They fear offending him."

"Then they do still speak."

"Or they suspect she's keeping an eye on him."

"Creepy," I say, slipping back a little further, beyond the firelight's reach. When Ashan joins me, I say, "We'll sneak around, take him when things get loud, and drag him out into the forest."

When I'm done laying out my plan, Ashan is staring at me like I've dipped my hand into honey and slapped a bear with it.

"What?" I ask.

"We'll wait," she says. "Until the only people upright are those moving through their visions. Even if we are seen, we won't raise concerns, nor will we be remembered."

I sigh, reach up, and pluck two mangos from a low hanging branch. I pass one to Ashan and tear into mine, careful to only eat the pulp and not the toxic skin. It's been a long day without much food, and little water. If we're going to spend the night awake and waiting for the Arawanti to get shit-faced, I'm going to need a few more mangos.

Time passes without a trace of boredom. The Arawanti know how to throw a shin-dig. The feast is composed of mostly fruits and vegetables, fit for even the most squeamish of vegans. The food is prepared with a wide variety of methods I have not yet experienced in the Amazon. Ashan and I cook over an open fire with only the machete to use as a tool. But the Arawanti have created a number of clay pots and stones, most likely gathered from the Andes mountain range to the west. Used in combination with a variety of spices, the air fills with scents that are new and unusual, but they set my stomach growling.

Just when I was beginning to think of the Arawanti as a jungle hippie commune, a blindfolded tapir is led into the village's center. It's an immense creature, easily five hundred pounds, capable of storming through a dozen people. But it's not only docile, it's stumbling.

How much of their ju-ju juice did they feed to it?

"Tikuna!" The oldest man I've seen since arriving in the jungle hobbles up beside the tapir with the help of a young woman and a cane. Framed by a blazing bonfire, he raises the cane above his head. "Tikuna!"

I watch, transfixed as the entire village chants Tikuna's name. He's not feared by these people. He's revered. And when he stands, I wonder if it has anything to do with his relationship to Mapinguari. He's a good five inches shorter than me, but he towers over the rest of the tribe. He's thick all around, not ripped like a bodybuilder, but no doubt powerful. Despite me being taller, he's got at least fifty pounds on me.

As impressive as Tikuna is, it's what he does next that makes me gasp. He draws a sword from a sheath hanging on his hip. The three-foot blade is double-edged and while it's speckled with rust, it looks strong and sharp. The blade ends at an ornate hilt of twisting metal.

"You know what it is?" Ashan asks. She's not at all surprised by the weapon's appearance, so she must have been aware of it. But she has no idea what it is, or where it came from. Or when.

"It's called a rapier," I tell her. "It was used by men who came to these lands a long time ago. Men who killed thousands using swords like that one, and even more by spreading disease. They were called conquistadors."

It's a simple explanation, and leaves out the mystery of how this weapon survived and made it this deep into the basin, far beyond the conquistadors' reach, but she seems to understand.

"There are more weapons like it where you are from?" she asks.

"Many."

"Did you have one?"

I shake my head. "There was no need, but I could have. They are common."

She taps the machete on my hip.

"You have this."

"I took it from a dead man," I say, and I don't bother explaining that it belonged to my pilot. I've never told the story of how I arrived in the jungle. She'd either think I was crazy, or think I'm some sort of deity, neither of which I want. Right now, she believes I'm from a far-off tribe and that I simply got lost while wandering in the jungle. She doesn't know about cities, and continents, and vehicles. And I like it that way. Telling her the truth might give her aspirations of leaving, and that's not something I want.

Not anymore.

Tikuna approaches the tapir. When he thrusts the rapier in the air, the village goes silent. The naïve tapir's nose twitches as it sniffs the air, perhaps wondering when it will get to eat all the fruit it can smell.

Tikuna grasps the sword in two meaty hands and swings it down hard with a loud, "Hoi!" The blade *clings* as it strikes, and passes through the tapir's spine. With a larger weapon—an axe or broadsword, I'm sure the strike would have lopped the creature's head off. Still, killing the tapir in a single strike through thick skin, muscle, and bone is impressive. He finishes the job by putting his weight into the sword and sawing it back and forth.

When the head falls away and blood oozes out, the party resumes and takes on a more primal feeling than the previous hippie, love fest. The tapir is roasted whole over the open flame. Rather than wait for the entire beast to cook through, members of the tribe peel off strips of meat over the course of two hours. Every time more meat is taken away, the raw flesh beneath is cooked. It's an efficient way of cooking and eating such a large animal.

When the tapir is reduced to meat on bones and the villagers are passed out or speaking to visions, Ashan and I step out of the shadows.

I'm tense, waiting for someone to shout a warning that will trigger a bloodbath at my hands. But the tribe is quiet, or delirious. An old woman sees me coming and just smiles. I smile back and pause at the tapir to pick off some still-warm meat. Ashan gives me a rapid-fire whisper snap until she sees how much I'm enjoying the meat. She joins me by the fire and for five minutes we eat, surrounded by people who'd like to see us dead.

When we've had our fill, we continue on our way toward Tikuna's large hut, which is still empty, aside from the big man. He sits alone, head leaned back on a basket, surrounded by fruit, as though he might wake at any moment and resume the feast.

Ashan stops short of the hut and puts a hand on my chest.

"What's wrong?" I whisper.

She points at the corner of her mouth, and then to Tikuna.

He's smiling.

But is he awake, or just drunk, dreaming of a voluptuous conquistador maiden polishing his sword?

When he speaks, I have my answer. "We have been waiting for you."

His eyes open and lock on to mine.

While his lack of concern or surprise at our arrival is disconcerting, the truly worrisome bit is his use of the word 'we.'

When every member of the tribe rises from the ground, fully aware and armed with bows, blowguns, and a variety of stone-tipped weapons, my fears are confirmed.

Instead of setting a trap, we've walked straight into one.

CATALYST

32

Tikuna isn't just some giant loner summoned to sever necks, he's the Arawanti's chief. The village stands ready to cut us down on his word. He rests his right hand on the rapier's pommel, but doesn't look afraid, and doesn't bother standing. He's relaxed. In control. If we make a move, we'll be struck by enough poison arrows and darts to make us look like porcupines.

"When did this happen?" Ashan asks, doing a decent job of masking her surprise.

"When turmoil dropped from the sky and infected the jungle," Tikuna says. "When men were slain in their sleep. When an outsider insults Mapinguari."

Upon speaking the monster's name, frightened whispers flow through the villagers.

"You're welcome," I say, forcing a grin to hide my own surprise. Tikuna is not only blaming me for the events that led to his ascension to chief, he also seems to understand that I arrived in a plane. While the sword is ancient, perhaps the Arawanti have made contact with the outside world? If that's the case, he thinks I'm nothing special.

He's wrong. I am becoming Mapinguari. It won't be long before he'll have to answer for *his* disrespect.

"This started when the Guaruamo killed my people," Ashan says through grinding teeth. "My mother. My father. My brother. The frail and young. All of them slaughtered."

"You should have married the—"

"I should have slit Juma's throat."

Tikuna offers a slow nod. "That would have worked, too. But that time has passed. Dalandala, Guaruamo, and Jebubo have all suffered wounds." When Ashan starts to speak, he holds up a hand and continues. "Some more severe than others, but it is *your* enemies who first paid tribute to Mapinguari, who summoned her wrath and set alight her hunger. It must be satiated, or we will all suffer."

"What does that mean?" I ask Ashan.

"If Mapinguari does not fulfill its task, it is driven to kill anyone and anything it encounters." Ashan frowns. "The river would run red with the blood of all living things."

Seems a little melodramatic, but I get it. No one would be safe, and since they all fear Mapinguari so much, they'd all be easy prey.

"She would kill her own brother?" I ask.

Tikuna squints at me and pushes himself up. Despite being shorter, his broad body is intimidating. I don't back down, but I do let my hand hang just an inch from the machete's handle. If he attempts to draw that sword, it will be the last thing he does. I'm tempted to get it over with now and strike him down, but that would result in Ashan's demise. That is something I will not allow.

"Mapinguari's blood changed the moment she was altered. She is no more my sister than she is human."

"Then you will not be offended when I kill her," I say, brimming with confidence.

The big man smiles. "Kill her? *You?* Seshanguami?"

Seshanguami?

It's not a word I've heard before, but it doesn't take long to break down the nickname into its distinct parts—sashan and quimi—and to understand its meaning: sleep-killer. It's meant as an insult. He's calling me a coward. Trying to prod me into action. But a war of words is a twenty-first century man's game. "Not all the men who died at my hands were sleeping, Chulabinsuat."

The name I've given him is a mouthful, but translates to "Docile, chubby, dung heap." It's juvenile of me, but this isn't an intellectual debate. It's a ruffling of feathers, showing our bright plumes, telling the other to back down before it's too late.

Tikuna doesn't flinch, but several of the Arawanti start whispering to each other.

"You are to both be delivered to Queshupa," he says. "Mapinguari waits for you there. But the blood she requires is Ashan's." He points a meaty finger at me. "You can die here."

I take a step back, resting a hand on my machete. I could dig into my satchel bag, draw the pistol, and put a few holes in the big man, but I've come to respect the laws that govern this ancient world. The gun may one day serve a purpose, but it will not be to kill this man, or Mapinguari. For me to become, for the alteration to be complete, I must fully embrace this world without technology. If not for Tikuna's sword, I might have even abstained from using the machete.

"And if I do not?" I ask. "If I kill you?"

Tikuna chuckles. I am a joke to him. The sleep-killer. "All who are present, hear me! Should I fall to Seshanguami, you will take them both to Queshupa and allow him to face Mapinguari in defense of Ashan."

No one speaks or moves, but they've heard the command. Whether or not they will follow it is anyone's guess. Also, I'm not done with my demands.

"And," I say, "You will tell me her name."

Tikuna is confused by the demand. "Whose name?"

"Mapinguari."

Tikuna knows what I'm getting at, but he decides to be a dick about it. "That *is* its name."

"That ounce of regret I felt at having to kill a good man just vanished like rising smoke," I say, and I'm pleased when his stone wall of a face shows a trace of concern. I point to the men and women around us. "I want the name of Tikuna's sister. The one who died to this life and became something new. One of you must tell me..." I point to Tikuna. "...because he will be dead."

"Let it be so," the very old man says with a tap of his cane. Tikuna might be the chief, but this man, and his opinion are respected.

"We are agreed," Tikuna says, like the conversation and civility is going to continue.

I'm not here to talk, or take part in a civilized trial by combat. I'm here to kill and become Mapinguari, and I'm going to pursue that the way Tikuna's own sister would.

"How would you like me to—"

I cut Tikuna short with a roar, charging the man while drawing my machete. One solid swing and this will be over. I can aim high, burying the blade in his neck. I lack his raw strength, but the blade is sharp and even if I don't hack through his spine, I'll sever his carotid artery. Or I could strike low, on the inside of his meaty thigh, severing the femoral artery. Then I'll just need to back off and wait as he bleeds out. Either way, it will be a messy, painful death, but it will get the job done.

I decide to aim high. I want to look him in the eyes when he realizes the depth of the mistake he's made. Want to watch his life fade. Want to laugh as the expression on his face goes slack and dumb. And I will tell him, 'You could have just pointed us in the right direction, given me her name, and lived a long life.' I'm not sadistic. I just want the people watching to learn, and spread that lesson throughout the Amazon. I will train these people as I have trained Oro.

Tikuna has other plans.

As I leap forward, machete already swooping down, he catches me mid-sternum with an open-palmed, straight arm that would have served him well in the NFL. Since the big man doesn't give an inch, all of the force is transferred to my chest. Ribs bend nearly to the point of breaking, but pressure is relieved when my feet come off the ground and he flies forward, as I spill back.

By the time I slap the ground, the air has already left my lungs. The second impact doesn't knock any more air out, but it prevents me from taking a breath.

As unblinking fireflies pirouette around Tikuna's head, he draws the sword, making a show of it.

He's a fool, I think after heaving in three breaths. He should have killed me without the bluster. He's used to an audience. To putting on a show. The big man who cuts down helpless animals.

I might be an animal, but I'm not helpless.

Tikuna raises the rapier over his head, preparing to swing it down on me like he did to the tapir. Instead of lopping off my head, he'd split me lengthwise. When a shout announces his swing, I roll to the side.

The blade slays the jungle floor, peppering my face with explosive soil as I scramble to my feet.

He recovers quickly and swings again, this time in a wide arc that forces me to leap back to avoid being eviscerated. I'm caught by a wall of hands that brace my fall, but then shoves me back into the fray, and into Tikuna's backhanded swing.

I've never been in a proper fight, even against all the men I've faced in the jungle. I've always been allied with darkness, surprise, or confusion. Against Tikuna, it's just me and him, which pits his fighting skills against my...what?

Ferocity.

That's Mapinguari's way. So it is mine.

And that means doing the insane. Leaving my humanity behind, I dive forward instead of aside. The rapier's double-edged blade cuts through the air above my bushy head of hair as I slide past Tikuna, slipping the machete blade against the side of his lower leg.

It's not a killing blow, but he howls in pain. I delight in the shocked faces of our audience and the approving eyes of Ashan.

When my toes catch, I bend at the knees and spring toward Tikuna's back.

With a monstrous shout, the big man spins around, throwing a meaty fist into my side. I manage to cut his arm as I sprawl away, but then I'm on my back and gasping for air again.

This time when he hacks the sword toward my midsection, there is no bravado. The show has become a fight for his life. The blood flowing from his leg and his arm have made that clear. I might be on my back again, but I'm not yet bleeding.

The rapier descends with a whoosh, but the strike doesn't end with the sound of sliced flesh. It ends with a clang, striking the machete.

I push myself back, but the soil slips beneath my feet, and I'm forced to parry another blow. The machete is nearly knocked from my hands, the vibration tingling my arm from wrist to shoulder.

He strikes again, this time with a scream, putting everything he has into it. With no time to move, I don't just block, I swing with a defiant shout of my own.

The sharp clang of metal striking metal is followed by a gasp from the onlookers, and a grunt of pain from me, as a red line of blood starts to seep from my midsection.

33

I'm cut. Can't tell how deep it is, but since my organs are not bulging out and the pain is a fierce sting, rather than a severe ache, I think the wound is skin deep. Despite the rivulets of blood streaked over my mud-covered torso, all eyes are on Tikuna.

His legendary weapon, probably passed down from one chief to another for countless generations, has broken in two. Ancient, rusted iron is no match for modern, hardened steel. The three-foot blade is now just a foot long, looking more like a gaudy knife then a warrior's sword. Given the grief in the villagers' eyes, I think they would have preferred Tikuna's death over the sword's breaking.

I intend to give them both, but my confidence wavers when Tikuna's face transforms into something hideous. His animal has arrived.

The big man dives at me, half-sword aimed at my throat.

With no time to move, I lift the machete, and place my left hand against the dull side. The blade strikes the rapier's elaborate hilt, preventing the broken sword from piercing my neck, but the big man is putting his weight and ferocity behind the attack. Antique iron inches toward my neck. In seconds it will push against my skin, break through, and slip through my windpipe.

Ashan kicks and fights, trying to free herself from the Arawanti men holding her back. She knows I'm screwed. Everyone watching knows that death is imminent.

What they don't know is that it won't be mine.

At the edge of the jungle, peering through the low hanging leaves of a mango tree, is a pair of rage-filled yellow eyes.

Had Tikuna been a smarter man, or not so lost to rage, he might have realized a simple twist would have freed his sword and sent it plunging into my neck. Instead, he just growls and pushes, lost to his animal so completely that my spreading smile doesn't register with him.

The others see it, though.

So does Ashan. She's stopped fighting, and is now watching with eager eyes. I'm not sure if she knows *why* I'm smiling, but she knows what it means.

I'm not dying.

"Not today," I say to Tikuna, and then I shout, "Oro!"

The Arawanti chief is undeterred by my outburst, by the cries of fear around us, or by the roar of an approaching feline. But he can't resist the force of a two-hundred-pound jaguar.

The only person surprised when Tikuna is sprawled to the side is Tikuna himself. All of his rage disappears when the first four red lines open up on his side. When he turns himself over to see what has attacked him and comes face to face with Oro, he screams.

The warrior becomes a child, gripped by fear, pushing himself away from the cat, who's low to the ground and stalking her prey.

My prey.

I roll onto my hands and feet and join Oro. She growls and hisses at me and I give it right back.

The Arawanti have backed away, giving us a wide berth. While they could still shoot us both, no one has raised a weapon. Oro's involvement, while technically unfair, is probably seen as even more of an omen than the breaking of Tikuna's sword.

The big man's blubbering is pitiful.

Embarrassing.

"Her name," I growl.

"W-what?"

"I want you to say it. Your sister's name."

Drool dangles from his quivering lower lip, and when he speaks, everyone watching knows he fears me more than Mapinguari. "U-Urpi."

If Tikuna believed telling me her name would save his life, he was wrong. "Oro..." I share a glance with the cat, offering a toothy smile that she matches with a snarl. Then we both roar and pounce.

Oro follows her instincts, going for Tikuna's head. Her massive jaws wrap around his lower face. The force of her bite breaks his jaw, but his high-pitched scream is muffled. She's going to suffocate him.

But Tikuna will be dead long before a lack of air does him in.

Much of what happens next is a blur, viewed from outside of myself. I see a man with shoulder-length, mud-clumped hair, his tan skin slathered in gray, his tendrilled beard tangling...

HE FEELS A warm spray. Hears a slurping whack. His arms burn. Guttural shouting turns his throat raw. He feels little more than a hunger that has nothing to do with food. Something in him is empty, the void filled for the moment, with savage violence.

He bathes in it. Revels. The life of another spills over him, granting him power, numbing him. For a moment, he is remade. Reborn. And then, as his energy waivers, he slips away as though into a fog.

WHEN FULL AWARENESS returns, I'm standing on two feet, machete in hand. Dark red blood covers me from head to toe, growing tacky as it dries. My voice is hoarse, each deep breath sounding like the grunt of a bear. At my feet is what remains of Tikuna. From the chest down, he's unrecognizable as a human. Pieces of him lie in the dirt up to fifteen feet away.

Oro keeps one protective paw on the former chief's chest, while licking out the inside of his cracked-open cranium. *This is mine,* she tells me with a hiss.

When I look up, the Arawanti people have fled.

Aside from Ashan, who's speckled with blood spatter and looking a little numb, and the very old man with the cane, the village is empty.

The old man looks sad, but he's unafraid. He leans on his cane, his help having fled with the rest. "He was wrong to insult you, Shawindo."

Shawindo... Cat-talker. My legend grows, but I am not yet Mapinguari. It's possible that my reputation might surpass that of the ancient beast, but the transformation Ashan began in me was not into something new, it was into something old. A legend more timeless than the broken sword. That is what I am to become.

The old man hobbles toward me, picking his steps carefully. One wrong foot placement and what used to be a man will squeeze up between his bare toes.

When he gets too close to the corpse, Oro hisses at him. The old man stumbles and falls, toppling toward the open mass of ruined flesh.

Without thought, I reach out, catch his arm, and pull him upright. While holding onto him, I crouch and retrieve the cane. I flick the blood from the wood and hand it back.

Tears in his eyes, voice quivering, the man says, "There is still a path back for you. Even the darkest heart can be remade."

"Even Mapinguari?" I ask.

He frowns and holds up his hand. "What do you see?"

"Your hand."

He puts his hand directly in front of my eyes. His closeness should put me on edge. Aside from Ashan, the only people to get this close to me since I arrived in the Amazon have lost their lives.

"Now what do you see?" he asks.

"Nothing," I say.

"That is where Mapinguari exists. She lives in a world that appears free of pain because *everything* is pain. She cannot see it because she is too close to it. Her darkness drowns out the world. Drowns out the past. It does not soothe, it erases."

Something in his voice, or perhaps his words, draws tears to my eyes. The pain he's talking about lurks just beneath the surface. I have pushed it down, I've obscured it with drugs, sex, and violence—the same remedy humanity has employed for millennia.

But it's not enough.

I need something more.

"That sounds perfect," I tell him, ignoring the tears.

An intense mercy fills the man's eyes. He tugs his arm from my hand and supports his weight on the cane. "Queshupa lies to the west. You will have no trouble finding it."

With that, he turns and starts trudging away. "Please take your jaguar with you."

"Oro will come when she is ready," I reply. "She is a friend. Not a slave."

The man just shakes his head and continues on his way, slipping into the jungle and abandoning his village.

Ashan approaches, wisely steering clear of Oro, and eyeing me with suspicious eyes.

"Where did you go?" she asks.

"When?"

She motions to the bloody heap beside us. "I did not see you..." She places her hand beside my eye. "In here."

I nod. "I don't remember doing it. Not really."

A voice from my past offers a diagnosis: dissociative break. I stopped being me. I viewed myself as a spectator, freed from the most visceral and disturbing event of my life. I have seen men die. I have taken lives. But I have never undone a man, body and soul, rending him to little more than a puddle. What does a man who can do such things feel like? I will never know.

I wasn't there. I didn't feel it.

I felt...nothing.

"It's perfect," I whisper, more resolute than ever to complete the alteration.

My hand on Ashan's cheek helps put her at ease. "I am here. Now." I offer her a smile. "Have you been to Queshupa?"

She gives her head a quick shake. "It is forbidden."

"But you know where it is?"

A nod.

"The laws of the jungle are ours to write. Forbidden or not. Right and wrong. Light and dark. These things are like clay to people like us." I look down at Oro, who's enjoying Tikuna's shoulder. "We are animals, traveling where we please, eating what we want, and enjoying the bliss that comes with freeing ourselves from this world, one way or another."

Her smile is unsure for a moment, but it returns when a raindrop strikes my forehead and runs down the side of my face. I turn to the sky where the stars are being blotted out by an invisible darkness. A deluge follows, chasing Oro away from her meal and cleansing the blood and mud from my body.

I stand in the rain, arms outstretched, feeling new.

Ashan does the same, until we're clean once more. Then she takes my hand and leads me to the dry interior of a nearby hut, where we partake in mind-altering substances and each other's bodies.

THROUGH IT ALL, his mind wanders through the jungle, seeking Mapinguari and the final bliss she offers. He will find her. He will kill her. And then he will finally become more, and less, everything and nothing.

34

For the first time since setting foot in the Amazon Basin, I'm relaxed without the aid of drugs—mine or Ashan's. That the hunters have summon-ed Mapinguari to kill us means they are no longer actively hunting us. As for the woman-turned-beast, she waits for us at Queshupa. I suspect her brother's challenge was not part of the plan. But he couldn't resist the temptation to inflate his own legend. Vanity has an uglier face in the jungle, but it is alive and well.

Oro's presence, once a source of nightmares, now provides security. As in tune with the jungle as Ashan and I might be, the cat's heightened senses will detect danger long before we can. She's out of sight most of the time, but she checks in on occasion, when she wants some more of the meat we took from the Arawanti village, or when I call her.

On the fourth night of our journey west, I woke to find her sleeping a few feet away. When she sensed my attention, she opened her eyes, yawned, and went back to sleep. She'd normally be more active at night, but she's traveling with us throughout the day, and hasn't needed to hunt. When I woke in the morning, she was gone, but she returned when the night grew dark. She fell asleep beside me as I scratched her head.

She's still wary of Ashan to a degree, but no longer bristles at her proximity.

It's now the tenth night of our journey. Oro leans her chin on my leg while I rub behind her ears. Her hair is soft and feels good between my fingers. With each squeeze, we both become more relaxed.

Ashan is squatted beside a fire, roasting a large catfish she caught. She and Oro had argued over the fish, the cat wanting to eat it on the spot. Ashan had won the argument after bludgeoning the fish and dragging it back to the fire—something Oro still avoids. But the jaguar hasn't left us since. Her tail snaps back and forth, impatient.

"Should I be jealous?" Ashan asks, when Oro begins purring. "I think she is smitten."

"You'll just have to share me," I say.

She smiles. "You've taken a jaguar as a lover, then?"

"Think of her as our daughter." I lean down to Oro and point to Ashan. "She's your mother now. Be nice."

Ashan's good humor fades. "And if I am her mother, and you her father, what does that make us?"

A mental stumbling block trips me up. I'm unable to answer for a moment. Something about this feels wrong. But why? Ashan is my life. What else is there? What is there to feel guilty about?

Nothing, I decide, and when Ashan flinches back, I worry that I've spoken the word aloud and out of context.

"You have to think about it?" she asks.

"I'm just not sure how it works here."

"How what works?"

"Marriage."

A trace of a smile returns. "A marriage must be recognized by a tribal elder. There is usually a ceremony."

"But it is not required?"

"It is also not possible. The Dalandala has no elder. Has no people."

"As long as you live, your people still exist. And if you're the last, I think that makes *you* the elder." I point at the fish, which is beginning to scorch. Oro's ears perk up when Ashan rotates our meal, but she doesn't move. "And maybe, someday, the tribe will grow again."

"Mapinguari does not have children," she says.

"Mapinguari does whatever he wants."

"I've noticed," she says, tearing off a piece of flakey catfish. She bounces the meat between her hands, cooling it down and capturing Oro's full attention.

Oro and I are both surprised when Ashan approaches us, meat in hand.

Before now, she's insisted that the cat receive our scraps.

While I don't think Oro cares about which cuts she's given, she is always tense about eating last.

Ashan crouches down, meat in hand. Oro sits up, licking her nose. "But first, our daughter must accept me, as she does you." She reaches her hand out to touch Oro's head. The cat bares her teeth.

"Easy..." I say, to both of them.

Ashan inches the meat closer and the snarl shifts back to eager licking. Both hands moving in unison, Ashan allows Oro to eat from her hand, while Oro allows Ashan to pet her for the first time.

"Good girl," I say.

Oro purrs at me.

When the cat finishes the meat and raises her head, she allows Ashan to rub their foreheads together. Ashan is so pleased by the contact that, with tears in her eyes, she continues to dole out the fish, giving the largest portion to Oro. I'm hungry, but I don't complain. It will reinforce their budding relationship.

Once I've eaten, I lean back against a tree trunk. Oro has abandoned me for Ashan. They're kindred spirits, strong and deadly women. My fingers aimlessly twist the ring on my finger. It had significance once, but that feels like another life, like a story I watched. I feel no value in it, and have trouble recalling why I ever wore it.

Feeling shamed by its presence, I pry it off my finger, working it slowly up and around my knuckle. I'm not sure why, but I don't want Ashan to notice. Don't want her to ask about it. I'm tempted to flick it away or push it into the soil, but I slip it into my satchel bag and let it fall to the bottom to lurk beneath the half brick of marijuana, the cash, the gun, and the bound paper. Of all the bag's contents, the pot, the paper, and the lighter have been the most useful. The rest I keep...well, because they're mine.

The lingering sun settles down for the evening, plunging us into firelit darkness. With the fish cooked and sleep nearly upon us, the embers burn down to a dull, hellish glow.

My thoughts turn to Tikuna, as they have every night since we left the village. I clearly remember our conversation, and the building tension, but I have no memory of our combat, of Oro's intervention, of killing the big chief, or of mutilating his body beyond recognition. I re-member *remembering* it, viewing the events from the outside, like an out-of-body experience. But those memories have faded in the same way the ring's history and importance has drifted away. It's like part of my life has been erased.

My mind is making space, I decide, for Mapinguari. My mind can't be remade and remain unchanged at the same time. Humanity is weak. Atrocities affect the soul and wound the mind. Part of becoming more means feeling less. Perhaps this is how it happens. A permanent diss-ociative break. All of the benefits with none of the negatives.

Sounds like bliss to me.

I hide my pain from Ashan, but while my thoughts of the past have dwindled, I still hurt on the inside. Emotions I would never admit to having reign chaotic in the quiet times between sleep and wakefulness. They're indistinct, without an accompanying image. It's like I've eaten something foul, but can't remember what.

So I press on.

I look forward.

As night settles in, I picture the impending confrontation with Mapinguari. I see a great fight. I smell blood. Mine and Mapinguari's. When it's over, she lies at my feet, begging for mercy. Then I wonder if I'll even remember the fight.

Whatever the case, when it is done—when I am Mapinguari—the ache inside me will be squelched. And then, I will just be. With Ashan. With Oro.

I want nothing more.

Sleep robs my growing smile and transports me to another world.

It's unfamiliar. A dwelling, bright and colorful with solid walls. The lack of trees confuses me. I see them through the windows... *Windows?*

I stumble as something bright and sharp stabs into my foot.

Where am I?

The world is a haze of unfamiliar smells that frighten me.

I'm not afraid of anything.

Thumping from above throws me to the ground, which is covered in a thin layer of light blue grass.

A rug.

A rug?

A luminous ball of light sways back and forth as the thumps return, this time coupled with a monstrous roar.

Where is the sky? The leaves? The surface above me is textured white.

A ceiling.

A scream directs me to a staircase. Where does it lead?

Upstairs.

What is upstairs?

A second scream, high pitched, forms a single word that bristles my insides. "Dad-dy!"

I don't know why it feels important, but I respond the only way I know how; I charge forward, ready to fight.

At the top of the stairs, I draw my weapon. It's a thin metal rod that grows when I pull on the end. I know what this is, and that it's not a weapon. A radio antenna. I push and pull the object, shrinking and growing it, fascinated by its ability to change.

A fresh roar centers me. Draws me through a doorway. I know what's on the other side of this door. I don't want to see it. I don't want to remember it. But when I step through the threshold, nothing is right.

Five large beasts bound around a crisscrossing maze of wooden beams. They swing and bounce, hooting like monkeys, but they're immense and tailless. At the center of the chaos is a massive beast clutching a small girl in his hand. Her face is obscured by thick fingers, but I sense her fear. Her desperation. Her sadness.

I want to make her feel better.

I want to save her.

When the beast begins squeezing, the girl screams again, launching me into action.

Armed with the radio antenna, I charge and stumble through the wooden beams, whipping the creatures in a futile attempt to save her.

"No!" I scream. "Noooo!"

The word erupts as a roar of my own. And then I see myself from the outside once more, hacking and slashing, clawing.

BLOOD SPRAYS, WARM and delicious.

He's lost in it, and quickly forgets why he's there. What he's fighting for.

Darkness consumes him.

Fills him.

And then, he wakes.

I STAND, HEAVING for air, exhausted and confused. Hands on knees, I scan the jungle surrounding me. To my left is a mutilated tree dripping sap. Ants are mixed in with the ruined bark, bodies on a battlefield. Some of them struggle to drag themselves free. Others are dismembered or squashed to paste. Ants above and below the wound are frantic, looking for any enemy.

I follow the irate mass of small bodies to the ground. A slow-moving river of twitching limbs and strong pincers courses toward my feet.

A few steps back frees me from danger for a moment, just long enough to turn toward the growl behind me.

Ashan and Oro stand together, both of them afraid and ready to defend themselves.

That's when I notice the machete in my hand.

"What happened?"

"You started shouting," Ashan says. "In your sleep. I think it was a name. Then you were fighting something. A spirit maybe. It was like with Tikuna. I could see you, but you weren't there. Oro came to help you when you attacked the tree. She was struck by your hand."

I drop the machete and approach the pair, head lowered. I drop to one knee and reach out my arms. "It was a dream. I would never hurt you. Either of you."

There is a moment of wariness, and then both of my girls approach and allow me to wrap my arms around them.

"You are all that matters to me," I say to Ashan, but it feels like a lie.

"That is good," she says. "But when the time comes, I want you to step out of yourself again. Can you do that?"

I'm not sure. I have no control over it. But I say, "Yes."

"Good," she says. "We are nearly there."

35

"You look tired," I tell Ashan, and I get a glower for my concern. While her inner strength is unaffected, her pace has slowed, and she's sweating more than usual. I've slowed my pace to match hers, trying not to push her, but her pride is doing that for me. "If you're feeling ill, we should rest."

"I'm not ill," she says, growing angry.

She's probably right. Sickness in the jungle is usually a result of toxic exposure to something derived by nature. Poison, mold, infection. But she hasn't been exposed to anything, and has no open wounds.

"Is it..." A glance at her crotch finishes the question. Ashan keeps a collection of cloth strips wrapped inside the sash around her waist. During menstruation, she uses them the way a modern woman might a pad. She washes them out in a stream or river, and lets them dangle from the sash before reusing them. She's not wearing one now, but that doesn't mean she's not cramping in preparation.

She pauses, hands on knees, murdering me with her eyes. "I'm not accustomed to the rise."

That makes some degree of sense. We've been traveling uphill all day, our first hint that we have reached the basin's fringe. The incline isn't steep, but it is persistent and working out muscles I haven't used in a long time. I'm feeling the burn, but it hasn't slowed me down. Ashan has led a physical life far longer than me. This shouldn't be hard for her.

When my look of concern grates on her further, she waves me onward. "Just...go!"

To argue would be folly, so I continue onward. The incline grows steeper over the next hour. Ashan doesn't slow, but I can tell she's pushing herself harder. She's not going to take care of herself. I have no choice.

With a grunt, I lower myself to the trunk of a fallen tree. I open my satchel, unwrap some meat, and begin eating.

"What are you doing?" Ashan asks, disappointment and relief at war in her voice.

"I'm hungry," I say. "And thirsty. Find us something to drink."

Telling her to find water helps diffuse her irritation. If I'm putting her to work, I can't be showing her pity, right? Pity isn't the word I would use, but it's how Ashan thinks. And though I might be more animal than man, I haven't forgotten how to love.

But I have forgotten a lot.

I close my eyes and shake my head. Memories scratch at the inside of my skull, seeking fissures. I seal them up with an irritated growl and accept a four-foot segment of vine from Ashan.

"What is on your mind?" she asks, tipping her own vine upward and drinking from it.

I drink from the vine. Once the water hits my tongue, I realize how thirsty I actually was. Memories of dehydration percolate, but are more of a feeling than an image. I never want to feel that desperate and helpless again. I am ashamed that I ever did.

"I am eager to complete our journey," I tell her. "To finish becoming."

"That is good," she says, genuinely pleased. On one hand, she is acting like herself. Sitting here, sharing a small meal, it is impossible to see that anything is wrong with her. But there is no denying her weariness. Perhaps she simply didn't sleep well. Whatever the case, I'm smart enough to know not to ask again.

"Do not let anything distract you," she says. "A lapse in focus will result in both of our deaths."

And there it is. The real reason she's not revealing the cause of her ailment. If I'm distracted by concern for her wellbeing—a very human emotion—how can the animal emerge? If Mapinguari defeats me, Ashan will be the next to die at her hands.

That is something I cannot allow, so I push all concern for Ashan from my mind. When my belly is full, and my thirst quenched, I waste no time striking out again. Ashan follows, but lags behind. An hour later, I can no longer see her, but I can hear her. Her feet have lost their feathery touch. She pushes through brush, rather than moving around it. Her breath heaves with each step.

While I am becoming more, she is becoming less.

A scent tickles my nose. The downhill slope carries the scent of something animal from above. I duck down, drawing my machete. While I still carry bow and arrows, I prefer the more visceral experience of a blade. I take a deep breath through my nose, and relax.

"Oro," I call. The cat doesn't reply. She never does. But I know she's there, waiting for me.

The hill grows steep, requiring me to proceed with my hands lowered to the ground. Despite the incline, I have no trouble climbing thanks to the tangles of tree roots and...rocks. I pause when I grasp the first rough-surfaced stone. It's dark gray and serrated by the elements. Something about the solidness of the stone underfoot feels familiar. Makes me smile.

I heave myself up over a tall root and roll into a clearing where Oro lounges. The cat gives me a glance, tongue hanging out as she pants. The climb has been hard for her, too.

Then I see the view.

I cling to the ground, head spinning from the vast openness ahead. Without realizing it, we've been climbing a mountain. We're nowhere near the summit, but the view is still staggering. The blue sky is pushed back by green peaks rising thousands of feet in the air. Further west, the jungle would give way to stone and snowcapped mountains.

But I don't think we'll need to go that far. We're already at the fringe of the Arawanti's territory, and far further than the lowland Amazonian tribes are comfortable traveling. The air is cooler here, and thinner.

Maybe that's why Ashan is struggling? Deep in the Amazon, she's accustomed to heavily oxygenated air. When I hear her grunting behind me, I lean out over the edge and peer down.

She looks exhausted, struggling to climb the steep rise.

"Hey," I say, ignoring her weariness. "You have to see this!"

After a pause to look me in the eyes, she gets back to work and starts climbing again.

She doesn't want an audience, so I don't give her one. I sit beside Oro and pet the cat's head. Seeing the open sky is a rare treat in the jungle. It's more common now, since Ashan and I never venture too far from water sources and the game they provide. But this…it is raw beauty. The world stretches out before me, and for a moment, I remember that the Earth is vast and its people diverse. Beyond our small Amazonian world, nations are at war, genocide is being carried out, and people with selfish intentions are making decisions for everyone else.

But not here.

Here we are free to live like we want, die on our own terms, and kill if we must.

"What do you think?" I ask Oro.

The cat's yawn infects me, and when Ashan drags herself atop the ridge, she's greeted by my open mouth.

"We can camp here," I say. There are still several hours in the day, but all of us are tired. Some more than others, but there's no need to point that out.

Ashan says nothing as she crawls up beside me and sits down to admire the view. "This is how birds see the world," she says with a smile, then wobbles and grips my arm for balance. "It feels strange."

I know what she means. I've seen things like this before. I can't say when. The memories are obscured. But I remember feeling dizzy and experiencing nausea upon seeing a great canyon. I had trouble comprehending its depth and breadth. Ashan has never seen anything like this before. Her mind struggles to cope with its vastness.

She turns to the side, heaves without any drama, wipes her mouth, and returns to admiring the view. "This will be our home." She looks at me. "After you take it from Mapinguari."

"It could take some time to find her," I say. "The jungle here is vast and steep. We need to settle in for a long hunt."

Ashan's brow furrows like she's concerned for my health. "We have arrived."

"In Mapinguari's territory, but it will take time to—"

Her lips spread in a knowing smile I haven't seen in a long time. When I was fresh to the jungle and naïve about most things, she would smile like this before explaining the situation. I've missed something.

I turn back to the view, looking at the mountains, and the trees, and the stones. But I see nothing else. I search the area around us, scanning for tracks or a path that I might have missed while distracted by the view. Still nothing.

The helpless feeling reminds me of the man I used to be, fueling a flash of anger. "Tell me," I grumble.

Her smile fades a bit and she pinches my cheek. "You were more fun when you were stupid."

I wait in silence.

She rolls her eyes and points to a distant peak. Then she lowers her finger slowly. "Follow the path down."

The mountainous slopes descend like giant steps intercut by massive rocks, on which nothing grows. Her finger comes to a stop in a deep valley. The far side of the valley rises up what could be a small mountain or a large hill. All of it, aside from the exposed rocks, is covered in green.

Ashan takes hold of my chin and redirects my gaze back to the valley's bottom. Other than a collection of small hills, there is nothing remarkable about the valley.

"There," Ashan says. "Queshupa."

"Ashan...I don't see any—"

But then I do.

While everything is green, not everything is tree growth. There are several clearings where grasses grow, but the trees do not. In the Amazon, that means someone is tending to the fields. But the small hills are what hold my attention. Not only are they not covered in trees, they're not hills at all—they're pyramids.

Stepped pyramids.

Here on the fringes of Peru, Mapinguari resides in the remains of a lost Incan city, queen of a long dead empire that will soon be mine.

36

Lying on the precipice's edge, watching the sun set behind the mountains to the west, I'm struck by a sense of wonder that is both relaxing and unsettling. Ashan sits beside me, bathed in orange light. She looks almost otherworldly, like the conjuring of some science fiction novel, luminous and transformative in her simple wonder. She's been smiling for a half hour, the exhaustion that vexed her throughout the day having faded.

She's not doing anything abnormal. Just being quiet, sharing some dried meat with Oro, whose fur is radiant in the half-sun's glow. They're like visions. Goddesses of the rainforest.

Are they real? I wonder. Or have I dreamt them this entire time? Am I huddled in the crook of a tree somewhere, hallucinating?

I reach out and slide my hand over Ashan's bare back. My fingers trace a line up over the bumps of her spine, skipping over familiar scars. Goosebumps rise on the backs of her arms, and I redirect my caress to her right arm. A shiver rolls through her body.

She smiles at me, says nothing, but stretches her back forward in a way that says, 'More, please.' So I oblige, and for the sunset's duration, I run my fingers up and down her back.

Will I be capable of such affection when I am Mapinguari?

I'm not sure, but I'm also not about to ask. We've come so far and sacrificed so much, I'm not sure Ashan would forgive me for turning back.

Oro rolls onto her back, giving Ashan access to her belly. We've become the most unlikely family imaginable, each of us a stranger to the other's world, but somehow connected in ways I can't explain.

I love Ashan and Oro. They are my family.

But will they still be when—

I close my eyes. Don't think about it. The animal might take over again, but it can't last forever.

In the midst of bloodlust, battle, or even pursuit, the idea of completing my transformation into a legendary beast is flawless. But here, on the cusp of our journey's end, doubt haunts me. Would I hurt Ashan? What about Oro? Will they even know me when I become?

If I knew I would lose them, would I still make the journey and pursue my mission to its end?

The question triggers a torrent of unexpected emotions. It feels old. Like a question I've asked before, and never answered. How long have I been pondering it without noticing?

I know the answer. It's why I avoid the question.

I would lay waste to the whole world before losing them again.

Again...

"Are you okay?" Ashan asks.

Her face is a silhouette, framed by the dark outlines of mountains and a muddy, purple sky.

I turn my head to the emerging stars and ask, "Do you know what they are?"

She opens her mouth to reply, pauses and then says, "Tell me."

"When you see a campfire up close, it is large and bright. But when you see it from a distance, it's just a point of light."

When she gives a slow nod, I continue. "The sun is a burning sphere of unimaginable size, but it is far enough away to not burn us. Our world—it's called a 'planet.' 'Earth.' It is like a speck of dust floating in a great body of water, spinning around the great fire. Those..." I point to a few stars. "...are the same as the sun, but farther away. Much farther. They're called 'stars.' And around those stars are other worlds like ours."

"With people?" Ashan asks, a sense of wonder in her voice.

"Maybe," I say, "though they wouldn't look, talk, or act like people. But they would be alive, like us. Maybe looking at our star from a distance and wondering who lives here."

Her fingers find mine and wrap around them, one at a time. "What is the lake called?"

"What lake?"

"The one we...the one Earth floats in."

"It's not really a lake," I say. "It's nothing."

She waves her hand back and forth. "Like air."

"Less than air."

"Huh... How do your people know this?"

I've avoided talking about the outside world, but I'm not sure how I can explain these things, without sounding like I'm making things up, without telling her the truth. "My people build..." There is no word for machine in her dialect. "...canoes with wings like birds that can fly through the sky."

Her grip tightens so hard and fast that I wince in pain.

"I have seen this!" she says. "Once, high in the sky. It buzzed like an insect. My father tried to shoot it down, but when it moved through the clouds, we knew it was out of reach."

"And the second time?" I ask.

"On the ground," she says. "Dead."

"They are not living things," I tell her.

"Its wings were broken," she says. "And it was bleeding. I saw its insides spilled out on the ground, though they had been scavenged. I did not stay long. I was afraid, and trying to hide from Juma. But it was dead. So it had been alive."

"It was never alive," I say, my voice small. Her description and time-line leave no doubt about where and when she saw the airplane. "But the people inside it were. The blood and remains you saw belonged to the men who flew the canoe. The canoes are called, 'airplanes.' The men died in the crash. And they weren't exactly scavenged."

Her grip loosens.

I have her full attention. "They were fed. To Oro."

A quick intake of air is as close to a gasp as Ashan can manage. "How do you know this?"

"Because the airplane carried three people," I say. "Because that was the first time I fed Oro."

"You fell from the sky?"

"It's nothing special," I tell her, hoping she won't suddenly think of me as some kind of deity. "Most people on Earth travel that way."

"Why have we not?" she asks. Her hand slips out of mine. "Why have you kept this from me? What *else* have you kept from me?"

"What I have left unsaid is what I left behind," I explain. "Who I no longer am."

"But you know about things like stars. And Earth. And Airplanes. The world is bigger than I knew. Bigger than any of the four tribes know. Tell me I am wrong."

I want to. "I can't. But I do know that life here is better."

"How?"

"It... It is more honest."

"Death is honest," she says. "But not always better."

"Life is simpler."

"Because my people are dead. Aside from you and Oro, my family is gone."

"That's why we are here," I remind her. "To become Mapinguari, and then to avenge your family. We will bring peace to the four tribes, and we will rebuild your family's legacy with children of our own."

"The children of a Mapinguari..."

"No one will hurt them," I say.

"No one will love them."

Her response silences me.

"Children should not be feared." Something has changed. In all the time I've known her, Ashan has been steeped in anger. Even when placated by drugs, her mind never wanders far from thoughts of revenge. How could she want anything else? What she endured was unthinkable. That the men who committed the crime still walk the Earth makes me ill. To think of any other course of action before we've killed Mapinguari, Juma, and the men who helped him is...wrong.

Unless...

"I'm not the only one keeping secrets," I say.

In the feeble starlight of a moonless sky, Ashan is nearly impossible to see. But I look at her anyway, recreating her image from my memory of her sunbathed body. I saw her as the sun set, but I didn't really look at her. Not with the eyes of someone trained to spot something wrong with someone.

Is she sick? Is she dying?

Aside from her weariness, there hasn't been anything else abnormal.

She did vomit, but after a day-long hike, and the nauseating effect of staring down on the world for the first time, it's not entirely unusual.

Then it's something else? A lie? She's been with me every day, all day, since our first meeting. What could she be hiding?

"You're right," she says, but I still can't think of—

Holy shit...

I see it all at once. The tiredness, the vomit, the change of heart, and the way she glowed beside me. It had nothing to do with the sun.

"You're with child."

Her silence is all the confirmation I need. I reach out and place my hand on her still-slim body. I didn't see it in the light, but in the dark, seeing with my hand, I feel the slight bump.

"*My* child."

"Not Mapinguari's."

"Is that bad?"

"It is not good," she says. "If you become. You might not accept the child."

Male lions sometimes kill the cubs fathered by other men. When I'm Mapinguari, will I see my former self as a weaker competitor? Will I be so separate from myself that I could murder my own child? I don't bother asking. Ashan doesn't know. No one does. Because Mapinguari doesn't have children. Perhaps this is why.

The unanswered question rises from the depths, where it lurks.

If I knew I would lose them, would I still make the journey and pursue my mission to its end?

"I shouldn't be here," I say. "I shouldn't have come. This isn't what matters."

Ashan's silence spurs me to explain further.

"Your family's murder is horrible. A crime of the worst kind. But taking revenge for them will turn us into monsters, too. Though we may live, we will not be alive. Not like we are now."

"What do you want to do?" Ashan's question puts the decision in my hands, but I have no doubt about how she wants me to answer. Standing on the boundary between justice at a permanent cost, and living with temporary regret, with our growing tribe hanging in the balance, it's not a hard call. Especially after making the wrong choice once before.

"We'll leave at first light," I say. "Head south, and then west, into Peru. We'll find a village on the outskirts of my world, where we can live at peace."

Ashan leans into me and whispers, "Thank you," as though speaking the words too loudly will let the spirits of her dead know she's abandoned them.

After thirty minutes of lying in silence, staring up at the stars, Ashan asks, "What is that?"

"What is what?" I ask. She doesn't sound concerned, but Ashan not being able to identify something in the jungle is a little disconcerting.

"You were humming."

"I was?" and then I hear the song in my thoughts, the words drifting to me from another lifetime. "It's a song."

The music composed by Amazonian tribes is rhythmic and powerful. The chanting often tells a story, and invokes powerful emotions, but it's rarely calm, never romantic, and reflects the primal life-and-death reality of the jungle.

The song that's found its way into my thoughts, as I lie beside Ashan, is in stark contrast. Despite that, and knowing she will ask, I sing her the chorus of Snow Patrol's *Chasing Cars*. I sing about lying here, her next to me, and forgetting the world. It's a simple image, but a big concept.

"What does it mean?" she asks, and I sing it again, this time translating it for her. Via the final lyrics, I ask her to lie with me and forget the world.

She holds me a little tighter and says, "I will."

We settle in for the night. With Ashan wrapped in my arms, and a smile on my face, I slip into a dream knowing that my life is about to evolve beyond the chaos of the modern world, and the darkness of the Amazon basin. I'm not sure what the morning sun will bring, but I look forward to facing it with my family.

37

"Daddy! No peeking!"

"I'm not," I insist, while looking through a gap in my fingers that's wide enough to provide a clear view of the park and the playground. It's a bright fall day, the air crisp and full of children's laughter.

"I can see your eyes!" Juni, dressed in a blue sundress, small fists on her hips, scowls at me with a deeply furrowed brow and pinched lips. She's a cute ball of demanding fury, which was my goal. She's rarely more adorable than when she's angry.

"Okay, okay. See?" I close my fingers and turn away. "See?"

"No peeking," she warns. "Count to forty."

"One, two, three."

I stop counting aloud when I hear the sound of small running feet. By the time I reach a silent ten, my hand taps my hip, my subconscious making sure the phone is still there.

Is the ringer on?

Did I miss something?

I dig out the phone and check the screen. Two missed calls. Two messages. I'm not on call today, but I have several patients who might need urgent advice. Juni's been waiting for our date for several weeks. I had to cancel our last outing because of a soup kitchen emergency.

The first call is from the office. The second from an unknown number.

I listen to the office message first. It's from the service that handles messages for my practice on the weekend. "Hello Dr. Zekser. This is Rachel from the MediCall center. Your patient, Mr. Phillip Clinton called regarding an expired prescription. The pharmacy won't fill it without your authorization."

The message continues with the details, but I'm familiar with Mr. Clinton's condition, his medication, and his pharmacy. The second call is from Phil himself. I'm not sure how he got my number, but he's the most resourceful eighty-year-old I've met—unafraid of technology and in love with Google.

My first call is to the pharmacy. After a few minutes of waiting, and then speaking to the pharmacist, the prescription is refilled. My call to Mr. Clinton, while good news, feels like a shouting match. Every word needs to be spoken loudly and clearly enunciated. I smile and nod to a few mothers watching me, attempting to put them at ease.

"Yes, Mr. Clinton. You can pick it up now. It's ready for you." I put a finger in my free ear to block out the sound of crying, listening to Mr. Clinton's questions, most of which have been answered in the past. "No, it's not a controlled substance. Yes, your son can pick it up. No, you have diarrhea because you won't stop eating dairy. The government isn't doing anything to the cows. I have to go now, Mr. Clinton. Yes. Okay. Have a…yes. Have a good day. Goodbye."

I hang up the phone fifteen minutes after checking it. Mental exhaustion directs me to a nearby bench. Head in my hands, I try to clear my head, but a child's grating cry frays my nerves.

As I open my fingers to find and level a cold stare at the child irking me, I remember what I'm supposed to be doing.

My hands fall away from my face.

Juni is thirty feet away, sitting atop a wooden castle. I can only see her dress, but it's *her* crying that I hear.

My walk of shame to the castle is observed by the same gaggle of mothers who watched me take the call. They weren't concerned by the volume of my voice, they were watching me ignore my child.

I'm an asshole.

It's the truth. I spend far more time at work than with my family. The money I make pays for a good life, but it's mostly without me. I take care of sick patients who need me. When half the people I see on a given day are falling apart, it's hard to remember that my healthy kid needs me, too.

But there's so much to do. The practice. The soup kitchen. In two weeks, I'm leaving for the Amazon. Those people need me, too.

I don't bother trying to explain this to Juni when I step up to the castle. She wouldn't understand. "I'm sorry."

"You forgot me," she says.

"I know." A list of excuses tries to bubble out of my throat. Right or wrong, she won't understand them. I swallow my self-defense and accept her verdict.

She stomps her foot when I reach for her. "You *always* forget me!"

Her claim riles my defensive nature once more. But she's right. This isn't the first time I've left her hanging to take a call, or to run to the office, or to help at the soup kitchen. Life is busy, but I'm helping people. She might not see it now, but someday she'll understand, and hopefully emulate the way I live.

"You're right," I say. "I'll try better."

My three-year-old daughter doesn't argue against the lie despite damning evidence to the contrary. She doesn't need to. We both know she doesn't believe me, and that she shouldn't. I scoop her off the castle and carry her to the car, checking my phone one more time en route.

When my eyes open to the morning light, I know what I've just seen was a memory, not a dream. The shift in my mission—from vengeance to survival—along with the knowledge that I am to be a father, has roused a part of me that had been dead and buried.

The part that is a father already.

I forgot her. *Again.*

Tears trickle down the sides of my face as I lie on my back, staring up at a cloudy sky. I lower my hand to my hip, searching for a phone that is not there. Feeling the bare hip, I consider trying the phone still in my backpack. But such a thing would disturb Ashan, and I'm not sure how I would handle it.

She's forgotten me by now, I think.

How long have I been here? How many seasons have passed? I've lost track. It doesn't matter. I can't go back. Not after what I've experienced.

Not after what I've done.

The animal I've become has no place in the modern world.

I drown out the memory with thoughts of my future with Ashan, our child, and Oro. To consider anything else, to give the memory of my past and the people in it my full attention, would tear me apart.

I wipe my tears and turn my head to the side. This close to Mapinguari's home, we're not safe. We need to strike out now and not stop for several weeks, taking great pains to cover our tracks. Only then will we truly be free of the darkness in which we've been steeped.

But Ashan is no longer beside me.

Oro is missing, too, but that's not unusual. She's typically up and hunting before the sun. Then again, Ashan rises early, too. I often wake to find a fresh killed or picked breakfast waiting for me. But in Mapinguari's backyard, that would be foolish. Something Ashan is not.

I sit up, scanning the area. "Ashan?"

Wind sifting through the trees behind me is the only response. I hadn't noticed the night before, but the jungle here is mostly silent, as though the animals know to stay quiet...or are missing.

"Oro," I call. If the cat is within earshot, she'll come.

"Ashan!" I flinch at the sound of my own raised voice. Any louder and it could echo through the valley below. "Where are you?" I whisper, and I decide that if she won't reveal herself, I'll have to go find her.

The memory of Juni slips past my defenses. I was supposed to find her, too.

I'm not that person anymore. I'll never put myself, or others, before the people I love most. The trappings of the modern world have lost their hold on me.

Instead of looking at the surrounding jungle, I turn my attention to the earth at my feet. The patch of compressed earth where Ashan had slept is easy to spot. As are the footprints disturbing it.

Two sets of footprints. There are no signs of a fight, but someone else was here, and now Ashan is not.

My heart races as I follow the prints, moving, one set in front of the other. The trail leads downhill, toward Queshupa.

The first set of prints leaves long, scraping depressions. *That's Ashan,* I decide. She's not injured, just leaving an easy-to-follow trail, which means she's in trouble.

Mapinguari has her.

It's the only explanation.

But why would a monster renowned for its ferocity not simply attack? If the beast found us sleeping, why not poison us as we did the men sleeping in the Arawanti village?

Because she is not a sleep-killer.

"Oro!" I call, but the cat does not respond. She is either out of range, or… I search the area for blood or signs of a struggle. Oro was not here when Ashan was taken. "Where are you, girl? I need you."

Seeing no alternative, I move to gather my meager gear. My bow and arrows are missing. The satchel and the machete on my hip are all that remain. Ashan's belongings are also missing. I open the satchel and check its contents, digging past the remaining pot, the scraps of meat, the money, the notebook, and my collection of jungle knick-knacks. The gun rests at the bottom of the bag, fully loaded.

Wielding the weapon goes against my heightened sense of nobility. If Tikuna were still alive, I'm sure he would mock me for using it, but fuck Tikuna. Fuck Mapinguari. Fuck nobility. I no longer want to become the monster, but I'll kill her if she forces me to.

I follow the path, gun in hand, telling myself that everything will be fine, that I'll find Ashan, that I'll kill Mapinguari, that we'll leave together and never look back. I tell myself this over and over, but I don't believe it any more than Juni did my promise to never forget her again.

38

The descent toward Queshupa is arduous. At times steep and covered in jagged rocks, I'm forced to return the gun to the satchel and concentrate on my foot- and hand-holds. Despite the natural obstacles, the path is easy to follow. Ashan drags her foot every few steps, leaving a broken line. While I'm glad for the trail, it's also unsettling. Mapinguari is allowing Ashan to leave a trail, meaning my pursuit will be expected.

Another trap.

Mapinguari is less of a monster than she's been made out to be. And that, I think, makes her more dangerous. To be a monster takes savagery. To be a hunter takes skill. But to fool entire peoples into fearing you, sacrificing to you, giving you tributes and a privileged life? That requires intelligence and cunning.

When the trees thin, I slow my pursuit. As much as I want to find Ashan, stepping on a poison dart isn't going to help either of us. The jungle is silent here. Even though I'm adept at moving silently, every footstep lets out a subtle crunch of dry leaves. The only sound aside from my feet is the gentle hiss of wind through leaves. Branches sway, pro-viding me with glimpses of the blue sky and the mountains surrounding us. The peaks are bathed in the morning sun, but the valley into which I'm descending is still cloaked in cool shadow.

Uneven ground trips me up as I watch my surroundings. The rugged terrain is different from what I've grown accustomed to. But it's also unnatural. The way the trees grow. The way things are spaced out. It almost looks cultivated.

Then I see it for what it is.

Walls of stone, crumbled over time, have been covered by earth and vegetation. Mentally removing the growth, I see foundations. Walls.

Streets. An empire once flourished here. The Incans populated much of Peru, up to the Andes, but they were adept at building mountain cities, like Machu Picchu. Finding a new city at the edge of their known borders isn't intellectually surprising, but it leaves my mouth agape until I remember why I'm here. The Incans are long since dead, and the woman I love—perhaps a descendant of the great Incan people—is at risk.

I push through the outer city's remains and follow the trail—now a worn path reminiscent of a game trail—around a tall hill contained by a wall of stone. It's not a natural formation, though. Massive rocks, pulled from the soil and smoothed down, have been fitted together like a perfectly seamed puzzle and raised as a kind of retaining wall. I look up at the steep rise. The wall could also be the side of a structure, now covered in plant life. I'm not sure, but the surface has been kept clean by human hands.

I'm getting close, I think, reaching into the satchel. My finger brushes up against the Ziploc bag containing all that remains of my previous life. I linger for a moment, and then grasp the gun.

The wall curves to the right, as I follow the path downhill. I slow when the smooth wall looks ragged ahead. Chips of stone litter the pathway. Is this a trap, meant to distract me? Is the stone concealing something? When I creep up to the aberration, I see it for what it is— morbid decoration.

Horizontal troughs have been gouged into the wall, ten inches deep and tall. There are three shelves spaced out between my waist and shoulders. All of them are filled with skulls. Some of them are turned sideways, bookends to even more skulls, all of them human.

The nearest bunch looks old. They're decayed to a degree, worn smooth by the elements and jaundiced by age. The lines of skulls resemble the ebb and flow of a song's soundwave, rising and falling. The dead on display are men, women, and children.

Some show no signs of how they died, but most have been crushed, cracked, splintered, and punctured. Violent deaths. But how long have they been here? They're not holdovers from the Incan empire. Skulls that old would be dust by now. And the stone fragments on the ground hint at a more recent creation.

Mapinguari has a hobby.

Ashan's trail leads through the loose stones covering the path. I continue forward, passing hundreds of skulls. Are all these dead at her hands, or do some of them belong to her predecessors?

The path ends at a line of trees so close together that they must have been planted. The thick growth creates an effective barrier to what lies beyond. I suspect the path had once been open, but now, the only way to see what lies beyond is to push through the trees and expose yourself.

Seeing no alternative, I slip between the trees and find myself at the edge of a clearing that had been concealed from view the previous night. Knee-high grass flows with the wind pushed through the valley by the still rising sun's warmth. A faint trail leads from the jungle toward what lies on the field's far side, several hundred feet away.

The Incan step pyramid stands out even more clearly from the ground. Still in shadow, but silhouetted by the sun's light on the mountains behind it, the moss-covered structure rises a hundred and fifty feet, and it's narrower than it is tall. Like the wall, and the structures at Machu Picchu, the stones have been carved with precision, interlocking in a way that seems impossible for primitive man. There are no skulls here, though the temple is ominous enough without them. In a land of wildlife and endless nature, the pyramid stands like an abomination.

The perfect place from which to create the legend of a god-like monster. Do they even know who built it? Who their ancestors were? How many people lived here? A thousand years ago, this would have been one of the great cities of the world. And now it is home to a monster.

A soon-to-be-dead monster.

Gun in hand, I start across the field, following the path of bent reeds straight toward the temple.

Eyes locked onto the temple, I almost miss the depression ahead of me.

Something is lying in the field, compressing a patch of grass.

Leading with the gun, ready to fire, I inch forward.

It's not Mapinguari. Of that, I'm sure. There's no sign of a struggle to indicate Ashan had gotten the upper hand. My heart pounds as I inch closer, expecting to see Ashan.

A stiff breeze tips the grass to the side, providing a glimpse of what lies ahead. It's a brief view, but it's enough to drag a sob from the depths of my soul.

HE STUMBLES FORWARD with **no regard** toward the possibility of a trap.

"Oro," he moans, falling to his knees by the cat's side. Tears seep from his eyes, his chest heaving with growling sobs. Oro, his most trusted friend and companion, is dead, her body cold and beyond the salvage of modern medical techniques.

He's never felt despair like this, and it coughs from him so hard that his ribs ache and his throat grows raw. A bellow rises like a volcano, erupting into the sky with all the fury of the Earth's interior.

Lost in a haze, his thoughts turn from Oro, to blood, and then, to Ashan.

CLUTCHING ORO'S SCRUFF, I wipe my tears into her fur. "I will not leave you here, daughter, but I must go now. Your mother needs me."

I scan the area for signs of what happened.

My imagination takes what little information I have and fills in the rest.

Oro followed Mapinguari and Ashan. Sensing her friend was in danger, Oro darted through the field and attacked. Rather than engage the jaguar, Mapinguari cut the cat down with a single dart. I pluck the poison-tipped projectile from Oro's neck and inspect it.

It's one of Ashan's, adding insult to injury.

With shaking hands, I lift Oro's face and place my forehead against hers. While we touch, I feel the calm confidence she brought to my life. "Love you, girl." Then I place her down and feel nothing but rage.

And fear.

Ashan...

I turn my head toward the temple and find her standing on the top step, naked and stripped of her belongings. Tendrils of dried blood coat her body, their paths leading to her head and a long gash on her forehead. She looks dazed, bewildered by where she is and what's happening.

This isn't how we envisioned this day. Even when our mission was to confront and kill Mapinguari, this scenario never entered our minds or our conversations.

Mapinguari is only human after all.

Right?

The demon rises up behind Ashan, appearing from the shadows of an open passageway at the temple's top. Even hunched, she stands taller than Ashan. The beast's face is concealed by a billowing mane. What little I can see of her body is covered in black scales, but they're not shiny, like on most scaled creatures. They're man-made matter, absorbing light rather than reflecting it.

Mapinguari sways back and forth, eager and excited.

I start toward the temple, gun in hand, trying to not show how much I want to kill her. With Ashan between us, that won't be possible.

With a nudge, Ashan starts down the steps. Using one hand for balance, she works her way down, her face disheveled and lacking the defiant anger that's been present since we met. Mapinguari follows, moving along the steps with the same fluid ease of a spider on a wall, brimming with energy.

Six young women emerge from the rooftop entrance. Adorned with bright feathers in their shoulder-length, black hair, and painted in bright red patterns from head to toe, they hardly look human. They follow in two lines, faces placid and indifferent to the drama playing out before them.

Mapinguari, the monster, has servants.

I stop when Ashan reaches the grass at the temple's base. She's held in place by a dark gray hand on her shoulder. Three of Mapinguari's long, black, pointed fingernails poke into her skin, drawing fresh rivulets of blood. Her index finger remains up and pointed at me.

It takes all of my strength to control the howling animal inside me, frothing at the mouth, but I manage it, waiting for the demon to speak first.

When she does, her simple message, "Drop the weapon," horrifies me, not because it will leave me unarmed, but because the words were spoken in English.

39

What is she? I wonder, inching closer, trying to make out the beast's face. There's a woman under there, but does she have the same dark tan skin and facial features as the other natives, or is she, like me, an outsider?

It's impossible to see her true skin color past the scales, which I can now see have been painted on, probably by the six women still descending the temple stairway, each delicate step taken in unison.

"Drop the weapon." Mapinguari follows the demand by placing the claws of her right hand over Ashan's throat. Her English isn't great. I suspect she hasn't spoken it in a long time, perhaps since childhood. And it's tinged with a subtle Spanish accent.

The memory of when I first learned about Mapinguari surfaces. I hadn't given it much thought at the time, but now it makes sense. She wasn't just Tikuna's sister, she was his *adopted* sister. Like me, she found herself lost in the jungle and taken in by the Arawanti.

Maybe all Mapinguari have been outsiders. Raised in the jungle, the natives might be too accustomed to harsh living conditions. But coming from the outside world and being forced to fight for survival is enough to strip away our modernity and humanity, leaving us as beasts.

But not entirely. Mapinguari's commands reveal her human mind is intact, sharing space with the animal that can, at times, over-take us both.

"Toss it. Over there." She motions to the side with her head.

I don't want to part with the gun, but I'm also certain I don't need it. With a casual flick of my wrist, the gun spirals away, disappearing into the grass ten feet to my right.

Mapinguari howls toward the sky. For a moment, I think it's a victory roar, but then the jungle all around comes to life. Men and women slip out of the shade and into the clearing. Judging by the variety of skin paints and ornamental piercings, and the sheer number of people, most of the adults from the Guaruamo, Jebubo, and Arawanti tribes have gathered to watch my demise.

Not one of them is armed.

They're not here to fight.

They're spectators.

When I see Juma, the animal stirs, twisting and clawing to come out.

The man tempts me further by grinning. The confidence in his eyes draws a growl from deep inside. When I bare my teeth, his confidence wavers, but it returns when he points past me, to Mapinguari.

"Who are you?" she asks, reverting to tribal language, her voice like tearing paper.

I flinch at the question. *Who am I?*

"I don't know."

Mapinguari nods as though I answered the question correctly.

"What do you want?"

The animal nearly responds with a threat. This is Oro's killer. I want to tear her head free from her shoulders. "To leave," I tell her. "With Ashan. We'll head west and never return."

Mapinguari squints at me. "You're not ready."

"Ready for what? Release her and we will leave. You have my word."

"The word of a man?" she asks. "Or a beast?"

She knows, I realize, *that I intended to take her place as Mapinguari.*

"A man," I manage to say, as my muscles tense to attack.

"I see it in you." She leans to Ashan's other shoulder, peering out from under her mane of dried reeds, her yellowed eyes and teeth glowing from the shadows. "I know you feel it. The craving. Death provides release. Life is yours to take…" She leans her face into Ashan's hair, sniffing. "Or spare."

Mapinguari's right hand slides from Ashan's neck, down her back and around her torso. The vile woman violates Ashan, clutching her breast before sliding her hand to Ashan's belly.

Why isn't she fighting? I wonder, watching Ashan's eyebrows turn up in fear. I know what Ashan is capable of. I can think of a dozen ways she could break free. But she stands motionless, allowing Mapinguari to defile her. Did Oro's death break her? Despite their rough start, Ashan had come to think of Oro as her daughter, born from the jungle's womb and adopted by us. Or is she simply concerned about the life growing in her belly?

When Mapinguari caresses Ashan's stomach, I'm sure she knows. But how? Ashan would never have told her.

She's been following us. Listening to us. She was there last night, invisible to even Oro.

Mapinguari gives Ashan's belly a pat. "A boy, I think." She grins. "Delicious."

She's messing with me. Trying to get inside my head. Of all the horrible things I've been told about Mapinguari, cannibalism has never been one of them.

"I'll beg if you need me to," I tell her, clutching my fists to keep the animal inside.

Mapinguari frowns. She's disappointed. What was she expecting? What did she want? A fight? To reassert her dominance over all the people watching us. Me begging at her feet should do the same. But I was not merciful with Tikuna. Why should I expect any different from a person so in touch with her animal?

"You *will* beg," she says.

"Please," I say.

"Not yet." She motions to the side with her head once more. "The machete, too."

I draw the blade and toss it to the side.

Ashan looks pained by my willingness to disarm. When our eyes meet, I see a new kind of desperation. She knows something, but can't tell me. Her eyes dart to the side and down, looking at Mapinguari's index finger. While the other black nails are still buried in Ashan's skin, the fourth digit and its pointed nail, remains extended.

When I look into Ashan's eyes again, she's apologetic. "I'm sorry," she mouths, and then she says, "Go! Escape! Live as the man you have become...not the monster she would make you..."

Mapinguari leans around Ashan's shoulder, the slow, sinister movement stealing her voice.

She licks Ashan's cheek, and then like a hungry dog, her own lips.

"Are you ready?" the beast asks me.

"No."

A smile spreads. "Perfect."

Her index finger taps down, the tip of it poking into Ashan's shoulder like a wasp's stinger. The movement is almost imperceptible. If Ashan hadn't pointed the poisoned digit out, I might have missed its significance.

"Love..." Ashan manages to whisper, but that's her final word. Her face twists in fear, and then locks in place. A wheezy breath is followed by silence.

She's paralyzed and helpless, at the mercy of the same poison that killed Oro.

I can save her. To the people of the Amazon, Ashan is already dead. But I can bring her back. I have before.

Mapinguari releases Ashan and lets her topple into the grass. "Not this time," she says before stepping over Ashan, lowering herself onto all fours and growling.

The message is clear. To save Ashan, I'll have to get past Mapinguari, and I'll have to do it fast. After five minutes without oxygen, she'll have severe brain damage even if I can resuscitate her, which is always a gamble, especially without a defibrillator. But if I can perform CPR...

I rush Mapinguari, fists clenched.

She ducks down lower and for the first time I understand the strategic value of her grassy mane. Here, in her home, she disappears into the yellowed grass.

I kick hard, aiming for her head. One solid blow should be enough to stun the women long enough to help Ashan. But I strike only her mane, which she's shed. When the mane topples through the sky, the gathered crowd gasps, but the maidservants don't flinch. They look numb. How much have they seen? How many people have been torn apart in this field?

A savage roar tears through the air to my left. I turn to throw a punch, but I'm struck from the side by a blur.

Two solid blows to my kidney fill my torso with agony even before I hit the ground. I swing a hard backhand, but again I strike nothing.

Mapinguari has the reflexes and cunning of a predator.

And I am fighting like a man.

Stop fighting like a man, the animal shouts.

I resist it. Becoming the animal might defeat Mapinguari, but it can't save Ashan. I need to do both, but I can't be both. I am either man or beast. For Ashan, and our unborn child, I choose to remain a man.

Reeds flatten around me as I flail my way back to my feet. I punch at the air around me, expecting another attack. Instead of Mapinguari, I find myself looking into Juma's confident eyes. His journey of hate comes to an end today. He's sure of it.

"Eargh!" Mapinguari launches onto my back. Her long, scale-covered arms reach around my torso, those long, hooked, poison-tipped fingers aimed for my chest.

I catch her wrists, lean forward and throw. Mapinguari crashes to the ground, landing on her back. She springs up as though I've tossed her onto a trampoline, twisting around to glare at me from her hands and feet. Low to the ground, her flexible body becomes more monster than human. Her scaled skin stretches over her slender muscles, twitching with anticipation.

I flinch when I see her face for the first time. Like her body, it's covered in scales, except for her forehead, where a large eye glares at me. When she blinks, her true eyes match the scales, giving her the appearance of a cyclops.

Some of the villagers see it, too, stepping back and gasping.

But it's just an illusion. Mapinguari is horrible to look at. Her jaundiced eyes and sharpened teeth are revolting. Her frizzy hair grows in patches, as though she tears it out on occasion.

She's not a monster, I realize, *just a broken person.*

Like me.

Instead of hate, I feel pity.

"We can leave," I tell her. "Together. Find your family. Your real family. You don't need to kill her. No one else needs to die."

"Beg," she hisses, drool flowing from the sides of her cheeks. "Beg!"

Tears flow. My legs tremble. And then I remember. I can turn this around with a word. "Urpi."

Mapinguari squints at me.

"Your family is looking for you, Urpi."

She looks disgusted.

"*You* killed my brother."

"Your *real* family. The parents who named you Urpi."

Her face scrunches in confusion. She doesn't recognize her own name. It's lost its power. She's too far gone.

A sob coughs from my chest as I look at Ashan's motionless form. She can't even fight for her life. "Please. God, please."

Mapinguari laughs. It's a horrible sound. Inhuman. "Urpi was my *mother's* name. The woman whose throat I tore away with my own teeth."

God-damn you, Tikuna...

She lets out a high-pitched giggle and then lunges for my throat.

40

I dive to the side, avoiding Mapinguari's attack, but the roll takes me further away from Ashan. I need to find the gun or the machete and put an end to this. Without a weapon, Mapinguari will eventually poke me with her poison-tipped finger and subject me to the same slow death already claiming Ashan.

Rolling to my right, rage surges.

She's going to die.

Only I can stop it.

When Mapinguari lunges again, I don't try to evade. I do the opposite, and unexpected, I charge like a bull, lowering my forehead into hers.

I hear a crack, but I feel nothing for a few moments. Darkness resolves into a blue sky full of spinning sprites. Then, pain. It pounds through my head and spreads down my neck and into my back. A concussion for sure, maybe worse.

Getting to my hands and knees is a challenge, but I manage it. The field spins around me, but I find Mapinguari lying a few feet away. She moans, but doesn't rise. I could kill her. I *should* kill her. But at what cost? Every second I spend fighting her, Ashan's death becomes irreversible.

I crawl toward the flattened patch of grass where Ashan lies. I close my eyes to prevent my spinning vision from filling me with nausea. When my hand bumps into Ashan, I open my eyes to find her wide-eyed face, frozen in sadness, staring into the sky. Her skin has already begun to pale and cool.

Sickening realization digs sharp coils into my gut. My counter attack on Mapinguari didn't just stun us both, it knocked us unconscious. But for how long?

Fighting back tears and sobs, I blow a shaky breath into Ashan's lungs. Then I link my trembling fingers and start chest compressions, gingerly at first, but then really pushing, the way you're supposed to. A wail rises from my chest when her ribs crack, a necessary evil.

Her body wiggles with each shove. There's no shifting expression. No signs of a struggle or discomfort.

Though the spinning stops, I can no longer see Ashan through the wetness in my eyes.

"C'mon. I can't do this without you."

Push, push, push.

"I can't live without you."

Push, push, push.

Inhuman sounds rise from my throat as the knowledge that the small life within Ashan is dying along with her. "No!" I roar. "No!"

Push, push, push.

I try to breathe into her lungs, but only manage to cough and sob.

My hands slip over her tear-slick skin when I try to resume compressions.

Her body goes limp, the expression of fear melting away. For a moment, hope. And then, her bowels void.

That's when I know it's over.

She can't be saved.

I can't save her.

And I am undone.

HE FALLS OVER Ashan's body, sobbing and screaming, unaware of the world around him. Lost in mindless emotion, the man who once was slips away into numb non-existence.

Love dies in his heart, taking mercy, sympathy, empathy, and compassion with it.

He sees Oro, feels her head against his. Then she's torn away, taking his skin with her.

Ashan is there for a moment, the smell of her hair, the taste of her skin. She fades away, sucking his insides out.

An image remains. An unborn child with his face and Ashan's eyes. It reaches for him, but is plucked away by a hooked hand. He's eviscerated. Nothing of the man is left.

Only the animal remains.

41

Tears dry.

Breathing slows.

When he looks up again, his vision is clear and his focus unwavering. A growl rumbles from his stomach and emerges from his mouth. Those watching inch away from him.

Mapinguari, his prey, shakes her head and levels her yellow eyes at him. Baring sharp teeth, she hisses.

Then she charges, running low to the ground.

Claws rake through grass, poisoned tips finding no flesh. The animal leaps over his enemy clutching her hair. Upon landing he yanks, intending to wrench her to the ground, but the hair pulls free, taking bits of flesh with it.

He stumbles forward, confused by the black strands in his hand. Then she attacks again, blood dripping over her face, into her eyes.

Vision obscured, she misses her first strike. The second strikes his satchel, snapping back the nail as it snags on the impermeable surface.

He stumbles back, catches himself on his hands and kicks out hard. Heel strikes chin, snapping sharpened teeth onto soft tongue. The severed meat falls to the grass, followed by a stream of blood.

Mapinguari doesn't seem to notice the injury. The large, blood-soaked eye on her forehead stares unblinking and unafraid—like the animal.

He charges with a roar, raking his claws over the monster's chest, drawing blood, but little else. The beast swings her right hand, wielding that horrible weapon, the poison that took the world away.

All of the animal's rage focuses on the limb. He catches it in his hands. Waves of rage and strength flow into his arms as he shoves. The wrist folds back with a snap and a wail of pain. It's limp and useless, but the animal's fury is far from satiated.

Blood fills his mouth as he tears into the tight skin of the folded-back wrist. His teeth gnaw through sinew and vein.

A high-pitched scream tears through the clearing as he twists and pulls, bites and tears.

He falls away, a prize clutched in his mouth. His prey stumbles away, clutching its barren wrist, blood spritzing the grass between them.

No poison, he thinks and spits the hand into the grass. It lands beside a modern weapon, one he knows how to use, but lacks the desire to wield. He steps on it as he stalks toward Mapinguari.

He feels her power flowing to him as he closes in.

The animal in her is fading. The spirit of Mapinguari is no longer hers. It has abandoned her in favor of another.

He has become.

Blood and drool dangle from his chin as he growls. The woman attempts to threaten him with a display of her own, but it is pitiful.

She turns to the people watching, pleading with her eyes. They remain motionless. Even her own people, whose skin lacks the red and black paint of the other tribes, remain stoic in her demise. Only one of the onlookers moves. A man. He stumbles back, fear in his eyes, and then he breaks for the jungle.

Juma, Mapinguari thinks. Memories elude him, but he feels nothing but hatred, loathing, and hunger for the man.

But first, the woman.

"Run," the man growls.

She stands on shaky legs, once powerful, now quivering with fear. Urine runs down her inner thigh. She has been unmade.

Blood flows from the wrist with each swing of her arms. Her legs pump hard. Her heart pounds, fueling her flight, putting pressure behind the blood in her veins, and the blood leaving them. The flow gives her strength, and then, when there is nothing left, takes it away.

A two-hundred-foot-long path of blood leads to the woman's body. He follows it at a walk, letting the bloody grass tickle his lowered hand. She lies in a bed of flattened reeds, gulping for air, eyes wide and unblinking. Without blood to fuel her, mind and body are slipping away.

And there is no one to save her.

He watches her life fade.

When she's gone, rage builds anew. He wants to kill her again. And again. And again. There is nothing he detests more than the weak mound of flesh lying limp at his feet. Darkness overtakes him, leaving only a vague awareness of movement. Of impacts. Of warmth moving through his fingertips. Of burning muscles and exertion.

He returns with a gasp, following it with heaving breaths. Confused, he searches the area. Men and women from the Amazon tribes stare at him. Some with reverent awe, some with horror, and others with approval. One by one, they bow and inch backward. The six feathered women standing at the base of the temple bow on one knee, heads lowered to the grass, where they remain, their devotion to Mapinguari unflinching.

This simple act of subjugation appeases him. He bears them no ill will. Most of them.

His eyes track motion at the jungle's edge where a man sprints into the foliage and disappears.

"Juma…"

First, the nameless woman.

He looks down to where the woman had lain, but in her place is a mass of flesh and bone, the stench of it pungent, but not unwelcome. A quick search of the field reveals nothing.

She's gone, he thinks, looking back at the gore. *Gone forever.*

For a moment, Mapinguari is appeased.

Then he remembers Juma, drops to his hands and feet, and tears through the field.

42

Reeds slap his skin. The sturdiest of them open small fissures. Blood drips from a dozen wounds. He doesn't notice the sting. Doesn't realize he's running on all fours. Doesn't notice the body of his dead daughter as he leaps over her still form.

His prey is all that exists.

The man is quick, skilled, and comfortable in the jungle. Mapinguari can't recall much about him other than his name—Juma—and that his death will be pleasing.

At the jungle's edge, Mapinguari scales the twisting branches of a tree covered in working ants. He pauses to watch them, always working, always the same. He's seen them before, somewhere else. At another time. There is no memory, just a feeling of having seen them before, during another emotionally charged transformative moment. He pushes past the ants to the higher branches, listening, looking, smelling.

A swaying sapling provides a starting point.

The distant slap of feet on earth gives him a direction.

Fear lingers in the air like a pheromone, fueling his hunger for death.

He's never sensed the world like this before. It's pure and invigorating, not held back by the constraints of civilization—modern or primitive. He's beyond such things. More. And less.

Branches sway as he moves through them, swinging from one to another as he'd always imagined trying, but never felt brave enough to attempt. After building momentum, he lunges between trees. He falls short of his goal, but clutches onto a smaller branch, which bends under his weight and lowers him toward the ground. Ten feet from the forest floor, he drops and lands with a roll.

A laugh sprays spittle from between his teeth.

His newfound freedom pleases him.

Juma…

Mapinguari races into the jungle, scurrying back and forth through the brush, searching for signs of his quarry's flight. A toeprint redirects him.

Juma has a good lead, but fear is making him sloppy. And sooner or later, his age will slow him down.

Moving with the newfound grace that comes with fearlessness, Mapinguari delights in the jungle. At the same time, he is not foolish. He doesn't remember where his knowledge comes from, but he knows what is dangerous to touch, or eat. The skills of his previous life have been retained, despite the alteration of what made him human.

And this knowledge guides him when Juma's path evades him.

The Guaruaramo tribe's territory lies to the east. That's where he will head, to the safety of home, where familiar territory will give him an advantage.

But we are many weeks travel from Guaruamo, Mapinguari realizes. *Juma isn't going home, he's—*

The whistle of an arrow would make most creatures in the jungle flinch or duck. Mapinguari charges onward, unconcerned with something like death.

When he reaches a clearing full of the various tribes' discarded weapons, he's tempted to take some for himself, but he wants to feel Juma's life slip away. Only then will he be satisfied. He can't remember why, but he craves little else.

Juma's retreat from Mapinguari's territory sets a troop of monkeys to screaming, warning each other of danger and revealing the old man's path. Far ahead, the twang of a fired arrow is followed by a shriek. The monkeys fall silent as one of their own has been slain by Juma.

Overhead, the fleeing monkeys make eye contact with Mapinguari and stop their retreat. The largest of them watches him, assessing. There's a subtle intelligence in the creature's eyes. The two primates come to an understanding. When Mapinguari strikes out again, the monkeys follow in silence.

Juma's trail disappears when the terrain becomes rocky, allowing the old man to leap through the forest. While Mapinguari growls in frustration, pacing low to the ground, smelling, searching, the monkeys shriek and leap overhead, leading the way.

As the terrain angles upward, Mapinguari alternates between running on all fours and on two legs. He falls into a comfortable rhythm, using both techniques to move through the forest with newfound efficiency.

A hundred feet ahead, the monkeys hold their position, bouncing in the highest branches. Their high-pitched shrieking is familiar. He understands it.

Here, they tell him. *Your prey is here!*

Little bastards, he thinks with a grin. Monkeys are always happy to point out a prey animal that isn't them, especially when it's someone, or something, that's killed one of their own.

Sensing Juma's exhaustion, Mapinguari launches uphill, oblivious to the burning in his legs and the pain in his chest. His pounding heart thumps behind his ears, drums inspiring the hunt.

A wall of brush at the hill's top explodes, giving birth to Mapinguari. Always in motion, the beast twists and turns, searching for Juma. The man is missing. The monkeys have betrayed him.

He nearly turns his ire on the small primates when he spots a large face looming down at him. Thrashing back in confusion, Mapinguari is torn between retreat and attack until what's left of his mind makes sense of the giant.

A statue, he thinks. A man made of stone. The scowl isn't real, nor are the fangs. Nor is the single eye glaring from its forehead. The fifteen foot, rectangular megalith has been worn smooth by time and the elements, but many of the details remain intact. It's old, but it has been tended to for generations.

This is where I was born, Mapinguari realizes, *thousands of years ago.*

I am immortal.

A god.

"Juuuma," he calls.

The old man doesn't reply, but the quiver in each labored breath he takes reveals his presence.

"Juma!"

A gasp. Mapinguari stalks around the statue's backside.

The old man has scaled a nearby tree and leapt onto the statue's back. A nocked arrow is aimed downward and released. It pierces the earth beside Mapinguari's side, tickling his skin when it vibrates from the impact. A near miss. But the monster doesn't flinch. Doesn't worry about its life.

"Wait!" Juma shouts, preparing another arrow.

"Your life belongs to me," Mapinguari hisses. "And I would like to have it. Now."

An arrow cracks against the tree trunk, splintering inches from the beast's hand.

Mapinguari pauses. Juma is missing on purpose.

The old man pulls himself higher, onto the statue's head.

"Did you think this would frighten me?" Mapinguari asks.

"It is…a reminder," Juma says, breathless. "Of who you are. Who you have always been and will be."

"Mapinguari."

"And you understand what that means? Who you are? What you are to do?"

"Aside from whatever I please?" Mapinguari grins.

"Yes."

Thoughts of tributes, of sacrifices and holy missions fill his mind. He understands the role. The horror of it, and the honor in it. Monster and legend.

"You will not live to see it." The beast paces below. He could scale the tree and tear the man down, but he knows he will not have to.

Juma relaxes, accepting his fate. "You understand why I had to—"

"I understand nothing!" The screamed words release a weight buried deep in Mapinguari's gut. The pain of it makes him uncomfortable, reminds him of dead feelings that bring discomfort. He doesn't know why, but killing Juma is the last step in silencing wisps of painful memories. Words. Faces. Names.

A sullen Juma lowers his bow and removes the arrow. "May Mapinguari's greatness increase until the ancient lights extinguish. If you require my life to begin your reign, I give it to you…willingly."

Juma stabs his arrow into his leg.

His eyes widen and then lock in place. His breathing becomes a wheeze.

"NO!" Mapinguari roars, furious at Juma's ultimate escape. Three leaps carry him up the tree's trunk and a fourth onto the great statue's head. A solid blow sprawls the paralyzed man to the ground. The beast drops down beside the old man as the monkeys reach a frenzy.

Juma is still breathing when Mapinguari rolls him over, seething. "I want you to beg!"

The old man says nothing.

"BEG!"

When the old man's chest falls still, the monster knows there are only seconds remaining in the man's life.

A gurgling of words from his old self surfaces. "Family is everything. You stole mine. Now, I will steal yours."

There is a flicker of terror in Juma's eyes, and then nothing.

Darkness claims Mapinguari as the last of his old self melts away and the animal takes hold once more. When he returns, the statue is decorated in the meaty remains of something that had once lived.

Covered in stiffening blood, he looks up at the monkeys. They sit in silence, watching. He feels neither their approval nor disgust. This is life in the jungle, and they are accustomed to it.

As is he.

But the jungle is no longer his home.

It is his kingdom.

43

By the time Mapinguari returns to the temple, the tribal representatives who had come to witness his undoing, but instead bore witness to his becoming, have wisely fled. Evidence of what occurred in the grassy field has been erased. No bodies remain. The grass has been groomed, standing tall where the dead, and the battles had flattened it.

He tries to remember the details of what happened here. He knows that he was involved. That he became Mapinguari only recently. But he cannot recall who lost their life or how he felt about it. He remembers only rage, but not at whom it was directed.

Flashes of his most recent conquest flicker through his thoughts, tickling him with feelings of satisfaction. But he cannot remember what was said. What was promised.

Mapinguari is a creature of vast skill, determination, emotion, and ferocity, but his memory and intellect have retreated, along with his sense of self. Lack of self leads to bliss. When he encounters the six young women waiting for him, clothed in bright feathers, he feels little.

He doesn't wonder who they are, how long they've been here, or even what their purpose is. But when they begin attending his needs, he permits them. Their touch on his body, scrubbing away blood and filth, is comfortable.

They've known me all along, he decides. Though he cannot clearly recall when he first saw them, he knows they've served him for as long as he can remember, which for a god, is eternal.

For weeks, they tend to his wounds, feed him well, ease his chaotic thoughts with bitter drinks, and satiate his urges with their bodies. He's lost in an abyss of base pleasure, where time has no meaning and life lacks any kind of substance. Visions come and go. Faces. Voices. The past, present, and future. Omniscient and omnipresent, he is and always has been.

Days repeat.

He soars over the jungle as vast cities beyond the trees burn to ash.

There are moments of clarity. The flavor of a new food. A great feast with bonfires and chanting. A woman writhing atop him, her sounding more like an animal than him.

But they are just moments, lacking any sense of context, time, or emotion beyond pleasure.

And then, it ends.

In the rain.

He stands atop his temple, beneath a torrent, the cool water dulling the day's heat. An old woman kneels before him, cowering in fear, holding a baby tapir by its hind legs. A maze of black lines covers her body, melting in the rainwater.

"You are Jebubo," he says. They're the first words he has spoken in…how long has it been?

The woman nods. "I seek your aid."

"I do not deliver aid," Mapinguari says. The words come from his mouth, but they do not feel like his. Whispers from the dark come and go. The voices of young women. His caretakers. They speak to him. Remind him of who he is. Eternity is a long time to remember one's purpose. They help him with that, their chants reinforcing what he's always known. "I deliver vengeance."

"At times," the woman says, her fear ebbing, "they are the same."

"Who would you have me kill?" he asks, as though reading from a script.

"Quecha of the Guaruamo." The name is followed by a warm spray of blood from the tapir's slit neck. The small animal bucks and squeals until more of its blood covers Mapinguari than flows through its veins.

The woman drops the carcass at his feet and a hunger awakens.

"Quecha of the Guaruamo," she repeats, backing away. He watches her slink over the top step and then descend from view.

He doesn't need to know what the man has done to earn the woman's ire. He doesn't care.

The man's life has been paid for in blood, and no longer belongs to him. All that he is and ever was now belongs to Mapinguari.

He remembers being told these words over and over, but cannot recall who spoke them beyond the pleasure the speaker brought him.

The mindless calm he's experienced slides away with the rain, leaving him with a building rage, an insatiable hunger, and a single name: Quecha of the Guaruamo.

He howls into the sky, his voice billowing into a clap of thunder that shakes the whole world. Scaled arms stretch up toward the raging sky, lightning arcing above him. This is his power, the beast awakening.

The scent of blood draws his eyes downward to the still-twitching body.

He sets upon it with ravenous, uncontained savagery. Six sets of eyes watch from the temple entrance, concealed in darkness, protected from the rain and Mapinguari's wrath. They have directed his path, and now set him free to follow it, wherever it takes him.

"Mapinguari," one of them says.

He glares into the shadows. A pair of hands extends into the muted light of a rainy day, wielding a weapon that is both formidable and familiar. He's had no need for it, and can't remember using it before, but it is his. He takes the blade, slides it into his belt—one of two items he has retained, the other being a satchel. The bag has remained over his shoulder, and unopened, during his long stay. He doesn't know why it's important, but he allows it to cling to him day and night. When the women attend to his body, massaging, pleasuring, grooming, or painting, they must work around it.

The women slide back into the temple's dark and dry interior, whispering their chants, fueling his rage and determination.

Mapinguari descends on the tapir's body, shaking it in his jaws, reducing it to pieces and consuming the most tender of its insides. He scurries down the temple's stairs and runs across the field on all fours, heading for the jungle leading south. He has no clear memory of how to reach the Guaruamo tribe, but instinct guides him through the hills to the south, and into the low, flat basin.

The journey is arduous and fraught with dangers. River crossings, stalking predators, and stinging insects are a constant threat. He handles them all with fearless resolve. The creatures that do not flee, become food. The itching of insect bites maintains the bright burning ire he feels for Quecha of the Guaruamo.

After many weeks, thirst drives him to the smooth waters of a lazy river. He searches for signs of danger, but finds none. Still, he waits. Impatient as he is to fulfill his mission, Mapinguari is no fool. He lingers on a branch, fifteen feet above the water's edge, waiting at a game trail's delta. A capybara approaches, but not from the trail. It comes from the river, alone and unconcerned. The large rodent rests by the shoreline, its eyes closed, confident that it is safe.

If a predator were lying in wait, this is when it would strike.

But nothing rises from the depths, slides through the water, or pounces from the brush.

The capybara is alone.

Well, not exactly.

Mapinguari drops from the tree, rolling to absorb the impact. Machete already drawn, he swings hard at the end of his roll, severing the capybara's spine. Allowing the creature to bleed out, he steps to the water's edge, intent on claiming a drink before he sets upon the carcass.

Despite sharing the capybara's confidence that he is alone, he creeps up to the water, machete ready. The water is still. The opposite shore is quiet. Low to the ground and lit in the setting sun's orange light, he turns his gaze to the water and comes face-to-face with a beast.

Three crazed eyes stare up at him, the largest of them in the center. Snarling teeth threaten to tear him apart. All of this is surrounded by a wild billowing of hair that flows with the water…or is it the wind?

With a roar, he swings the machete down, carving both water and beast in two. When no blood flows, he assaults the water with a series of blows, screaming with each strike. The battle rages for several minutes.

Exhausted, Mapinguari stops the attack. His chest heaves with each breath as he looks down, expecting to find his enemy floating as bits of gore. Instead, he finds the monster similarly exhausted, catching its breath…underwater.

What is this? he wonders, reaching down to the water. His fingers slip through the river—and the monster.

Mapinguari stares at the image, watching it solidify as the water settles. The creature matches his movement, staring back. And in the water, he also sees trees and sky.

A smile spreads as Mapinguari realizes the truth.

He is the monster.

A laugh bubbles up and bursts into the jungle.

"Mapinguari," he whispers to himself, pleased by the sight of himself. He stands tall, gazing at his body, his scales, and the wide, sharp-toothed mouth on his belly.

Then he rends the capybara and feasts.

The following day, he encounters a man whose forehead is painted red. The man shakes in fear as he bows.

"Quecha of the Guaruamo."

The man points without hesitation. The directions aren't very specific, but they don't need to be. Mapinguari finds another man thirty feet away, eyes wide, lips trembling. Despite being armed with a bow and arrow, the young warrior turns and runs.

With a howl, Mapinguari pursues his prey.

It is his last memory before finding himself seated beside a puddle of gore, his rage satiated, his sense of duty fulfilled. The journey home to Queshupa takes weeks, and is not without its challenges, but Mapinguari enjoys every moment. The struggle. The fight for survival. The power he wields over the life and death of all the rainforest's creatures.

Upon returning to his temple, his wounds are treated, his body restored, and his mind numbed by the pleasures of the six.

Time loses all meaning until, once again, he is summoned to the temple's entrance by the promise of spilled blood. This time, when he steps into the sapling light of a new day, he is greeted by not just one tribal woman, but several dozen men and women representing the basin's three remaining tribes. A smile creeps onto his face as he realizes his subjects aren't requesting a simple killing, but a war.

44

Bathed in the blood of many sacrifices and empowered by a night of tribal drums, hard drink, and feasting, Mapinguari ventures into the steaming basin. The men he has been sent to kill are called Guagin—*the nameless*. All he really knows is that they are men with strange clothing accompanied by large, growling monsters. They arrived several weeks previous, laying waste to the southernmost edge of Arawanti territory. Orchards were destroyed. Valuable food lost. And what affects the Arawanti's food production affects all the tribes.

Warriors were sent and turned back by loud weapons, the kind only encountered once before, by a man they also refer to as nameless. Mapinguari is certain he's heard the story of that man before, but the details have drifted away with time.

His path, as always, is challenging, but manageable. He kills, eats, travels, and thinks only of the Guagin. But he is not alone. Several times along his journey, Mapinguari encounters members of the three tribes. They offer him food, water, and places to rest.

He's never seen the people like this before.

They are frightened, but not of him. The terror of the jungle has become a beacon of hope. The attentive care from others beyond the six both revolts and pleases him. Fear-driven worship buoys him, but adoration…is intoxicating.

He wonders if he's ever felt it before, but cannot recall.

Two days journey from where the Guagin were last encountered, he closes his eyes, listening to the gentle singing of an old woman and her daughter. They met him along a game path armed with fire, meat, fruit, and drink. The elder said the meal would be his last and was prepared to give him strength.

What it did was make him sleepy and content.

The women continue their musical chant, voices flowing like the wind, like the river. He can feel the Amazon moving through him, carried by their words. Their delicate voices sing the history of the many tribes that once were and their slow demise to a creeping invader. Smoke and ash, bone and blood. When the Guagin come to the forest, entire tribes disappear.

But not Mapinguari. The beast endures. He has driven the Guagin away before. He will do so again.

Mapinguari smiles. That is his destiny. His purpose. Vengeance brings him pleasure, but defeating another legend of the jungle, one that harms those who bend their knees and heads to him, will bring him glory.

Placated by song and drink, slumber pulls him into the darkness.

He dreams of blood.

Of screams.

Of a face, pale like a ghost, smiling at him. He reaches for outstretched hands, but falls short as darkness claims the spirit.

He wakes from the dream feeling raw frustration, but the smell of acrid smoke disperses his thoughts.

Tendrils of gray snake through the jungle, trapped beneath the canopy. The familiar scent of burning wood comingles with something else. It's both foreign and familiar. Memories flicker, but fail to surface. The scent leaves him feeling confused, which in turn, fuels his growing rage.

His kingdom is being defiled.

This is my jungle, he thinks. *My people.*

All those who think otherwise…

He hooks his fingers and blacks out for a moment. When his vision returns, the foliage around him has been ravaged, the soil beneath him raked. The creatures hiding in the branches high above have gone silent save for the occasional cough.

Blood and soil cling to his fingertips. The stinging focuses him.

Rage, instinct, and knowledge find a comfortable place to coexist. While he wants nothing more than to charge into the unknown and tear it to pieces, Mapinguari is more than that. His enemy is not a lone man or woman, it is an entire tribe, and while it goes against his baser instincts, his task calls for a strategy.

He returns his hands to the earth, clearing out a hole. Then he squats over it and relieves himself. The scent of his urine is pungent, containing traces of the previous night's meal and potent drink.

Memories flicker again as he mixes the thin mud and coats his body, becoming a shadow. Feelings from a time long ago surface with a smile. Someone taught him this. He cannot remember who, but he is filled with a sense of longing, a moment of despair, and then a rekindled rage.

He slips into the jungle, moving low to the ground on all fours, where the air is still fresh. After just a few miles, he pauses at the sound of voices. Men. Several of them. The Guagin have made quick progress.

A tapir emerges from the jungle, eyes wide, limbs jittery with fright. Mapinguari pauses and relaxes his stance. He motions for the animal to pass, and it does. The tapir's obedience stokes the flames burning inside him.

All of this is mine, he thinks. *The land, the people, and all the creatures.*

Defying his building rage, he scales the tallest tree he can find. Its power-ful, twisting limbs carry him through the smog, toward the sunlit sky above.

He emerges from the canopy, coughing and lightheaded. Head and shoulders above the trees, he finds a world he never knew existed. Though it looks solid enough to walk on, he knows the layer of leaves would never hold his weight. But it does support several troops of monkeys and brightly feathered birds who have fled the smoke, which seeps through several gaps, towering into the sky.

As otherworldly as the view is, it doesn't hold his attention. To the south, the jungle just ends. It's been erased from the world.

A buzzing fills the air, like a colossal insect. Mapinguari flinches, looking for danger, but there is nothing in the trees, and nothing below. Despite the noise's volume, the source isn't nearby.

A tree at the jungle's new edge shudders.

Birds take flight.

The monkeys taking shelter in the broad branches shriek. Some leap into neighboring trees. Some stumble and fall from view. When the tree topples, a lone mother, clutching her baby, falls with it, her eyes locked onto Mapinguari's, as if asking why he is allowing this to happen.

Then the mother, and a large segment of the canopy, are gone. A bill-owing of dust and smoke takes the tree's place as it crashes to the ground.

Voices rise up, some victorious, others giving orders. He doesn't understand the language, hearing only threats.

They're here to take the jungle.

To take what's mine.

To destroy all that I have.

They won't take it…take her…my kingdom.

Mapinguari shakes his head, smothering confusion. He lowers himself beneath the green ceiling and leaps through the branches. Cloaked in shadow, moving in silence, he closes the distance. He can't see the Guagin yet, but they're loud enough to send even the bravest jungle denizen running.

All but one.

A slice of yellow locks Mapinguari in place. There are flowers and birds in the jungle, whose colors match the luminous sun-like hue, but none so large. Black smoke coughs in front of the swatch of color, breaking his trance.

Buzzing cuts through the jungle again. The grating sound sends tendrils of tension out through his back. Wood splinters and another tree falls, shaking the ground. Men shout again, and more buzzing fills the air.

Mapinguari heads for the light left by the fallen tree, stopping high in the branches.

A hundred feet below, the Guagin toil over the fallen trees. Bright red headdresses shade their faces, but they are men. The way they speak, and move, with two arms and legs, is unmistakable, even if their clothing is strange…and yet familiar. Has he seen these men before, during his ancient life, and forgotten them?

A lone man wielding a squealing sword cleaves the tree's branches away with the same ease Mapinguari's machete trims fat from an animal. It is a powerful weapon being used to kill trees.

Why would they do this? he wonders, surveying the rest of the scene.

A large patch of jungle is missing. It is just gone. The smoldering remains of branches stretch to the horizon. The Guagin are a blight, eating the jungle itself.

He counts twenty men and more beyond. A burst of smoke and a deep growl draws his eyes back to the bright yellow thing. It's a beast of some kind, lacking legs, but still powerful enough to drag the fallen tree away.

I will wait, he decides. *When night falls, their heads will follow.*

"Seshanguami," he whispers. The sleep-killer. Someone called him that once. Someone who is now dead. If Mapinguari cared about what people thought of him, it might change his plans, but his only concern is that every one of these men offers their blood to the earth they have defiled.

Only then will my kingdom be whole.

Only then will I deserve the praise of my people.

The buzz fills the air again, even louder than before. A vibration cuts through the air, making his limbs feel strange.

He searches for biting ants, but the branches are empty.

Far below, Mapinguari sees one of the Guagin, roaring blade in hand, carving into the trunk of his perch.

Frothing with anger, he lunges down through the branches. This man will be the first to fall, night or not.

The tree quakes with a loud pop. The jolt loosens Mapinguari's grip, but he catches himself on the next branch down. As the ancient trunk twists in its death throes, he works his way through the ever-shifting path of branches, racing the tree toward the ground.

As the branches of neighboring trees shatter under the tree's falling weight, Mapinguari leaps free, rolling to his feet.

Behind him, the tree slaps the ground, coughing a cloud of detritus all around him. A gust of wind, flowing freely over the cleared land, sweeps the dust and smog from the air, revealing Mapinguari to the Guagin. They stare with fearless fascination, whispering to each other. Several of the men hold up black rectangles.

Are they weapons?

One of the men, dressed in striped yellow clothing, points at Mapinguari's nakedness and laughs. The other Guagin join in, but their attempt to humiliate the great jungle god sends him into a rage that explodes from his lungs as a roar that dwarfs the giant yellow creatures and the buzzing blades.

The Guagin fall silent, and when Mapinguari draws his mythic blade, they run.

And are chased.

45

While most of the men flee down the large dirt path carved through the forest's skeletal remains, the closest of the Guagin—the man foolish enough to cut down the tree in which Mapinguari stood—follows a different route. Gripped in panic, he flees *into* the jungle, sealing his fate.

After shedding his tree-slaying blade, the man bolts headlong into the shadows. His red head-covering falls away and bounces to the ground. Mapinguari watches the man, curious about his clothing and his strange behavior. Despite being deep inside the Amazon basin, the man seems out of place.

A roar pulls Mapinguari's attention back to the wide path. A monstrous creature billows smoke as it carries the other men away. Cowards, all of them. He'd expected more from men who could cleave their way through the jungle, who wield the power of buzzing blades and enormous creature-slaves.

But even these men see and respect the power of Mapinguari. Basking in the glory of himself, the beast smiles, and then remembers his quarry. The man has a significant lead, but he tramples through the forest like a falling stone. With only one enemy to track down, Mapinguari decides to take his time, to draw out his vengeance. The man will wear himself down and then beg for mercy, of which he will find little.

Footprints, broken branches, and the smell of something foul make the man's path easier to follow than a well-worn game trail.

Mapinguari follows in the man's wake, watching the monkeys overhead. They linger in uncommon silence. He imagines they under-stand what's happening, that the great beast of the Amazon is defending the homes of all its creatures, man and animal alike.

Heavy breathing from the far side of a tree reveals the man's presence long before Mapinguari sees him. He's hunched over a tall, twisting root, fear-clutched eyes dripping tears into the earth he sought to destroy.

He looks like a man, Mapinguari thinks, *but has the strength of a child.*

Mapinguari sniffs, alerting the lone Guagin to his presence.

The man stumbles back with a squeal. Holding up a hand, he begs in a language Mapinguari can't understand, but recognizes.

Have I encountered the Guagin before? He imagines it was possible. His life *has* been a long one.

I'll ask the six upon my return, he determines, and then he steps closer to the man, casually swinging the machete back and forth. Like a serpent hanging lazily in a tree, the blade's relaxed posture does nothing to diminish its deadly potential. Even the stranger recognizes its threat.

The Guagin backs away, speaking fast-lipped nonsense. Despite not being able to comprehend the words, Mapinguari understands.

Don't kill me.

Let me live.

Have mercy.

These are the final words of all men and women who face the animal.

Then the man says, "Please."

The lone word locks Mapinguari in place. He doesn't recognize the word, but he understood it.

The Guagin's eyes widen. "English? You understand?"

Mapinguari does, but he refuses to answer.

What language is he speaking? Why do I understand him?

It is at that moment that Mapinguari realizes the Guagin speaks the language of thought, the language that no one outside the confines of his inner self can speak or understand.

Mapinguari's eyes narrow. "Demon."

The man shakes his head. "No, no, no. I am man. Like you. Like you!"

Muscles tense. Fury builds. Mapinguari lowers himself to his hands and feet, a growl building in his chest. "I…am *not* a man."

The Guagin backs away, fear returning. With one hand raised and the other reaching into his garments, he says, "I no want to hurt you."

Mapinguari's laugh raises goosebumps on the man's arms. "You could no more harm me than a baby could a jaguar."

A weapon appears in the man's hand. Its presence confuses Mapinguari because, like the language they are speaking, it is both unknown and

known. He has seen it before. Used it. He understands its power—and its
limitations: the man wielding it.

Mapinguari lunges to the right, slipping through some brush before
springing off a tree trunk and lunging toward the man.

The animal surges.

Darkness takes over.

For a moment, he feels the bliss of violence and vengeance, but it
is cut short by a series of loud booms, and a deep pain.

Darkness gives way to light. The morning sun cuts through the canopy
where monkeys scream in dismay. The slap of feet announces the flight of
his prey, but pain keeps Mapinguari rooted to the earth, unable to pursue.

What happened?

The weapon. The...gun.

I've been shot.

When he pushes himself up, pain erupts from his shoulder. Blood
pulses from a hole in the front, and in the back. He lifts his left arm, growling
against the agony it produces. The limb can move, but not without cost.

As anger builds, the caution and pain fade. The Guagin wounded
him. His death will be slow and agonizing.

Back on his feet, Mapinguari searches for his machete and finds it
several feet away. The Guagin was not smart enough to take it when he fled.
The man's trail remains easy to follow. It's a twisting path that covers miles
of terrain without putting too much distance between them and the clearing.

Is that on purpose? Mapinguari wonders. *Does he believe his chaotic wanderings
will confuse me? Is he trying to stay close to the large path, hoping to be rescued?*

Mapinguari slows his approach when he hears the man speaking
in his foreign tongue.

Is he with someone? Have more Guagin entered the jungle?

The beast slides along the forest floor, slipping between plants to find a
small clearing in which a strange large body lies on the ground. The dirty, white
surface is strangely smooth and covered with minimal growth, all of it new.
He follows the red stripe along its side, where he finds strange text. While he
recognizes the individual characters—BE-TTY-074—they are meaningless.
The man's voice comes from inside the strange structure, which is canted up
at an angle, the top of it torn open.

Mapinguari crawls into the clearing. His stomach churns with discomfort as another wave of familiarity washes over him.

Did I kill this beast?

His eyes linger on its familiar surface before taking in the surroundings. Images of a jaguar flood his mind.

I fought the beast here, he thinks, imagining a great battle between two warriors. His memory disagrees, offering up flashes of a terrorized man flinging meat to the cat.

He winces in disgust. That man had been a coward, like the Guagin, taking refuge in the remains of some ancient thing. Men such as these have no place in the jungle. *In my jungle.*

He prowls closer, low to the ground, hidden from view. He can feel the man's fear emanating from inside the white walls, can sense the quivering of his body. If not for the gun, Mapinguari would dive inside and let the animal consume them both.

Instead, he proceeds delicately, climbing atop the fallen tree supporting the vessel.

A trail of ants marches across the logs, carrying leaves, oblivious to the nearby destruction, the man's fleeting life, and the presence of their protector. The hardworking insects trigger more memories, fluttering images, and ancient feelings of poignant moments, somehow forgotten. He does not miss the memories. Desiring to live and fully experience the present, he chases the images from his mind and focuses on his prey.

What comes next will require fearless timing and surprise. The man fired his weapon three times. He can fire it three more times. Mapinguari isn't sure how he knows, but he does. The round cylinder containing the weapon's projectiles holds just six. Once they've been fired, the man's only defense will be screaming in horror.

Without making a sound, Mapinguari rises toward the opening, pausing at the edge. The man inside is still, clutching himself, trying to control the trembling wracking his body. In one hand he holds the gun. In the other, a black rectangle.

He looks at the strange device.

Like the gun, it is familiar.

Where have I seen it before?

His hand reaches back, touching the satchel bag that has not left his side. He doesn't register its presence. To him, it no longer exists. It's a part of him. Just another appendage.

The Guagin's eyes flick to the opening, wide with fear.

Knowing he's been spotted, Mapinguari springs up, hooked fingers raised to strike, teeth bared, a roar exploding.

The man raises his weapon and fires. The first shot buzzes past, an angry insect, its passage warm on his cheek. The next two hurt Mapinguari's ears, but that is all. Safe outside the metal nook, he assesses the pain in his cheek. Warm blood trickles down the side of his face. A near miss of little consequence.

When he climbs back up, the man has discarded the useless weapon and taken refuge in the back. Mapinguari pauses to regard a skeleton seated to his left. The headless body wears the tattered remains of clothing similar to the Guagin's.

They've been here before, he thinks. *This isn't a chance encounter. The Guagin are invading.*

Seething, drool dangling from his clenched teeth, Mapinguari climbs into the small space.

A memory flickers to life. Similar circumstances, but seen from below.

The cat.

A name.

Oro.

The dead. Two men.

A crash. The mighty bird that had carried him to the jungle. He doesn't remember it, but recalls telling someone about it.

Someone important.

Another detail returns. An image of an unclaimed weapon. A knife.

Mapinguari's gaze shifts to the dead man's belt. It holds an empty sheath. He reaches for his machete, but is too late.

The Guagin lunges up, striking hard with the knife, plunging it into Mapinguari's flesh.

46

Darkness comes in pulses as he flails, claws, and scratches. When it fades, the animal is gone, but the pain remains. Mapinguari thrashes about, searching for his adversary, or what's left of him, but the man is gone. Head throbbing, he wonders if the man was ever really there. Perhaps it was the spirit of the headless dead man resting above him.

Looking up through the moss-covered insides, he's struck by a new sense of familiarity. He's seen this before. In a dream? In his imagined wanderings?

A deep churning pain keeps him from lingering on the subject. Fighting waves of nausea, Mapinguari twists around to find the knife impaled in the satchel bag. He eyes the pack, unsure about how it got there or what it contains. All he really knows about it is that it saved his life, or at least delayed his death.

At least an inch of the knife passed through the leather pack, stabbing into his side. The initial pain of that wound was enough to release the animal, which carried out a mindless assault on nothing. In his blind rage, the knife came loose and punctured his flesh three more times.

The collection of wounds oozing blood down his side need to be treated.

He wrestles with the idea of seeking aid. Humility, the most powerful foe he's ever faced, keeps him rooted inside the strange cavern, bleeding his life force into the cracked fabric beneath him.

I can't die, he thinks. *I am Mapinguari.*

But he remembers being injured before. Being sick. Being tended to. Someone helped him then.

"Where are you?" he whispers, and he is caught off guard by warm liquid running down his face.

Am I bleeding?

He dabs his face and is confused by the clear liquid.

Tears?

Mapinguari doesn't die, and certainly doesn't weep.

The Guagin will escape if I fall, he thinks. *They'll return in greater numbers, with weapons the three tribes can't stand against.*

I am the only one who can defeat them.

He pushes himself up, grunting with pain. Back on his feet, he takes a deep breath and waits for the spinning to stop. Centered, still living, and with a newfound resolve, Mapinguari climbs. A new kind of darkness threatens to overtake him as he scales the slippery interior.

A growl and a burst of adrenaline chases the black nothingness away. He pursues it, tears it to shreds, and then tumbles out into the daylit jungle. The fall knocks the air from his lungs, leaving him breathless on his back. How easy it would be to lie there.

"And just forget the world," he mumbles.

Get up.

He looks for the voice's source and finds the monkeys high above, watching their last hope languish in a near-death stupor. He can sense their disappointment.

Get up!

Mapinguari obeys the voice, pushing himself to his knees. Every motion brings about waves of agony from his wounded side and shoulder. The animal rages. It wants to take over, to gnaw at the pain until it stops.

Quiet, Mapinguari urges. *Let me think.*

A crunch of leaves tickles his ears and sets the animal into a frenzy, scratching at the remains of its feeble cage.

The Guagin is coming back.

GET UP!

Mapinguari's legs shake as he stands.

His right side, coated with tacky blood, is warm. The rest of him feels cold. A shiver convulses his torso.

When the jungle separates, he reaches for the machete. His fingers wrap around the handle, but he lacks the strength to draw the blade.

The animal digs into him.

It's all he has left. He's about to let it loose when a timid voice says, "Mapinguari?"

The animal calms.

It is not the Guagin.

"Show yourself," he says.

An aged woman with a red half circle on her head and whiskers protruding from her nose steps into the clearing. He can't take his eyes off of her. He's never met her. He's sure of it. But there is something familiar about her.

"I know you…" he says.

She smiles. "In a way. Is it safe?"

She's not asking about the Guagin, he realizes. *She's asking about me.*

He nods.

The woman whistles and several more people emerge from the forest. They're a ragtag group of women, children, and a single old man, all of them with red foreheads and whisker piercings.

A name slips into his thoughts.

"Dalandala."

The fourth tribe.

"You're spirits," he says. "I'm dying."

The woman smiles again and something about it puts him at ease. "When death came for us, we eluded it. Far to the south. Hidden by friends in the Arawanti. When we learned of your ascension and Juma's demise, we returned to claim what was ours, including this land."

"Why didn't I know?" he asks.

"It is not your place to know, only to feel, and act, when you please, or when we summon you." She squints at him. "The way you look at me… Do you remember her?"

The animal mewls, a pitiful thing. "Remember who?"

"My granddaughter," she says, "The woman who kept you alive, who took a Guagin and made him Mapinguari. She was the rarest of creatures, blessed with intelligence, ferocity, and a heart for wounded animals."

"Guagin?" He grits his teeth and attempts to stalk toward the woman. Dropping to one knee, he is brought low before her, incapable of defending himself even against the frailest.

She puts her hand on the back of his head, her touch calming him. "You really don't remember her, do you? How would she feel about that, I wonder? You are everything she hoped for, and yet nothing like the man she loved. So I am told."

The shaking in his body doubles as emotion forms an alliance with weakness. "Her name. What was it?"

The woman leans in close, her breath tickling his ear. "Ashan."

Images flood his mind. A woman with whiskers, body bathed in sun, a smile on her face. Smoking a joint, sharing a meal, laughing at a joke. Then a cat, the woman's kindred spirit, his daughter, prowling, hunting, but not for him. *With him.* A belly, swollen with the subtlest bump. A child. A son.

'Live as the man you have become…
Not the monster she would make you…'

Ashan's last words put a spear through his heart.

Mapinguari is brought low by returning memories held at bay by the animal, but he is not unmade. The jungle-beast is stronger than that, but still lacks the resolve to stand.

As despair drags him toward the ground, he's caught by a pair of hands that becomes a dozen. He's lifted up, carried by the extended family he never met and believed dead.

Lifted over their heads, he watches the jungle's underside pass by above. Held by a raft of hands, he flows down a river, drifting toward unconsciousness, until a finger shoves something bitter in his mouth and the old woman says, "Stay awake, or you will not return."

High above, the sentinel monkeys follow, watching their fallen champion. When he reaches for them, the old woman says, "They favor you."

"I am Mapinguari," he says.

The woman has a hearty laugh, the kind that mocks, but it is not loveless. He knows that laugh. It might be diluted through generations, but it is still familiar. "If they follow you, it is because of their respect for her."

He doesn't need to ask who 'her' is. They're still speaking about Ashan, though he wishes they weren't. The old woman has brought discord to the bliss of rage and fury. She's inserted doubt in the form of memories and emotions of the past, along with the memory that he was not always Mapinguari.

Not a god.

The woman whistles into the trees. One of the monkeys leaps ahead of the others, descending with fearless grace. It pauses five feet above him, until the woman pats his chest. Then it leaps down onto him, and allows the woman to stroke its head.

"This," the old woman says, "is Kaxuyana."

A hiccup of sadness embarrasses him, as a fresh wave of memories returns. *This is Ashan's monkey, another survivor of Juma's assault.*

"She is the matriarch of these monkeys," the woman explains. "Like her mother, she was too strong-willed to resist."

Another name bubbles to the surface. "Yabuti?"

A hand moves from his back, to his arm, squeezing. "Here."

He can't see the young man, but he doesn't need to. Ashan's brother lives. Her family lives, and family is everything. A deep pain that has nothing to do with the holes in his body or the blood flowing from them, is birthed in his chest. It moves through his body and out through his limbs.

There's something else, he realizes. Something contained by Mapinguari, by Ashan, by the jungle.

I was Guagin, he realizes. A shameful thing. *I don't want to remember.*

The pain thunders, lighting his muscles on fire.

"He is nearly lost," Yabuti says.

"We are nearly there," Grandmother says to him. "You must remain strong."

"You're unmaking me," he complains, angered by the weakness she has revealed.

"Mapinguari has failed. He is not strong enough for this. We need you to be something else. Something more."

He's offended, but curious. "What is that?"

They lower him to the ground beside a blazing fire. Grandmother leans over him, whiskers twitching. She smiles, touches his hairy cheek, and says, "A man."

47

A drug-induced stupor keeps Mapinguari docile and dreaming while awake. Chanting and thumping drums enhance the effect, transporting him to another plane of reality, while his wounds are tended to. He's aware of the pain, but experiences it from a distance, hovering outside himself.

But he is not alone. Another presence lurks in the painless void, hiding in the shadows.

"Who are you?" he asks, unafraid.

When the shadows stay quiet, he turns away from his supine body, surrounded by Dalandala healers. He hears himself scream, as the glowing hot tip of his own machete is placed against his skin, but he does not feel or smell the searing agony.

"Show yourself," he growls.

A shadow at the jungle's fringe shifts, but its source eludes him.

"You cannot hide from me." He creeps closer. "Step into the light."

"I remain hidden, not for me," an indistinct voice says, "but for you."

"I fear no man."

"I am not a man."

"A god, then?"

"Neither."

Mapinguari shakes his non-head. "Then what—"

"It is not important. *I* am not important. Leave me be."

"I am Mapinguari." His whispered rage rises into a shout. "I cannot be dismissed! I will not be told what to do!"

Leaves part, giving way to an indistinct figure of a man. He steps into the clearing, immaterial, like smoke slipping through the people in his path. While in the shape of a man, the air around him vibrates, blurring all his features save for his pale skin. "You are in *my* home. You have no power here. And you have something that belongs to me."

Mapinguari flinches when Ashan is suddenly beside him. She steps through the fire, heading for the pale man, her belly swollen, Oro by her side. They're silent. Placid. Drifting memories.

His memories.

"No!" the beast rages, reaching for a machete that is not there. He looks to his body for weapons, but he is naked, washed clean of his scales, his third eye, and his second mouth. He carries no blade. No satchel.

But he is far from defenseless.

Ashan reaches for the pale man, her fingers inches from his ghostly digits.

"Gwaaarr!" Mapinguari lunges, raking his long nails through the man's throat. Though his enemy is not flesh and blood, the strike peels him apart. The cloud disperses, but reassembles just a few feet away, hand still extended toward Ashan.

Realizing the fog-man isn't alive to kill, Mapinguari turns his attention to Ashan. His memories of her are clouded, nearly as indistinct as the man beckoning to her, but his feelings for her remain powerful, including how he felt in her absence.

"I miss you," he says. "Where have you been?"

She doesn't acknowledge him. Doesn't even glance in his direction. Hands on belly, she continues toward the stranger.

"Why are you leaving me?" he asks. "Again?"

She stops walking, locked in place, but somehow still moving forward, hovering over the ground.

When it is clear Mapinguari is powerless, that he will lose her again, he falls to his knees.

"Wait." The new voice belongs to Grandmother. She's both seated by the fire, eyes closed, enveloped in smoke, and standing beside Oro, a hand on the cat's head. Like the pale man and Ashan, she appears as smoke, her body transparent and drifting with the breeze.

Ashan's hand hovers just above the figure's, her betrayal nearly complete.

"You cannot have her," Grandmother tells the pale man. "Not all of her."

"It is too much," he says. "The monster cannot—"

She silences him with a raised hand. "Just a touch. Enough to center him. Enough to tame him. To unlock his potential."

"And that is all?" the figure asks. "More than that would—"

"A touch," she says. "Nothing more."

The figure withdraws his hand from Ashan's and she comes to life once more. When she turns to Mapinguari, her face is alive with all of the emotion and beauty he now remembers. She is young and vibrant with the body of a warrior and the eyes of a hunter. Her image is exactly how she would want to be remembered. She squats down in front of him, hands on his cheeks.

Her touch makes him weep.

He feels his life with her as though for the first time.

When she leans in to kiss him, he closes his eyes and accepts the gift. Emotions surge when their lips connect. Memories surface. Of their time together. Of the things she taught him. Of how he felt.

And then, it all disappears.

Her lips have retreated.

When Mapinguari opens his eyes, Ashan is already approaching the jungle with the pale man. As darkness envelops them both, the man looks back, and Mapingauri sees his own face, but cleaner and at peace. Then he is alone once more. As most of his memories fade, so does his anguish. He remembers her, and what he learned from her, but the power of their connection is dulled, leaving him with a sense of duty more than anything else.

A soft nuzzle pries his head up.

"Oro," he says, smiling. "You're still here."

Memories of the cat surface. Their first encounters. Their slow-formed trust. Their friendship and finally kinship. He learned as much from her as he did from Ashan. He welcomes her back by massaging the short fur between her shoulder blades, watching the black spots stretch and bend. The content cat sits beside him, and they linger in that place together, separate from the world, but not alone.

By the time Mapinguari thinks to look for Grandmother, she has gone, from the dull place and from the fire's edge.

The others have gone, too. Like the pale man, the Dalandala have faded back into the jungle, leaving him with Oro for company, and a fire to keep the night at bay. As the night wears on, Mapinguari settles down, Oro snuggled up close, and falls asleep.

He wakes to sunlight and pain. Every movement is stiff, but he has endured worse. He reaches for Oro, and when he does not find her, he searches the area. The cat is gone. *Probably fetching breakfast,* he thinks, and then, with a punch of sadness, he remembers that she is dead.

Like Ashan.

The pair of them linger in his thoughts, indistinct memories not powerful enough to unmake him, but potent enough to fuel his sense of duty—not just to the jungle, but to the Dalandala.

Mapinguari has no tribe. No people. But he knows now that he isn't just a beast. He is also a man, with a people to call his own, if he can turn the Guagin back.

Sitting up, he takes stock of his body. His wounds have been seared shut and slathered in ointment that will aid healing and prevent infection. He will not die from his injuries, but he is too weak to even stand, let alone fight.

He discovers the solution to this problem wrapped in leaves. The package lies on the ground beside his still-closed satchel bag, machete, a bow, and a quiver of arrows. He peels open the leaves to discover a variety of fresh fruit, recently cooked meat, and a metal container full of water.

He picks up the bottle and looks it over. The metal is scratched and old, but no one in all the tribes knows how to create such a thing. It is an object from the world beyond. From the Guagin.

How far south did the Dalandala venture?

Who did they encounter?

He ponders these questions without answer as he devours his meal.

Hours later, still feeling weak, he is prodded to his feet by the distant buzz of Guagin weapons and the crack of falling trees. His enemy is both powerful and relentless.

Mapinguari retrieves his gear, carefully plucking the items from the ground and stowing them on his naked body. He pauses to look at his skin. The scales have fallen away. When a breeze sifts through the trees and cools the skin of his face, he probes his cheeks with his hands. The long beard is missing. He checks his head, feeling the prickle of shaved hair on the sides and slightly longer hair on top—the cut of a Dalandala.

A quick dab of his finger on his forehead reveals red pigment. *They've made me one of the tribe,* he realizes, searching his nose for whiskers, but finding none.

Buoyed by their acceptance of him, not as a fearsome monster, but as a member of their tribe, Mapinguari sets a careful pace through the forest. While he wants nothing more than to charge into the Guagin midst, lost in a haze of claws, and screams, and blood, he resists the urge.

Grandmother said a man would save them, not a beast, so that is what he will be…until there are no other options. He is still Mapinguari, after all.

As the buzzing grows louder, he takes to the trees, moving through the branches with careful grace, both to remain hidden, and to show his body mercy.

The Guagin have returned in larger numbers. While many of them still wield the tree-slaying weapons, others carry guns, patrolling the jungle's shrinking fringe, providing protection to the workers.

How many? he wonders, counting. He stops at forty-three, but suspects there are more beyond his sight. Instead of fleeing from Mapinguari's appearance, they have doubled their efforts.

This is because I failed, he thinks, *because I let the Guagin wound me. They have no respect for the jungle, and now, none for Mapinguari.*

Resisting his growing wrath, he plots out a plan of attack. Rather than raging into their midst and assaulting them head on, he needs to remain concealed. In their eyes, he won't be a man or a beast, he will be an army.

Those with guns will die first. Fifteen of them. He takes stock of his arrows. Twenty. *Enough,* he thinks. And when the gunmen have fallen, the workers will fall, first the tree-killers, and then the rest. And when they have all died, the rest will come. But he will not kill them. He will let them collect the bodies, returning home to lick their wounds, mourn the dead, and spread word that the jungle's protectors are stronger than they had imagined.

Content with his plan, Mapinguari climbs to the forest's new edge, finds his first target—a man holding a long gun—nocks an arrow, takes aim, and lets it fly.

48

The arrow slides between branches and leaves, carving a straight and silent path through a complex maze of soon-to-be-cut-down life. Gravity tugs it downward in an accounted-for arch. A saw buzzes, filling the jungle with its wood-eating grind. Somewhere in the distance, a tree cracks and roars to the ground.

The arrow strikes flesh without a sound.

The man's scream is drowned out. He looks down at the projectile protruding from his chest, eyes wide, mouth agape. His expression of shock and pain locks in place. Strength fails the man and he topples back, sprawling to the ground. His chest continues to rise and fall, but the interval between breaths is slowing.

He's not dead yet, but he will be soon.

Mapinguari smiles. This will be easy. He picks his targets, starting with a man walking toward the dying worker. When he sees him, the alarm will be sounded, and secrecy lost.

Part of Mapinguari longs for that outcome. To attack from the shadows, in secrecy, is cowardice. It does nothing to satiate the animal. But it *is* effective, and the man who loves Ashan, who has been accepted by her family, is driven by responsibility. He is both man and animal. And yet, he does not feel whole.

Something is missing.

Ashan.

Oro.

His unborn son.

And something else...

Mapinguari nocks another arrow, draws the string back, and leads his target. The man is moving, but his gait is steady and the range unchanging.

An easy target.

The distant buzzing stops. Mapinguari waits for the pop and rush of leaves, but no trees fall. For a moment, the jungle falls silent.

Then men begin to shout.

His target stops walking, listening to the shouts.

Mapinguari adjusts his aim. He'll put the arrow in the man's neck. The poison will subdue him before he can shout in pain.

The bow string rolls over his fingertips. It will be another smooth and calm release, every gust of wind, swaying branch and external factor accounted for—except one.

A gunshot rips through the forest.

The bullet tears through air, and leaves, and finally flesh.

An unbidden shout of pain bursts from Mapinguari's mouth, just as the bullet passes through his thigh. The arrow fires, sailing harmlessly into the side of a metal beast. The bow falls away as he twists, left leg numb and useless. Hands reach, but find nothing upon which to grasp. Mapinguari falls.

Five feet closer to the ground, a branch collides with his shoulder blades. Momentum catapults him forward and down again, where a second branch careens into his gut. Though now breathless and wracked by pain, Mapinguari knows the tree is no longer a refuge.

Head spinning, gasping for air, he lunges down, weaving through the branches. Shouting grows louder as men approach, hunting him. They grow louder still, pitched with worry, when they reach their fallen comrade.

When Mapinguari hits the ground, the man reborn as a Dalandala is jolted back into the recesses of his mind, leaving only the animal—only the legendary beast. Rather than flee from the overwhelming numbers with powerful weaponry, he rushes toward them.

Shame fuels Mapinguari's raw frenzy. He runs on all fours, heading toward the Guagin. A group of them rush toward the tree from which he fell, while several more panic and shout over the poisoned man, whose lungs have, by now, stopped working.

When several of the men hunting him begin firing at shifting shadows high in the tree, Mapinguari realizes that his fall was unseen. The element of surprise is his again, and he doesn't waste it.

Bursting from the underbrush with a thunderous bellow, most of the men flinch. The two who *don't* get Mapinguari's full attention. The first is driven to his knees by a solid blow to his groin. He catches the second man by his ankle and yanks. The man flails backward, his head striking the ground hard enough to stun him.

As the rest of the group starts to react, he leaves the stunned pair behind and dives into the Guagin ranks. He punches, kicks, and claws, keeping himself close to his adversaries. Too afraid to use their weapons so near to each other, he whittles the armed men down. He doesn't kill any of them. First, he must disarm and subdue them. Then the slaughter can begin.

And when it does, the animal will have blood enough to bathe in.

Mapinguari senses the men's strikes on his body, but he is numb to their punches and kicks. Each impact fuels his rage, increases his thirst for violence, and pushes him closer to the darkness that will consume them all.

The last man standing raises his gun in a shaky hand. With no one left between them, Mapinguari is exposed. But the man is a coward. He stood clear of the fight, hoping the others would do the job for him.

The Guagin's finger twitches. Mapinguari lunges to the right, the bullet humming past him. Three more shots ring out, all of them missing. When Mapinguari adjusts his course, running low to the ground over the fallen men, the coward stops firing to avoid striking his comrades. Then he does the only thing he can—he runs.

But not fast enough.

Mapinguari tackles the man from behind, hooking his fingers into the man's shoulders. Knees crack ribs when they strike the ground, drawing a high-pitched scream from the coward.

Machete slides from sheath, rising into the air.

One strike will silence the man.

Will stoke the burning in his heart.

Set the beast loose.

Unleash the flow of blood.

Mapinguari's vision narrows toward darkness. His muscles tense. The blade cries for flesh and bone. He can hear its song. A manic grin spreads on his lips and a laugh gurgles from his chest. He is Mapinguari, not a man. Forgetting that nearly got him killed.

Eyes locked onto the back of the man's neck, the beast roars and strikes.

"Stop!"

The machete's course ceases just inches from the man's spine.

That language again. The one he does not know, but understands. He turns to see who spoke the word, who will die first in the coward's place. He finds a tall man with light skin and hair on his face. Like Mapinguari, the man is an aberration in the jungle. He's dressed in strange clothing, mostly because it's so clean. The man stares at Mapinguari, the blueness of his eyes disconcerting and foreign.

"You understand me, don't you?" the man asks.

Mapinguari growls, tensing to strike, to finish what this man interrupted. Then he will die, too.

"My name is David Wellcome. I'm from the United—"

"Gwwaaarrrgh!" The machete rises and falls.

"Greg Zekser!"

The machete's blade stops again, this time a millimeter inside the now-weeping man's neck.

Waves of nausea roil through Mapinguari. What did he say? What curse did the man use? *Dark magic,* he thinks, snarling.

A convulsion starts in his feet, working its way toward his head.

Mapinguari grips the machete tighter, grinding his teeth, as he pushes the blade down.

But the weapon doesn't move.

Something is resisting him.

He looks for the person clutching his arms, but there is no one.

When he growls in frustration, the man beneath him wails once more, but still, Mapinguari cannot silence the man or end his life. The darkness has fully retreated.

He twitches at the sound of weapons being readied. The beaten and bloodied men he subdued have risen anew, guns in hand, all trained on him.

Why haven't they fired?

Do they know he can't move?

"Greg Zekser," the white man named Wellcome says again, this time pleading.

"Greg Zekser is dead!" Mapinguari screams. "I devoured him, and I will—"

"He's not breathing," someone calls out.

The Guagin gathered around the poisoned man part. They've plucked the arrow from his still chest, but there is nothing they can do for him.

"Please," Wellcome says. "You are a doctor, yes? Doctor Gregory Zekser."

MY HAND SNAPS up, releasing the machete. I'm repulsed by the weapon and the blood, both new and old, staining its blade.

The man beneath me cries out in relief, slapping his hands over the bleeding wound on the back of his neck.

A wave of disorientation sweeps through my body when I attempt to stand. I stumble and fall onto my back, staring up at the blue sky surrounded by jungle trees. Monkeys dance about, agitated by my defeat.

Memories and self return in painful waves, comingling with vivid recollections of my time as Mapinguari. An anguished scream tears from my throat as I remember...everything. Ashan's death and my failure to not just save her, but to mourn her passing, and that of our child, arches my back in pain as I gasp in a raspy breath. The memory of Oro's limp body reduces my screaming to sobs. And then, the moments of darkness concealing my worst deeds clear. I see, for the first time, how Juma, Mapinguari, and Tikuna died at my hands. How I desecrated their bodies and bathed in their remains.

Despair becomes horror.

I truly was—am—Mapinguari. A monster. A man-made beast.

And then the rest of my life arrives in a sudden, mind-numbing explosion.

Gwen and Juni's faces return to my memory in high-res clarity. I can hear them, see them, smell them. Even worse, I can remember how much I love them and they love me, and I fully realize just how much I have betrayed them both. I remember Juni's birth, my wedding day, the deaths of my parents, my childhood. All of it comes back, and with it, more pain.

I writhe in the mud as though struck by madness. I don't want to be seen. Don't want to exist. Drowning in shame, hands clutched over my eyes, I weep for the life I lost, the loved-ones cleaved from me by fate and violence—and the lives I ended.

How many people did I kill? How many did I enjoy killing?

"Doctor Zekser?" Wellcome asks, his blue eyes staring down at me, hands on his knees, surrounded by a bevy of guns aimed at my forehead. "Is there an antidote for the poison you used?"

I try to focus on his words, but my body continues to convulse, clutched by the horrors of my own creation.

"Doctor Zekser," Wellcome says, worry raising the pitch of his voice, "if this man dies at your hands, I will not be able to get you home."

Home.

"Home?"

"Yes!" the man shouts, now with tears in his eyes. "Home! To your family! Your wife. Your daughter."

When I sit up, the men with guns rush in.

"No, no, no!" Wellcome shouts. "Let him be. His mind has come back."

I nod my thanks to the man and crawl toward the Guagin...a logger just doing his job. A swipe of my arm sends the nearby men scattering, and I descend on the fallen man with all the ferocity of Mapinguari, but with the intention of saving a life, not taking it.

The man's ribs crack as I perform CPR, pumping blood through his veins, filling his lungs with oxygen, keeping his mind alive until the paralysis wears off. It's impossible to know if he's dead beyond rescue, or simply too frozen to show signs of life, so I continue for ten minutes, weeping and begging, "Please, please, please," to anyone that's listening.

The man's return to life is subtle. He doesn't gasp. Doesn't open his eyes. I simply feel the resistance of his lungs rising on their own when I try to compress them. I lift my hands up and away, watching his chest rise and fall. Relief rushes through me, overwhelming my already frayed nerves.

This time, when darkness overtakes me, it's the merciful nothing of unconsciousness. I hear Wellcome shouting my name, again and again, and I feel his smooth hand patting my face.

And then, nothing

49

I wake to the sound of distant chainsaws. The loggers have already returned to work, deforesting a swath of jungle that has belonged to the four tribes for thousands of years. Revulsion for this desecration wages war with the fresh memories of my own despicable acts. Who am I to judge the actions of anyone?

"You're awake?" Wellcome asks.

I open my eyes and glance at the man. He's seated, elbows on knees, beside my cot. We're in a trailer, something old, something that's spent too many years fending off the jungle. It smells of mildew, and feels a lot like a cave, the ceiling's closeness oppressive.

"You changed your clothes?" I ask, noting the dry, unsoiled Hawaiian print shirt. In the jungle, he'd stand out like a beacon for all kinds of trouble.

He looks down at the shirt. "You think I'd be able to handle the humidity by now. I've been here enough."

"You work with them?" I motion toward the sound of the saws.

He chuckles. "Hell, no. I'm a private investigator. Honestly, looking for you, out here, it's a bit out of my wheelhouse. But I speak the language and I need the money. So here I am. That I found you, now, is something of a miracle."

He waits for me to ask why, but I just stare. It's been so long since I've held a conversation in English, it feels strange. The cadence of the language sounds off. I'm having trouble distinguishing honesty from sarcasm. Is the man disappointed he's found me? Is he relieved? Indifferent?

"I've been down here a dozen times, networking with local governments, unsavory types, farmers, and logging companies. I even made friends with some Indians. The civilized variety. Not the guys you've been hanging around with."

"They *are* civilized," I say, and I must be glaring more than intended because Wellcome leans back and looks ready to bolt.

"They wanted to strap you down," he says. "Was I wrong to stop them?"

I relax in the cot. "Yesterday, you would have been smart to kill me."

"And today?"

"I'm me," I say, and when he doesn't look convinced, I add, "You're safe."

"What happened to you?"

"Plane crashed," I say.

He nods. "That's the one thing I know."

"After that..." Memories flash past. My descent into madness, and love, and mercy, and primal violence is a story that's not easy to tell, and somewhat unbelievable. There are also people to protect. The four tribes, including Ashan's family, need to be protected. Their traditions, sacred locations and myths must remain a secret. At the same time, my capture has exposed them. No one will believe that I survived the Amazon rainforest on my own, developed my own tribal paints, self-taught the use of poisoned arrows and cut my hair like...

I rub my hand over my head. It's been shaved down to stubble. I glance down at my body. I've been dressed in cargo shorts and a T-shirt. *My* cargo shorts and T-shirt.

"Your wife had me bring them, along with..." he digs into his pocket and pulls out a Snickers chocolate bar. They're my longtime favorite, what Gwen calls my 'one and only vice.' I take the candy, unwrap half, and bite down. The sweetness is overpowering. I fight to not spit it out. I wrap the rest, pretending to have enjoyed what now feels like fake food.

"I thought it a bit strange," he says. "Honestly, I usually just eat them myself. They melt down here, you know. I was about to eat that one when I got this." He digs out a smart phone, and after a few flicks he turns the screen around for me to see.

The man captured in the photo is a stranger...if he's a man at all. His skin is covered in scales and mud. A large eye glares from his forehead. A mouth gapes from his midsection, matching the snarling maw on his face, which is surrounded by a gnarly mane of hair. He stands low to the ground, on all fours, like an ape, the motion blur blending it all so that he looks like a true beast of legend. He's horrifying.

"You don't recognize him?" Wellcome zooms in on the photo, shifting it around with his thumb until the man's face fills the screen.

My face.

"That's…"

"You. Pretty nasty, right?"

"I was in a dissociative state," I say. It feels like a lame excuse, but it's also the truth. I was both me, and not me. The jungle made me more, and less, revealing my true self and the monster all men are capable of becoming.

He tries the word on for size, speaking slowly. "Dissocia… What is that?"

"When you become disconnected from your own memories, thoughts, feelings, and actions. For me, there were layers. At first, I was disconnected from everything that came before, but I was still living my life. When things got…unbearable, I was separated from myself entirely. It's like…watching yourself on TV. Living in third person. Some of it I didn't remember until yesterday, and now I wish I could forget it again."

"Sounds like a foolproof diagnosis." His tone a mix of distrust and compassion. "I can see it. The man in this picture is you…but it's also not. The man I'm talking to now is not the…"

"Monster I was before."

He gives a slow nod. "That's fair. The point is, you're definitely not the same guy now. Honestly, when the logging company e-mailed this—" He gives the phone with my image on it a shake. "—to me, I didn't think it was you, but Gwen…"

I clutch my stomach and lean forward.

"Please don't puke," Wellcome says. "This isn't my trailer, and I don't want to clean you up again."

"She saw this?" I grip the phone, crushing my shame into it.

"I had to be sure it was you."

"Where is she?"

"In a plane by now," he says. "From Manaus."

"What was she doing in Manaus?" It's the largest inland city in Brazil, and the base of operations for many cultural and relief organizations dealing with tribal people, but why would she be there if she didn't know I'd been found?

"She's been living there for two years now."

Two years...

"She sold the house in Massachusetts and came here. She's really something. Never gave up hope. The Brazilian government stopped searching for you after a month. She never did."

This news brings tears to my eyes. She never gave up on me. Never moved on. But I... A heavy sigh leaves my body shrunken.

"I get it," he says. "You did things out there. To survive. I don't need to know. No one needs to know, especially your wife and kid. The only real problem we need to clear up is the man you nearly killed. He's hurt pretty bad, though it's more from your effort to save him than to kill him. I'm not sure they're going to let us leave, no matter how sad your sob story is."

"Is Gwen coming *here?*"

Wellcome shakes his head. "Iquitos, in Peru. That's where we'll be headed if they let us go. It's a few hundred miles closer than Manaus." He squints at me. "Do you even know where we are?"

I shake my head.

"Vale do Javari. State of Amazonas. And if that doesn't mean anything to you, it's the wordy way of saying, 'the middle of nowhere.' You're damn lucky you didn't spend the rest of your life in this green hell."

My instinct is to argue with his assessment of the jungle. There is plenty about life in the Amazon that is hellish. I became my worst self here. But I also learned things about myself, and my life's priorities, that I couldn't have learned in the sterilized world outside. Life in the modern world might be more cosmetic, but there are enough desperate junkies, hungry thieves, and ruthless murderers to know Mapinguari's darkness roams all corners of the Earth.

"How long *have* I been here?" I whisper.

"You don't know?"

"Lost track of time."

He flicks his phone on, taps the screen a few times, and then looks up. "You want exact number of days, or—"

"Just tell me!"

"Four years, two months. Roughly."

Invisible leeches suck away my strength, leaving me numb. Four years. Why didn't Gwen move on? Why didn't she give up? Her stalwart dedication is inspiring.

"This needs to stop," I say, turning toward the sound of a tree falling. "There are several uncontacted tribes in this region. If they keep logging, it won't just be one man sent to stop them. It will be an army. They'll all be killed."

"And then the tribes will be wiped out," he says, sadness and understanding in his voice. "But that's not going to happen while we're stuck in this camp. A battle for the trees might be fought in the jungle, but the war won't be won here. You need to get back to civilization for that. You...wait, the tribal people sent you to stop the logging? *Just* you?"

I nod.

"What were you supposed to do against that many men?" He's genuinely bewildered, and for some reason I decide to trust him with the truth.

"Kill them all."

He swallows and glances at the door. "But that was dissociated Greg Zekser, yeah?"

"Mapinguari," I say. "That was my name. I was a monster. A legend."

We sit in silence for several long seconds before he clears his throat. "Well, the Brazilian government is protective of indigenous people. With your story, I'm sure it won't be hard to get their attention."

My story... I don't like the idea of telling anyone what really happened in the jungle, but if a watered-down tale of peaceful tribes will save them, that's what I'll give the world. "What will it take? To get out of here?"

"Money," Wellcome says. "Of which your wife has little."

"That's why this was your last trip?"

He shrugs. "I have bills to pay, too."

"My satchel, did you open it?"

He shakes his head and searches behind him. He leans back and plucks the old leather bag from beneath a soiled towel. "Didn't look inside."

Wellcome puts the worn strap in my hand when I reach for it. I open the satchel and pause. At the top is a leaf-wrapped meal, a surprise gift from Grandmother. I can smell the fruit and meat within. I hand the bound food to Wellcome and dig a little deeper. A small portion of the marijuana brick comes next.

"Is that?" He takes the bundle of pot and smells it. "That will help, I'm sure, but it's not enough to—"

I remove the $5000 stack of cash.

His eyes widen. "How much?"

"Five thousand."

He nods. "That should do it. Though we'll offer less to start. We still need to secure travel, food, and lodging. Getting to Iquitos won't be easy."

I look down into the satchel and hold my breath.

The notebook. Nearly all the pages are missing, pillaged for joints or starting fires. But the pages that remain… I lift it from the satchel and place it on my lap. Wellcome watches in silence as I open the cover with shaky hands to reveal a page with four words written on it in charcoal.

Gwen.
Juni.
Home.
Purpose.

I choke back a laugh-sob, but fail to stop fresh tears.

I have been given all four, and the last of them drives my hand back into the satchel. The bag falls to the floor, empty as I lift the zip-locked phone from inside. I tear the bag open and reassemble the phone, my whole body shaking. I press the power button, but nothing happens. "C'mon, damnit. C'mon."

Wellcome places a gentle hand on mine. "Hey."

When I look up, he's holding out his phone, swiping to a saved contact that reads: Gwen Zekser. "Your number is different, anyway."

I snatch the phone from him, hit the call button and nearly have a panic attack as several clicks are followed by ringing.

On the sixth ring, the phone is answered. "Hi, Mr. Wellcome. Mommy forgot her phone, but you can—"

When I sob at the sound of my daughter's voice, she stops speaking. It takes all of my strength to reign myself in and say just one word.

"J-June-bug?"

There's a pause. Several loud breaths. And then...

"Daddy?"

EPILOGUE

One Year Later

"Careful," I say, reaching for Gwen's hand. "It's steep here."

"You're sure this is the way?" she asks for the tenth time today. It's a question I've grown accustomed to over the past few weeks. With no path to follow and no maps or compass to guide us, it's not hard to understand her fear of getting lost.

From her perspective, I was lost in the rainforest for four years. But that's not entirely true. For a time, I was lost, and then I was home. Even when I don't know where I am, I know how to get where I want to be. It's hard to explain. It's instinct, I suppose, but that's not the answer she wants to hear, and it's not the one I want to admit: that some part of me that was Mapinguari is alive and well, guiding us through the Amazon rainforest not far from the Peruvian border.

"It's just ahead," I tell her, lifting her from atop a boulder and placing her beside me. She looks at me with bewildered eyes, impressed by my strength. We've been reunited for a year now, but she's still getting accustomed to my new physique, which I've maintained by hitting the gym.

Our reunification was one of the most joyful and painful experiences of my life. I've never felt anything quite like it, though I experienced it again, when two days later, we returned to Brazil and I saw Juni. I was wrong about her forgetting me. She ran into my arms while I blubbered like a fool. She and Gwen had looked at photos of me, watched videos of me, and told stories about me every day I was gone.

Juni will never know the truth about what happened in the jungle.

Neither will the outside world.

But I told Gwen—everything.

It was about six months before we recovered from the revelation that I'd been with another woman, who'd been pregnant with my child before her demise. If not for the photo of me, looking like a wild, mindless monster, I'm not sure she would have forgiven me. But she believed my story—all of it—including Ashan and I saving each other's lives on multiple occasions. Without Ashan, I'd be nothing more than a skeleton. When Gwen came to that conclusion on her own, she felt more endeared to Ashan than angry.

In my absence, clutched in desperation, Gwen had started attending church, and praying. She prayed for my safety and return. That's it. Every day for years. In her eyes, Ashan had been the answer to her prayer. When I told her about my own, offered just once, and showed her the piece of paper, she broke down in tears, freed from the pain and anger of my betrayal.

It wasn't long after that Gwen had asked to meet my extended family, the Dalandala. Struggling to survive jungle life after Juma's assault, the withered tribe revealed themselves to the outside world, with me serving as both mediator and translator.

Logging in the area has been suspended, and millions of acres protected. For the four tribes, it's a happy ending, though the Dalandala have already begun interacting with the outside world. Some now wear clothing. Others have taken up smoking cigarettes. Ashan's family will survive, but it won't be long before their tribal names, customs, and history are forgotten.

But I'll never forget.

And that's why we're here.

To remember.

To pay our respects.

Juni is at home in Manaus under the watchful care of Gwen's parents. Over the past year, I've loved and doted on her more than any parent should. She and Gwen are my life, my purpose, and I'll never put the world, or my position in it ahead of them again. I volunteer as a doctor working with tribal people, though my motivation has changed. But my days of putting charity and work ahead of my family is over.

A book deal telling my watered-down story is paying the bills. It'll be another fourteen months before it's published, but the publisher has high hopes. That's part of the reason I've returned, to take photos and check in on the Dalandala, several of whom are escorting Gwen and me through the jungle. Some of the tribes would still react violently to Guagin, and we've encountered Guaruamo and Jebubo hunters, but their tune changed when they learned who I am—that Mapinguari has returned.

They no longer believe in the monster, or the legend. The return of my self proved to them that I am and always have been just a man. But they all know my story, and unlike the outside world, they know the whole truth. Know what I'm capable of. Gwen asked about it when the first group of hunters we encountered fled upon hearing the name Mapinguari and looked at my face, which is now covered in a trimmed beard. At that moment, seeing the fear my name and face produced in a group of armed men, the story became reality for her.

It's been a long journey. Difficult work. But for the most part, it's been pleasant enough and without significant danger. Gwen has watched me scale trees, hunt for food, and forage fruit she didn't know existed. Seeing me in the jungle has been eye-opening for her. She's spent a lot of the time hidden behind a camera, snapping photos and videos of me in the jungle, interacting with the Dalandala, who still view me, and treat me, as family.

But today, for the last leg of our journey, they've left us alone.

What comes next is private.

When I step into a small clearing atop a rise, overlooking a massive valley, I stagger to a stop.

Gwen catches my arm. "You okay?"

I stare at the ground where Ashan and I slept on our last night together.

When I start crying, Gwen understands. "We're there?"

I point into the distance. "See the steps?" It's been just a year, but the temple is overgrown with vegetation. With the time of Mapinguari at an end, his six attendants, who also maintained the temple, returned to their own tribes.

"I see it," she says, but she's not falling for my redirection. She puts her hand on my chin and turns my face to hers. "Tell me."

"This is where Ashan told me she was pregnant."

Gwen gives a slow nod and rubs my back. "Thank you for bringing me here. It's helping me understand. What happened. How you changed. Everything that happened. It wasn't what you wanted, but it was what you *needed.* Ashan didn't just keep you alive, she sustained your soul, even when your psyche was lost."

I smile and wipe away my tears. "We're almost there."

We descend together, walking in silence as my emotions roil. When we reach the curved wall following the path down into the temple valley, I stagger to a stop and catch myself on the smooth rock. I've become soft again, driven by emotion, my ability to wall off and control feelings diminished by safety and comfort. "I can't do it..."

"You need to," Gwen says. "It's important."

"What if they're not here?" I ask, looking for any excuse to turn back.

"Grandmother said they were here, right?"

She waits for me to reply, but I've got nothing to offer aside from hiccups of sorrow.

"She wouldn't lie to you," Gwen says. "Not about that."

She and Grandmother hit it off, despite not sharing a language. Unified by their affection for me, they became close, and for that reason, both of us now bear the red half-circles of the Dalandala on our foreheads.

Gwen takes my hand, and despite never having been here before, she leads me along the path. Hours later, she slows when we reach the first skulls, their aged appearance now sporting the first signs of moss growth, as they stare back at us.

"All of them are family members?" she asks, looking closely at a skull.

"Of Mapinguari," I say, remembering the somber tone in which Grandmother spoke when she told me about the tradition.

"How many were there, before you?"

I shrug. "Hundreds. Maybe more. The older skulls would have dissolved by now."

We continue past the columns of skulls, slowing again when the end is in sight.

My legs quiver as we near the whitest skulls. I do my best to avoid looking at the last of them. I hold on to the wall, arms shaking, and I take several deep breaths.

"What happened to him?" Gwen asked. The question and her tone are almost light. She's redirecting me again, calming me down. It nearly works until I look at the skull in question and note that it is the third to the end, the skull and part of its face crushed in.

With a somber sigh, I face the hollow eyes. "This...was Tikuna."

I don't have to say anything else. She knows the name. Knows who he was. And how he died.

"I'm sorry," I tell the dead man, and then I push past my fears to the next skull in line.

When I see it, I can't stop my sob. My whole body shakes as I pick up the only skull on the wall that isn't human. "This was my girl."

Gwen is crying now, too, nearly as hard as me. She places her hand on the feline skull. "Oro..."

I kiss the skull between the eye sockets and put her back in her place of honor. Then I step to the side, eyes closed. When I open them, I stare into the empty eyes of Ashan. So much of her is missing, but I recognize the bone structure.

My legs fail me when I try to lift her up. On my knees, lost in sorrow, I hear the words, "I have her."

When I look up again, Gwen is kneeling beside me, Ashan's tear-soaked skull in her hands. "This is her? Ashan?"

My blubbering is all the confirmation she needs. There are so many things I want to say, so many ways I've pictured this moment, but I can't bring myself to speak.

Gwen holds the skull like it is the most precious thing in the world, and then with more grace, mercy, and love than I've managed in my entire life, she kisses the top of Ashan's head and says, "Thank you."

A NOTE FROM THE AUTHOR

For some reason, when I'm going through a tough time, I tend to put my characters through the ringer. It happened with *Infinite*, as I wrote the book while in the midst of an emotional breakdown and the news that I had a brain tumor (spoiler: turns out I didn't). The result was an emotionally charged story that went on to become my bestselling novel ever. A year later, and it's still doing amazing.

About a year after writing *Infinite*, I started having strange symptoms, which I learned were neuropathic. Burning skin, shooting pains, constricting muscles, numb arms and legs, micro-spasms through my body, tingling all over, and my old friend: panic. I couldn't be touched. Couldn't take showers. Physical contact of any kind felt like a hot flame. Turns out the emotional breakdown from the summer before was the same problem: a tick-borne disease called Bartonella, for which I am STILL being treated and making slow progress in defeating. Instead of just attacking my peripheral nerves, it spread to my whole nervous system. Fun!

While this was all going on, and I was bedridden, I wrote *Alter*. My discomfort fueled Greg's painful journey, each page acting as catharsis. The result is a novel that, I think, is as emotionally charged as *Infinite*, and hopefully just as good of a story. If you think so, please post a review for *Alter* on Amazon and/or Goodreads. *Infinite*'s success is thanks to the many readers who posted reviews—more than 300 on Amazon and nearly 6000 on Audible! The power to make or break a book resides with the fans, and I hope you'll support *Alter* in the same way.

So where is my health now? Confused. I still have the neuropathy, and struggle many days just to do normal things. But I'm writing every day now, and starting to get out of the house. I take about 20 pills twice a day, including two different antibiotics. I've been on four since October. While I'm pretty discouraged about feeling crappy still, it generally takes 1–2 years to kick this thing, so I'm in for the long haul and trying to learn what I can from the ordeal, including how to write better characters, and how to show mercy to people who are suffering.

Thank you very much for coming along for my own personal journey. It's been an interesting one, and has only been possible because I have awesome readers (that's you!).

—Jeremy Robinson

ACKNOWLEDGEMENTS

Thanks to Kane Gilmour for the awesome edits, as always, and to the best proofreaders an author could hope for, Heather Beth, Roger Brodeur, Julie Carter, Liz Cooper, Dustin Dreyling, Donna Fisher, Dee Haddrill, Jeff Sexton, and Kelly Tyler. Thanks to my family for not just supporting my creative endeavors, but my journey back toward health. Love you guys.

ABOUT THE AUTHOR

Jeremy Robinson is the international bestselling author of sixty novels and novellas, including *Apocalypse Machine, Island 731*, and *SecondWorld*, as well as the Jack Sigler thriller series and *Project Nemesis*, the highest selling, original (non-licensed) kaiju novel of all time. He's known for mixing elements of science, history and mythology, which has earned him the #1 spot in Science Fiction and Action-Adventure, and secured him as the top creature feature author. Many of his novels have been adapted into comic books, optioned for film and TV, and translated into thirteen languages. He lives in New Hampshire with his wife and three children. Visit him at www.bewareofmonsters.com.

CPSIA information can be obtained
at www.ICGtesting.com
Printed in the USA
LVHW031502160119
604152LV00005B/914/P

9 781941 539392